Furball

Chris Parthemos

Furball is a novel wherein mostly good people begin to do very bad things. These aren't meant to be heroes. It is as such dedicated to the good people who manage to have bad things happen to them without it ever even starting to change who they are.

Part 1

If I was a junkman
selling you cars,
Washing your windows
and shining your stars,
Thinking your mind
was my own in a dream,
What would you wonder
and how would it seem?
Living in castles
a bit at a time
The King started laughing
and talking in rhyme.

Singing words, words
between the lines of age.
Words, words
between the lines of age.

from "Words" by Neil Young

THE DOG
Tony

EVERY SUNDAY EVENING TONY PLAYS chess with Mrs. Misery in her apartment overlooking the Arno, and every Sunday evening Tony loses. That's not her name, obviously, or at least it's not her real one. The inside joke started when he was a tenant in an apartment she managed on *Via del Corso*. Tony introduced himself and immediately butchered the pronunciation of her name. *It's Mee-zoo-ree,* she told him, *Misuri.* Try as he might he could never stick the landing, and eventually the name was just the name. Even after they ceased to be landlord and renter, that part of their relationship remained immovable. Tony moved out of that flat almost two years ago to a little place on the river's south side. The new apartment smells like algae and rat shit, but it's quiet and very nearly tourist free. If you know the right angle, you can just barely see the cupola of Brunelleschi's dome from his bedroom window. Even buried under hotels and Prada outlets, the thing is still massive. In his head, Tony thinks of the city of Florence as a wedding cake, and the *Duomo* as the little plastic bride and groom on the top layer. It's the garnish that tells you what the whole thing is for.

Tony likes the walk back from Mrs. Misery's place for two reasons. The first is an alley a few blocks from her home, where his favorite street musician is out most nights. The man's got to be seventy-five years old, and his acoustic guitar is at least twenty years older than he is. He doesn't draw the crowd that the Armani model in the *Piazza della Signoria* does, but he also manages to play something other than James Taylor and Simon and Garfunkel every once and a while. For Tony, it's a win-win. When the old man sees him, he smoothly changes songs. Tony recognizes the chords after the third bar: "Birds" by Neil Young. They haven't spoken much, but one of the few things the old man knows about Tony is that Tony feels about Neil Young the way an aspiring chef might feel about Julia Child. His aged, wavering voice meanders through the chorus of the song – in Tony's mind, one of the finest ever written. He sings along.

When you see me fly away without you,
shadow on the things you know,
feathers fall around you,
and show you the way to go,
it's over, it's over.

It's sort of strange to hear it sung with an Italian accent, but it's sort of charming at the same time. Tony waits for the song to finish, and when it ends he drops six euro in coins into the old man's guitar case. He's not always this generous, but this is his favorite song and, oddly enough, he's in a good mood. The old man smiles and goes back to something different as Tony walks away. It's a Lou Reed song, if Tony's not mistaken. Charlie's Girl. He thinks about staying longer, but he doesn't.

The second reason Tony likes his walk home from Mrs. Misery's place is that it takes him straight across the Ponte Vecchio. By day the place is a nightmare, tourists crowding it like coconut on a wedding cake. By night, though, it's mostly empty. Sometimes he even gets the whole place to himself. Nights like that he'll sit on a bench and listen to the river pass below, gurgling happily. Sometimes five minutes will go by, sometimes forty. When he's alone on the bridge he forgets about the jewelry stores stuffed to the gills with gold and diamonds, and the couples snapping padlocks onto the railings, and everything else he hates about being here when the sun's out. When he's alone it's just stone over water, but tonight he's not alone.

It's black mostly, the dog – the kind of blackness that absorbs light, that sucks in warmth and sound and good intentions. There seems to be a pigeon in its mouth... correct. It's looking up at Tony with these big eyes, proud eyes, as if to say *Yes, I've killed this pigeon. Why? I'll tell you when you're older.* Tony smiles. He likes dogs, Tony, and this is one of those medusa-headed dogs that looks like the business end of a mop. A Bob Marley dog. Puli, that's the name. He's pretty sure it's a Polish breed, and he's seen a couple of the gypsies outside town with them – but they're Romanian, aren't they? This dog, though, this one's a mess. A stray. It's got mud in its stiffened dreadlocks, and big clumps of dirt or maybe even blood. Its eyes are one-hundred-percent invisible under its tangled mats, and it smells the way the Arno smells when you get right down close to it. It's not a wet dog smell, it's closer to piss and old man's cologne.

I wonder how long the thing's been out here, Tony wonders. From the looks of it, probably a few weeks or more but it's hard to say. For all its history and culture, all its past glories and present fame, Florence remains a city. Like all cities, it exerts strong entropy upon the unsheltered. Still, the dog's cute. It's cute covered in ugly, but cute nonetheless. He decides to feed the thing. Give it a bath, maybe even take it to the vet. He's pretty sure they've got no kill shelters now, so he won't have to feel too bad about leaving it someplace like that – anyway they can find it a home or something. Get it back to whoever lost it, or do whatever comes next. He's never thought about it before, but there must be animal shelters somewhere in Italy. Right? Gingerly, he accepts the proffered pigeon only to toss it reluctant-fingered to the curb. It lands with a stiff thud, as though it had come out of a freezer.

"Let's go inside," he says.

The dog says nothing.

Later, after the omelets, the dog will perch on the arm of Tony's couch with the long-standing permanence of a gargoyle. Like he owns the place. But at the threshold, where wood meets tile and that inexplicable feeling of belonging begins, it stops. Whines, even. The noise comes out like the scrape of a dentist's drill, and Tony is quick to say *what do you want, a formal invitation?* Like that, like it's a joke, but the dog's not laughing.

"Well alright, come in then."

With the dog and himself both fed and a little extra for the house, Tony begins to relax. Work had been a toothbrush and a statue, the latest in a long line of graffiti-related restoration jobs. The gigs pay well but there's only so many times you can see the Madonna and Child with their eyes blacked over without starting to get creeped out. The dog curls up by the sofa and Tony turns on the television. This is a nightly ritual for him. It's not that he's an addict or even a fan of anything in particular. TV is his go-to source for learning Italian. He'll watch cooking shows, crime dramas, whatever's on. Slowly but surely he's learned how to navigate most situations, especially if they involve food or police procedure.

The TV cuts to an infomercial and Tony mutes it and goes to put on a record. Tony's got a modest, but expanding, vinyl collection, and the prime star is a limited press copy of Neil

Young's *On the Beach*. He drops the needle on it and lets it spin. It's almost imperceptible under the dreadlocks, but he swears he sees the dog's ears perk up. After a few seconds of crackling static the opening jangle of "Walk On" kicks in. If he didn't know better he'd swear the dog was wagging in time. Tony snags a seat on the couch next to him and, cautiously, scratches him behind the ears. Tony's pretty sure it's a he, at least. Only one way to be sure, but he's not in a hurry.

"I should give you a bath," he says.

The dog says nothing. Tony's still thinking about the limp body of the pigeon it had in its mouth when he found it. He's known the occasional stray cat to catch birds, but never dogs. Either Tony's stumbled upon something smarter than the average canine or the dog had stumbled upon a particularly stupid pigeon. Given the state of the average city bird the latter seems more likely, but watching the dog half-nod its head to the kick drum, Tony can't help but wonder. But not too hard. One way or the other it's most likely a fluke. The dog's clearly been on a hard road for weeks, and hunting down a bird was just what it had to do. If he hadn't found the thing, brought it inside, and given it a plate of eggs, that bird would have just been dinner.

"Don't get used to it," Tony says. The dog looks at him. "The couch, I mean. I'm not trying to keep a bird murderer as a pet."

The dog snorts and, as if on command, falls asleep. Neil Young's changed his tune to something slower and less personal with "For the Turnstiles" and Tony's starting to zonk out.

"Ok, you win," he says. "We'll talk about it in the morning."

THE AMBULANCE
Paolo

ALOUD, SHE SAYS, "YOU'RE NOT GOING to try and stop me?" She actually says this.

After a moment the impotent wailing of a siren splits the silence. Red and blue light settles in pools on the hardwood, scattering around piles of clothes from the night before and clashing with the gunmetal glare of a pair of handcuffs. In the street below, street muck and cigarette ash slosh audibly under the wheels of the screaming ambulance. Paolo can't move.

She's getting dressed now, pouring herself into ten year old jeans with worn-out knees. One moment he's counting vertebrae, the next there's a black t-shirt – Pixies logo circa '89 on the back, but it's blocking the view. She's left her strapless jammed in the corner of a dresser drawer, forgotten, or else abandoned by design. A little lace *memento mori*. Her voice is as vacant as the silence that preceded it, but at least it's a woman's voice. Anyway he can't stop her: he's cuffed to the bedposts. Cuffed to his bedposts.

"I can't," he says. "You've locked me to the bed."

"Well you could say something."

He could. He could ask her to stay, but she wouldn't listen. He could ask her why, but she wouldn't answer. He could ask for a chance, for a shot. He could make a battle out of a retreat, if he wanted. But she would always win. She would leave him tattered and bloody and strewn across the floor, and all without loosening the cuffs.

The ambulance fades into the afternoon and Paolo's gotten to thinking about the Doppler Effect, trying to remember how it works. Something about sound or volume – sound changing at certain distances or sound remaining the same. It doesn't matter now. Her bags are packed, both of them. She had never brought much.

"How long did I live here, Paolo?"

She says his name, but she could just as easily be saying 'toaster' or 'bowl of soup.'

"Two months," he says. "Maybe three."

"What a fucking waste."

It had been three months, almost exactly. That first day, she'd shown up with her guitar and a stack of records. She didn't even ask his permission to come in, she just sat down. She'd slept on the couch for a few days. Like everything else, that didn't last. Now she's standing by the door, framed in the entrance like a knockoff Caravaggio backlit by the flickering exit sign. Take your shot, Paolo, he thinks. Give her something to remember you by.

"Wait," he says.

She stops with one bare foot in the hall and the bells of *Santa Maria dei Fiori* ring out. Arrogant bells. Like anyone cares it's three o'clock. Like anyone cares at all.

"Don't I get a kiss goodbye?"

A smile splits her face into a momentary quivering rictus. Then comes the fauvist snarl of a stiff zipper – her fingers find the button on her jeans and release it with an empty click, like the safety on a pistol.

"I guess a kiss wouldn't hurt," she says with a smirk, and the door slams shut behind her.

THE HOTEL
Jacob

THE SKY OVER FLORENCE IS HAZY WITH FOG of mixed origins: exhaust fumes from a fleet of Vespas, carcinogens from cigarette ash and factory smoke, the steaming stoves of a million white-tiled kitchens, and a storm just barely forming at the edge of the constantly looming smog. The blinding lights of the runway cut through the haze like a hatchet through an oak. The crowd applauds as the plane lands safely on the tarmac. As always, Jacob is the only one disappointed. Out in the fog, strangers scurry around slinging suitcases with a confidence born out of ignorance to their contents. The sign says it is alright for him to remove his safety belt. Jacob is the last off the plane, and the stewardess no longer smiles as she waves him off.

No one stops him at customs. He could be carrying anything. No one waits for him beyond the gate; no mother, or sister, or tuxedoed chauffeur. There is only the overweight cab driver he had called from the gate, standing outside smoking a cigar. He shows Jacob a picture of his kids as he throws the bags into his trunk.

"Not half bad," Jacob says, but he's not sure the cabby gets the joke. He gives him the address to the hotel. The driver has done this no less than ten thousand times this year alone, Jacob knows, but he feigns surprise and interest very well.

In the car, he asks Jacob why he's come to Florence. Jacob

says he's here for a story, which is true. The cabby wants to know what the story is, and he's not sure he should tell him. Jacob's here to write about gypsies. Specifically, to write about why people in Italy seem to hate them so much. He's not sure how the cabby feels about gypsies, so he decides to say nothing.

"It's a travel piece," Jacob says. "I'm profiling a couple of restaurants and museums for a write up on Florence."

The cabby nods with a knowing smile. Jacob can barely hear him over the Euro-pop blaring from his speakers and the clicking of the meter adding up the fare.

"My wife loves to read stories like this," he shouts into the back seat. Jacob smiles. Who doesn't? The conversation falters and dies in its infancy, but then there's only so much common language between the two of them to begin with. It's just as well. Jacob doesn't take to being misunderstood. He stares pointedly out the window at the road. Somewhere beneath the chaos of spinning wheels are clearly delineated lanes, but the drivers pay them no mind. A moment later he's dizzy. He focuses on the little details: the empty container of air freshener dangling from the rear view mirror, the Koran sitting open on the passenger's seat, the spider-web fractures obscuring the screen of the GPS.

"Have you read it?" Asks the cabby.

He's asking about the Koran, not the GPS. Jacob shakes his head no.

"We have a saying," he continues, "that God is closer to us than the veins of our necks."

He jabs two fingers into his jugular to demonstrate. Jacob realizes after a delay that he is meant to respond to this.

"Do you believe it?" Jacob asks the cabby.

"Of course I do," he replies, "I'm Turkish."

"But not all Turks are Muslims."

And nor are all Turks expatriated in Italy. Jacob's done no research on the subject, so what does he know?

"You don't have to be Muslim to know God."

Jacob doesn't argue. He wouldn't know where to begin.

"Do you believe it?" The cabby asks him. He shakes his head. "You will. Before you leave, you will."

Jacob closes his eyes and tries to sleep. He's certain he won't succeed, but maybe if he pretends that he has the cabby will stop talking. Begrudgingly, the cabby takes the hint.

Lightning strikes. Thunder pulses, haltingly, through the city's cobbled capillaries like a cardiac arrest. Jacob's hotel is six weeks' worth of shitty at best, but not eight. He'll have to call someone.

There's a cat underneath the car on the curb, a little white one with eyes as gold as the pictures Jacob's seen of the Doors of Paradise. For a second he's sure it's watching him, but when he pays the taxi it speeds off in a drippy blur. Jesus Christ, it's cold. The sign over the place – Hotel Romanza – blinks in syncopated spurts, and it's giving him a headache. When his feet hit the pavement the cat dashes past him and brushes against his leg. It only touches him for an instant but Jacob feels like his heart is going to leap out of his chest and follow it down the sidewalk. God, he thinks, do I need to sleep.

The inside of the place is better, marginally. Typical marble; clean, vaulted ceilings only lightly cracked with age. Charming would describe it, but less than aptly. There's no one here but him and the man behind the long mahogany desk, who wears a grin plucked straight from a Jehova's witness recruitment pamphlet.

"Shall I have someone take your bags?" The desk clerk asks

in his best fake English. There is still no one else here.

"No, I'd rather get them myself."

"Very good sir."

The clerk reeks of hair gel, which means the lobby reeks of hair gel. When the whole room is barely the size of a closet, smells carry. It takes him nearly fifteen minutes to process Jacob's information, which is just long enough for Jacob to get his hopes up that his reservation had gotten fucked up enough for his boss to pay for a new place. No such luck.

"I'm going to be here for about eight weeks," Jacob says, "and possibly a bit longer depending. Is it possible I could get a more permanent solution for an internet connection? I don't want to be paying per day."

"You won't have to pay at all, sir!" Exclaims the clerk. Jacob's about to breathe his first sigh of relief before the man finishes his thought. "We don't have internet available here. May I suggest, in walking distance, the city library, the hospital, and the McDonald's closest to the train station. All have publicly available wireless."

Jacob wants to fight, but he doesn't have the energy. He's torn between wanting to sleep, and wanting to eat. Jacob's been a passionate eater since he was a kid, which is part of why he took the assignment. Tell the truth, he has not one iota of interest in the plight of the Italian gypsy, but it gets him to the land of *Chianina* beef and *Brunello di Montepulciano*. It's a compromise he's willing to make.

"Can I use your phone?" Jacob asks.

"Of course," says the desk clerk. "I'll take your bags to your room and give you some privacy."

As soon as he leaves, Jacob hops the counter and sits down in the chair. It's not great, but it beats the airplane and the taxi. The first thing he's got to do now that he's landed is hook up with his fixer. This is always the diciest bit. Some of the people the magazine sets him up with are consummate professionals, they do nothing but work with magazines and newspapers and TV networks, helping them navigate the inevitable eccentricities of their home country. Some of them are friends of friends of local contacts that mean well but don't know enough to do anything more than recite a list of the local tourist traps and, if you're lucky, their favorite bars. Of course there's no motivation for them to be any better than that. They get paid the same for being terrible as they would for being great. With a sigh, Jacob punches the numbers into the phone, which is an honest to god landline. One evolutionary step from a rotary, and another from a carrier pigeon. The line on the other end rings so many times he thinks he must have been given a wrong number. He's about to throw the phone aside when the voice on the other end, nearly out of breath, responds.

"*Pronto*," says the voice, "or maybe I should say Hello, judging by the time. Are you Jacob? This is Tony, Tony Ducati."

Jesus Christ, Jacob thinks. Another goddamn idiot.

THE GUITAR
Kitsune

IT'S A WHITE STRATOCASTER. Black pick guard, black neck. She's had it for years now. The thing is more or less invincible. She had a dream, once, that it had taken a bullet for her. She gave it a strum, even with the bullet hole, and it sang perfectly, so loud its screeching burned her would-be assassin to a crisp. It was just a dream, but it had a ring of truth to it.

She scans the crowd; a few familiar faces, but mostly strangers. It's always like this in the spring. Tourists flood Florence from every corner of the globe, and they love to stop for street musicians. Of course, they're expecting an old Italian man picking arpeggios with a somber air of quiet dignity, but they'll stop for her and her guitar just the same. She sees an old friend at the back. Tony's here, she realizes. That's all it takes to make a show out of a street gig, one face. One smiling face and a beer bottle.

She tunes up and starts her first song. "Ohio" by Neil Young. It's the only song by the guy she even likes, but Tony loves him. It's a great number, honestly. The drums jangle like spurs on boot-heels, the guitar crunches and rambles, and the voice line rages and wails and bemoans a grand social injustice she's too young to really know anything about. She's only got the guitar for now, but she loves to scream the lead part, and she loves this solo. Tony emits a big goofy grin, and she knows she got it right.

Truth be told, though, the thing's always had some problems. The D string gets knocked out of tune ever so slightly any time her strumming moves beyond Glam into Metal. The paint's worn around the edges of the pickguard, and no matter how long she spends trying to make it behave, it never sounds right in anything other than standard tuning. It barely tolerates capos. Still, there is not a human being that she loves more than this guitar, much to her mother's chagrin.

On one occasion, the man she'd been sleeping with had bought her a new one. She'd come home and it was sitting there on his kitchen table, laid out like a corpse in a casket in its case. He'd bought her a Red Fender that looked like it had scraps of glitter in its paint and she hated it the second she looked at it. They didn't split right away after she made him take it back, but when they did they both knew the guitar was what had killed it. She'd always had a thing about presents as a general rule. Guys buying her things always felt like they were trying to pay her for sex, when a simple yes or no question would usually have gotten the job done.

"Ohio" comes to a crashing halt, and she slides into a new number. She changes it up with "Ziggy Stardust", and half the crowd leaves. Florentines are used to their street artists being a good bit quieter than this. They're used to little British expats singing James Taylor in the apses of the Uffizi, or old Austrians showing off on classical arrangements – Mozart, Schubert, Chopin. They're not used to something you can hear more than a block or two away. They're not used to the Clash, at least not at eleven in the morning. To be fair, it's not for everybody.

"Alright, little lady," she says, "let's go ahead and close shop."

She pushes the equipment into a tiny alcove as the first taxi passes by, and pantomimes smoking a cigarette. The driver checks her out in passing, but he's not looking at her guitar. She starts to cough. She would almost say she'd taken the fake smoking bit too far, but it feels real. It hurts, deep in her chest, in a way that lingers for a while after it's done. Try as she might to think of anything else, the cough reminds her of her father. He had smoked three packs a day until he couldn't smoke any, and he always used to call his cough 'the first sign of the apocalypse'. He never got to decide what the second sign was. Anything else, think of anything else. The cops, she decides. Typically she figures she gets about fifteen minutes before someone calls the cops. Her math hasn't been wrong yet.

"Kitty!" Tony calls to her from across the crowd.

He started calling her Kitty instead of her stage name a few months ago, and at first she figured she'd just ignore it. Then she realized she kind of liked it. Then she started to insist on it. Most of her friends, or the guys she met at her gigs, couldn't get their mouth around the full name – Kitsune – and she'd yet to let anybody other than her mother in on her real name. She'd come close with Paolo, but he'd disappointed her one too many times. Besides, she liked Kitsune. It reminded her of her sister, which most days was kind of nice. The name was Japanese, of course, not Korean, but beggars can't always be choosers.

"What's up, Tony?"

"I heard you plug your amp in from half a block away, so I came over. What've you got it cranked to, eleven?"

She makes a 'ha ha' face at him, but doesn't laugh. He's not funny, and anyway she knows as well as he does that he's got the times and places she sets up for 'impromptu' shows more or less memorized. She knows as well as he does that he's here on purpose, and he's seen her go through these motions a hundred times. He's her biggest fan, like it or not.

"What are you on your way to, then?" She asks.

Truth be told, she doesn't want to know. Tony's nice, and loyal, and on the rarest of occasions even funny, but most of the time he's just boring. He's a glorified librarian for the British

Institute and when he's not editing a journal he's touching up a painting that looked perfectly fine before he started scrubbing it. Not even he seems to like his job, but he never does anything to change it.

"Actually," he says, "the institute gave me a new gig. Some visiting writer's supposed to be doing a big piece on the city, and I'm supposed to show him around."

He's like a kid with candy. He knows he's got something interesting for a change and he wants her to see it, too. The only problem is he's told her this so many times she's lost what little interest she had to begin with. It's not his fault. She's learned the hard way not to invest, over the years. It never ends well.

"So you're on your way to meet him?"

Tony nods, "we're supposed to have lunch in a few minutes."

She waves him on, and starts boxing up her amplifier. She gets about halfway through her routine before she hears a siren. Right on cue.

THE CART
Jacob

THE CROWD SURROUNDS THE OPEN DOORS of the *Santa Maria dei Fiori*, pulsing with expectant religious fervor. Jacob, having arrived early, sits near the front with his eyes on the festivities. They've been doing this since the Crusades, apparently. They call it the *Scoppio del Carro*; the 'explosion of the cart'. The priests have set up the massive wood and metal cart on the cobblestones in front of the cathedral, loaded with fireworks. It looks like it'd burn, the cart, or burst entirely. But that isn't what usually happens. At the appointed time a dove – mechanical, of course – will fly along a wire out the church doors, colliding with the cart and triggering a massive pyrotechnic display. That's the plan at least.

Generally, Jacob hates being packed into crowds this tight. It's an occupational hazard to be surrounded by people, but to be this close drives him a bit batty. He's looking for every angle of escape, but it's too close-knit. There's no way out so he looks for a distraction, anything tangible. He doesn't have to look far. The woman in front of him has her hair bleached blond and strung up with a hawk feather and an assortment of beads. He can feel her stranger's shoulders digging into his chest as she leans into him to get a better angle for her camera. He can smell the perfume she spritzed over her hair and neckline: citrus and verbena. There's a little rumbling in the pit of his stomach.

Another occupational hazard: he's nearly always hungry.

A gasp from the crowd. The bird flies. There's a squeal like a birthing baby's squeal, volume competing with pitch and peaking with the immediate peripheral discovery of mortality. The newborn blob of volatile sulfur has a moment to think – I'm going to explode – before sizzling silent with a puff of smoke and tumbling, invisible, to earth. He watches the fireworks. There's a very strange rhythm to them. They fluctuate between bursts of intense multi-colored sparking and slow, single cracks of a consistent dull yellow – an inconsistent sine curve of noise and color and fire. The whole thing lasts about a minute, and leaves the square smelling of smoke and chemicals. Bits of paper and ash clutter the ground and blow in the slight breeze like detritus in the tide. He brushes some out of his hair.

The woman in front of him has put her camera away, but she hasn't moved from her position unintentionally nestled into his chest. At least he assumes it's unintentional. She may know full well what she's doing, and a part of him hopes she does. Part of him hopes she'll let her camera fall and reach her hands behind her to pull him closer. For a moment Jacob is struck by the intimacy of their position. He considers wrapping his arms around her waist but leaves them planted firmly at his side. This takes a surprising degree of self-control. His stomach growls again, loud enough that he's certain she can hear it. He shakes his head and tries to think about something, anything else. Fireworks. Citrus. Christ on the cross.

Time passes. A few last fireworks squeak through, deliberately or not. Eventually there's a long enough silence that it's clear all the ones that work have done their thing. Slowly the crowd starts to thin, and slowly the mess is cleared. The debris is swept up and the cart dragged away. The square seems empty, and the crowd alien, in its absence. The feeling doesn't last long. Much of the crowd follows a procession of chanting priests onto the next station of their Easter tradition, whatever that might be, but a few remain. This has always been the part he likes best of any kind of ceremony – the recessional. He likes watching the brooms erase all evidence of any activity, likes watching the few remaining souls spin their wheels and twiddle their thumbs as the crowds disperse. Usually, he's the last man standing, which is just how he likes it.

Against his better judgment, he's thinking about the woman from the crowd. He doesn't usually go in for Asian women, but there was something about her that he responded to. Or at least something that his body did. It could have been the perfume. Maybe it was the sleek black dress, or maybe it was what the dress let show. Hell, maybe it was the tattoo. Watching her as she walked off, he'd seen it wrapped around her calf. It was a foxtail, mostly in black outline, but with a little bit of white around the tip. It was a beautiful piece with a bit of a water-color feel to it, inked well beyond the caliber he's used to seeing, and he's seen his fair share. He has a thing for girls with tattoos. There's no point thinking about it, he tells himself. There's no point guessing if she's got any more, and no point wondering where she was going dressed like that. You're never going to see her again in a city this size. With that in mind, he remembers his job and makes a decision. He's come all the way here, he might as well pretend to be a tourist, at least for a little while. He decides to climb the dome.

Like it or not, the *Duomo* is Florence's most enduring landmark, a behemoth of renaissance architectural masterwork said to be so beautiful that when St. Peter's Basilica was under construction in nearby Rome, they'd agreed to keep it just a few inches shorter than Brunelleschi's dome out of respect. At least that's what his idiot fixer had told him. There's a door on the building's right-hand side that they leave open with a ticket taker during the day, leading to a staircase. It's some five hundred steps, little shallow stone ones worn shiny and flat by centuries of footsteps. Aside from being a ridiculous twelve Euro to enter, climbing the dome is the exact sort of touristy bullshit Jacob usually avoids when he travels, but he's decided to make an exception. He's decided to look at Florence like a foreigner, instead of like a citizen. Maybe the view will be perspective he needs.

At the top he's part of a crowd that feels absolutely no smaller than the one he'd just left. On a rational level he knows it has to be. It's at most twenty people, because that's all that the space can accommodate. There are absolutely no Italians to be found, which he expected, but he's surprised by the diversity. A couple of ruddy-faced Brits won't stop moaning about the heat and complaining in advance of the steps on the way down. A pair of limber Australians is planning their next adventure, passing what looks to be a mostly-drained flask back and forth between mouthfuls of their ridiculous accent. An old Japanese woman who Jacob is genuinely impressed could make the climb does nothing with the view but take pictures. And then there's the kid.

Jacob hates kids. Always has, at least since he was done with being one himself. Kids, to Jacob, represent the amazing difference between humans and the rest of the world order. Even deer, which people think of as helpless little creatures that leap almost purposefully into the grills of their SUVs, can walk within minutes of their birth. Predators will practice their hunting skills on insects and in play with their siblings, only days after emerging into the world. They're not helpless, not totally. They're not yet as strong as what they will be, but they're not helpless. And they know their limits. Human children seem to be totally oblivious to their vulnerability. If Jacob picked that child up right now there would be nothing stopping him from tossing him off the building. The kid certainly couldn't. Maybe his mother could, but probably not in time. These are the kinds of intrusive thoughts he gets constantly around children, and which make it so difficult for him to be around them. Also, they smell.

Jacob looks out at the view, desperately seeking a distraction. Florence from the air is a gridded mess of terra cotta rooftops and white marble. It's beautiful, but it's a cliché. It's a postcard. He's glad he saw it, but he wouldn't look at it again on purpose. What surprises him most of all is how far he has to look to find green. It's miles off, on the far side of the river. He makes a mental note of this in case he needs the fresh air, and then the kid starts to scream. He wants to go down, he says. This is boring, he says. Why did we come here, we could have gone skiing, he says. They could have. They should have. One more time, Jacob closes his eyes and thinks about heaving the kid from the top of the cupola, and his bones shattering into a jigsaw puzzle when he crashes into the cobblestone below.

"You got a problem, mister?" The mother asks him.

He doesn't say anything. There's no need to state the obvious.

On the walk down, Jacob's mind wanders back to the girl. He's got a meeting with his fixer, Tony, around the same time tomorrow. There's no chance he'd know her, right? Jacob smiles. There's a chance. And if not, it can't be that hard to find her. In a city like Florence, a girl with a hawk feather in her hair stands out like a bloody corpse on the sidewalk.

THE GIRL
Paolo

THE GIRL WITH THE EGYPTIAN EYELINER takes a pull on her glass of Aquavit. She's been making punctuated eyes at Paolo all evening, no nonsense eyes. He's trying to tell if they're question marks or exclamation points, but either way she's forming a complete sentence. Her dress is V-cut deep enough to get her burned at the stake in some countries, but on further inspection there's something about her that pushes the eye away. A certain coldness he can't put into words. She's at least eight years his junior, though, and American. In other words, she's his type.

She slides her firewater down the bar, arriving on his right. From the vacuum of her dress she produces what appears to be a business card.

"That's not my real name," she says.

Paolo grunts and points to his glass. The bartender refills it with a bleary wink. He opts to wait for her to continue.

"I judge a man by his drink," she obliges. "And I don't waste my time on men with martinis."

She's serious. Paolo takes a sip of glorious twenty-four karat whiskey and wonders what it says about him. He wonders if she keeps a list of this information somewhere in her purse, or if she has it committed to memory.

"What about tequila?" He asks.

"Bad for the breath."

"Gin?"

"Old women and country club owners drink gin."

There's definitely a complete table of all this data somewhere in her possession, and probably a small folder with scientific data backing each claim. Nothing else would justify that level of confidence.

"Whiskey?" He says, pointing to his glass. She doesn't respond.

They don't flinch when they drink, but the similarities end there. She's taller than average, but not tall. Pale but not sallow. Her eyes are deep and colorless, and they lock onto Paolo's like targeting computers. She must blink, but he can't seem to catch her at it. Her drink is empty. Paolo calls for the bartender. They sip in silence for a minute.

"You're a local." She isn't asking.

"Yes," he confirms, "I was born at a hospital about a block from here."

"The big one."

He nods. Everyone knows the building. Its ambulances are a constant nuisance throughout the city center, but he's always loved it. It's less ornate than the other landmarks – there's a solidness to it that makes the rest of the city stronger by association.

"So what about you?" He asks her.

"What about me?"

He points to the fire-water in the tumbler in front of her.

"Aquavit is clean. It's strong. It's unpretentious."

Paolo snorts. On any other night he wouldn't entertain this labor-intensive of a flirtation, but he's eager for the distraction. Kitty's on his mind. A waste, she'd called him. If he was a waste, he might at least get wasted.

"No one drinks it." He prods the Girl with the Egyptian

Eyeliner. "You might as well wear a sign that says 'look how much I know about liquor.'"

"The drink is unpretentious. You could call drinking it a pretentious act, but that's got nothing to do with the substance itself."

She probably has a point, but he doesn't understand it, nor would anyone else in this bar. This bar's the sort of place that still plays Italian radio hits from the seventies when every other dive in town's at least switched to Bon Jovi to pull in the Americans. It's the sort of place you'd never expect a girl like this to drink, but she's got an answer for that too.

"I come to this bar because they have it on the shelf," she says.

"I come here because nobody else does," says Paolo.

He gestures. There are five people in the bar, including the bartender. He's been coming in for years, and tonight is the busiest he's ever seen it. The place only stays in business because its few regular patrons drink enough to keep it open. Paolo suspects the mob may also be involved, but he's never confirmed it.

"Alright," he says. "Alright I'll bite. Why me?"

She downs the last of her drink and begins to gesture, but Paolo stops her. He raises a hand and the bartender slides a new glass down the bar without delay.

"I didn't say you could buy me a drink."

"You also didn't answer my question."

"Well, as you've pointed out, there's not a wide array of options on display here."

"The night is young. There are other bars, lots of them."

She smiles around the rim of her glass. Her teeth are impeccably clean, and possibly a touch sharper than normal. It might be his imagination. It's the sort of smile you'd see in a black and white movie rather than a dive bar in Florence, but only he seems to grasp the significance of the gesture. That said it's not a light up the room kind of smile, at least not fluorescent. It's more like a candle. It's the sort of smile that an art critic would spend a couple dozen pages explaining in flaccid prose, ultimately saying nothing.

"I can leave if you want me to," she says.

"I didn't say I wanted you to," he says. "I just asked why me?"

"And I told you."

"No, you didn't, but you were very clever. Was it the whiskey?"

"Not exclusively."

Well, it certainly wasn't his staggering good looks. Paolo checks out the room. She has a point about the options on the table. The only other man in the room under forty is just barely that, and the years have done him no favors. His belly seems to be colonizing the bar stool next to it, and the locals aren't putting up a fight.

"Truth be told," she says, her voice dropping to a conspiratorial whisper, "truth be told I picked you for a very simple reason."

"Do go on," he says.

She smiles again, and the light blows out entirely. Her voice drops so low that he can barely hear it over the sound of the bartender waxing the counter.

"I picked you because I knew if I came up to you and told you I was going to fuck you into a stupor you'd listen."

He gestures to the bartender to clear his tab. The old pervert gives him a wink and a nod, and Paolo tries to pretend the man won't be thinking about this for the next week or longer.

"So," he says, leaning in closer, "where are you staying?"

The Girl with the Egyptian Eyeliner answers his question by leading him on a whirlwind tour of the city's darkest allies. By the last one, he's moving a hand to unfasten her bra through the back of her dress, which he's started to unzip. She's not wearing one. Her apartment's on the same block as the San Lorenzo chapel, just above the street that turns into the leather and knickknack market by day.

"One more thing," she says at the doorway. "If you see any of my roommates, do not engage. They're just sycophants."

It's an odd word choice, but Paolo's less interested in examining that than he is in dragging her back to her bedroom to finish what they've started.

"I'm serious," she says.

"Your wish is my command," he says, and pushes her up against the door. She likes being pinned to walls, but she's good at wiggling out, too. She likes to be in charge. Paolo likes that she likes that.

"I'm going to give you my number now, because I'm going to forget later, and you're not going to ask if I don't give it to you."

He's not going to call her. She must know that. There's a twinkle in her eye that says she does, but she doesn't care. She fumbles with the key while he slides his hands up the inside of her dress. No underwear, either. She's definitely his type.

THE CAT
Tony

"CONSIDER FOR A MOMENT," SAYS Jacob, grinning like the big cat in question, "Consider for a moment the jaguar."

Tony nods at him in that way that he's pretty sure will come off as encouraging. Jacob's always talking about cats, like there's nothing better he could be doing with his time. He talks like he's a cat expert, but near as Tony can tell, he's not an expert in much of anything other than talking.

"The jaguar is ninety percent muscle. The jaguar can drag an eight hundred pound bull twenty-five feet in its mouth, uphill. The jaguar kills by piercing the brain of its prey with exceptionally strong jaws. It's a beautiful animal."

"Of course," Tony replies. Some of these statements might even be true.

"But at the same time, it's a killer."

Jacob's always making points like this. He's always talking about Survival of the Fittest and Natural Order. Tony, he never talks about anything. At this exact moment they are sitting at a little table on the street, waiting for gnocchi and white wine. He hasn't said anything, but Tony picked the place so he could wait nearby for the dog to get groomed. He could have told his lunch guest, but he wasn't sure how to broach the subject. In spite of himself, Tony's starting to like Jacob. He's good at his job and he takes extra steps to get a good taste for the city. His passion is clear enough that Tony's willing to put up with a little bit of the eccentricity that emanates from him like heat from asphalt. He can even deal with a little bit of aggression.

"What I mean is," Jacob continues, "Its aesthetic derives from its desire to kill. Does that make sense? It's beautiful because it's a killer, not in spite of that fact. The spots, the muscles, the fur, the teeth - they're all adaptations, all designed to make the perfect predator, the perfect cold blooded killer."

They're filling the time between courses with debate, apparently. Mostly, Tony doesn't like to discuss these sorts of things, but Jacob's good company and he was the one who brought it up.

"So what's your point," he says.

"My point is that humans are no different."

Tony smiles expectantly, and takes another mouthful of bread. Traditionally, the bread in Florence has no salt. This is the result of a now-defunct rivalry with Pisa that spanned centuries of insults, politics, and outright warfare. Pisa set up an embargo, denying the Florentines salt, so they made their bread without it to spite them. Tony would much rather be telling these kinds of stories, but they're not what Jacob wants to hear.

"I mean Christ, Tony, do you even read the headlines these days? I wrote a true crime piece, years ago, on a man that ate his dog. He skinned it, and ate it with some of his buddies."

Jacob used to write for a newspaper – for The Newspaper, as far as it goes in the states – but these days he's hitched his wagon to a relatively reputable magazine. This of course is why he's here to begin with, and why he's talking to Tony at all. In his role with the British Institute Tony's often asked to entertain writers, artists, and journalists, and point them towards the things they need to see for their story. Unfortunately, this particular subject is not his area of expertise.

"Why'd they do it?" Tony asks.

As he speaks, a plate of gnocchi slides into view in front of him. Without meaning to, Tony thinks of the little black dog getting its dreadlocks cleaned in a sink basin a block away. He wonders what sort of owner it might have escaped from. He wonders if maybe trying to help it get back to them might be a mistake.

"What do you mean why did they do it, it's what people do! Jesus, do you think you're any different?"

"I've never eaten a dog," say Tony, and takes a big bite of gnocchi.

"But you've eaten cows. Birds. Pigs. Insects, probably, on accident. You're a predator, Tony. We're a predatory species."

Whenever he says that word, predator, his lips pull back and a tiny rush of air lights past the gums, the incisors, and his razor-sharp off-white canines. His are the jagged teeth of a print journalist: they're too pointed and useful for television. His voice sounds like fresh asphalt smells. You wouldn't trust it to tell you the weather if you were standing outside, but you wouldn't want it to stop, either.

"But what this guy did, that's different," Tony says. "Dogs are different."

"How? How are they any different?"

"We have an obligation to them. We domesticated them. They were predators, and we domesticated them, and now they're fun-loving little toys for people."

"You think a dog couldn't kill a man?" Jacob asks.

Tony thinks about the pigeon, resting unbloodied between the dog's jaws.

"That's not what I'm saying." He says. Still, he hopes it's true.

"It could, and you know it. Look at the teeth. It's adapted to be a killer, a fighter, a predator."

"And what about you?" Tony asks. "How have you adapted?"

Jacob gets this look like a magician peering over his cape, or a vampire about to go for the throat. Tony counts three sleazy jumps of his bushy brows. His eyeteeth shine with fresh saliva.

"I saw a girl today," Jacob says.

Tony waits for him to elaborate, but he opts to attend to his gnocchi instead. It takes him five minutes to alternate between savoring and inhaling it, and to drain his wine.

"A couple years back," Jacob says, "I was given what I guess you'd call a black box for an airplane that crashed, only it wasn't the black box. The black box is part of the plane, it belongs to the airline. It's just people talking to each other about how to keep the plane from crashing, and then screaming, and then silence. This was video that had been shot by a passenger. It's thirty seconds long, and twenty seconds of it is him talking about the woman half an aisle away brushing her teeth. Can you imagine that? Can you imagine knowing your death was minutes, moments away and thinking to do that?"

Tony would prefer to be silent, but long speeches like that sort of demand some kind of response. Instead, he changes tack.

"Listen," he says, "I've got a handful of people for you to talk to. You're writing about the Roma, yes?"

Jacob nods, sullen. He wants to talk about the girl, either the one he saw or the one with the toothbrush, but Tony frankly has no interest in either.

"Well I've got a few contacts you can talk to. There's a policeman we work with at the Institute that I know has had to handle a few raids on gypsy camps outside of the city. There's a vendor I know at the market who trades with one of the camps directly, and he might be able to set you a meeting. I don't know any gypsies myself, unfortunately."

"How do you feel about them?" Jacob asks.

To be totally honest, Tony's never thought about it. They're a constant presence but not the kind you spend any energy thinking about, because thinking about it would make you sad.

"I don't know that I feel anything," Tony says truthfully. "I guess they're kind of tragic, really. I think there's a real chicken and egg thing with their reputation and their situation. I'm not sure if the ones you see who actually are pickpockets are doing it because it's what they've always done, or because they basically can't do anything else. Almost no one will hire them, so what are they supposed to do?"

Jacob nods, and he writes a few terse notes in a little spiral notebook he produces from seemingly nowhere. Tony makes out 'chicken and egg' and feels a flush of pride. He'd thought that was a sharp line.

"Listen, Tony," he says. "I'm glad you've got those contacts, really, they're a big help. But I need another favor, too."

Tony nods. He's paid well enough for this that as long as the guy doesn't want to sleep at his place, he's willing to be flexible.

"I need you to help me meet some people that have nothing to do with this. I need a baseline feel for what the city is like, you know? How does a Florentine talk? What do they do when they go home. How do they fuck? Stuff like that."

Tony swallows, hard. This is one area he can only be but so useful in. Truth be told he doesn't know very many people. Truth be told, he's never tried to. He's about to say as much to Jacob when the man completely loses focus. He's staring off across the street with a look somewhere between curiosity and – is it fear? Of course not, but Tony's not sure what else to call it.

"I've seen that cat before," Jacob says. The feline in question is all white, with eyes that somehow read as golden from all the way across the street. It's sitting on top of a Vespa someone parked haphazardly half-on half-off the sidewalk, and it really does seem to be looking at them.

"When did you see it?" Tony asks.

"The night I landed," says Jacob, "It was right by my hotel. That's blocks away from here."

"It's probably just a stray," says Tony. "God knows there's hundreds of them here."

"Of course. Right."

"Listen," says Tony, "I've got to get back, the British Institute's hosting a conference on restoration and I've got to be there. I'll get back to you on local color contacts, ok?"

Jacob hasn't broken eye contact with the cat. It seems like a bit of an overreaction for a glorified case of déjà vu, frankly.

"In the meantime, if you want local color, check out some of the museums. I'll make you a list."

Jacob's nodding like he's still distracted, but he manages to take the piece of paper Tony hands him with names and places scribbled on it.

"I'll get the bill," Jacob says. Tony's got no complaints there. "But before I forget, the girl. She was stunning, Tony, I mean honestly. I don't say this lightly, but easily a perfect ten. I saw her at the Easter thing they do by the Duomo."

Tony's always hated the numeric scale. There's so many variables in attraction it can't possibly account for, and it's so reductive. But still, he knows what Jacob's saying.

"*La scoppio del caro*," Tony fills in.

"Yes, that. She was there too, watching. She was Korean, I think, maybe Japanese, I'm not really sure."

Tony feels a pit growing in his stomach, because somehow, he knows what's next.

"She had these beads strung up in her hair, and a hawk feather. And this tattoo of a foxtail curled around her leg."

Tony's never been good at poker. He must be showing his hand, because Jacob stops his description right there.

"You know who I'm talking about, don't you. You know her?"

He does. It's a damn shame he never learned to lie properly.

"Yeah, actually. That's Kitty – Kitsune. She's a musician in town, I've been to a bunch of her shows. I don't know if she'd call us friends or not but we've definitely hung out."

Jacob's got a look on his face like a dog that's smelled something good in another dog's yard he can just barely reach through the fence.

"You got a number?"

Tony sighs. All the possibilities fly through his head at once, and none of them are good. Still, Jacob's only going to be around a couple of weeks. Eight total, one of which is almost done. Maybe it won't be so bad.

"I do," he says, "but she's pretty private. I tell you what, I'll tell her about you and if she wants to call you she'll call you. Does that work?"

Jacob seems satisfied, and goes back to looking for the cat. His eyes widen, but it's not the cat he's looking at. The groomer's carrying the dog across the street like an armed warhead, and the man looks for all the world like it exploded in his face. He's bleeding from dozens of cuts and scratches, but the dog's clean.

"Jesus Christ," Tony mutters. "You must be miserable at grooming if he went after you like that."

He drops the dog in Tony's lap, and shakes his head.

"*Mai piu, capisce?*" He more or less growls. "*Giammai.*"

Jacob's staring at the dog, now. It's not the same look that he gave the cat, but they could be cousins. The weirdest part is that the dog is looking back at him. If it wasn't impossible, Tony would have said they'd known each other.

"This is my dog," says Tony, "I guess. He found me on the street a few nights back."

"I've got to go," Jacob replies. To the point as always, and quick. He doesn't even put his chair back, he's gone so fast. To Tony's surprise, the dog's growling. It's the sound of gravel under tires, and it leaves him empty. Against his better judgment, he thinks about the pigeon.

THE PAINTING
Jacob

TONY'S SENT HIM TO ONE OF FLORENCE'S smaller museums, hollowed out of an old *palazzo* on the *Via Ghibellina*. He's supposed to be experiencing local culture at the micro level. The big museums are for the tourists, the small ones are for the locals – that's what he'd said. Jacob didn't argue.

The place is hosting a big exhibit on Goya; a complete retrospective. Jacob knows the name, but he's never seen any of his pieces. Older Florentine men stand in neat semi-circles around aquatint prints with ominous titles. A piece called What More Can One Do? shows a soldier slicing the cock off of a naked man with his saber while his comrades watch. It was made as part of a series, Goya's chronicle of a bloody civil war in his home country of Spain. The Disasters of War, aptly named. Frankly a little on the nose for Jacob's taste, but most art is.

He's never been the sort to bother with decorations. Back in the states, the walls in his place are bare. Spartan is the word the girls he brings home use for it, at least the smarter ones. Some of them get ideas like they can put their stamp on it. They'll bring pots with flowers, they'll hang pictures of the two of them or of parks or mountains or rivers on the walls. One girl mounted an entire series of Japanese kanji in his living room, and a huge print of The Great fucking Wave. The best part of kicking them to the curb is chucking that shit out the door after them. The girl he'd told Tony about — Kitsune, he'd said? — that one he'd let decorate though. She could hang some of those awful posters of kittens hanging from flowers or getting out of bathtubs with motivational phrases stamped on them and he wouldn't mind.

The next room of the exhibit's got a different tone. They have simpler titles — things like Goat and Old Men Eating and The Dog. The Dog is two toned, with maybe ninety percent of it made up by a long swathe of sepia stained sky. At the base of the painting is the dark curve of a hill, with the head of a dog just barely peeking over. It's black, mostly, the dog, though there's highlights of sepia that show the direction of the light. The Goat shows a huddle of poorly defined people in Biblical-era getups huddled around a dark robed figure with the head of a goat and the barest white outline of an eye shining from it. They're disturbing images, somehow more so than The Disasters of War. A sign posted at the entrance of the room reveals that these were the last paintings Goya had done before his death. found on the walls of his home, and removed carefully to be preserved as they were. They spoke of insanity and depression. They spoke of a genuine lack of hope. For the first time in his life, Jacob's found art he understands.

Walking around the room, though, there's one that really resonates. It's not Asmodeus or Atropos with their warped faces and mythological allusions, or The Duel with its uncharacteristic pops of blue and impending violence. It's Saturn. Jacob's heard the story of Saturn before — the God, not the planet named after him. Known to the Greeks as Cronos, he was Zeus's father, and the first in a long line of Gods in that pantheon to attain power by killing his father. There's any number of versions of the story, most involving a sickle and castration, but Goya was interested in something else entirely. Goya depicts Saturn as a colossus, occupying the bulk of the scene. His eyes wide, he shoves a bloodied body, already decapitated, into his maw. He looks helpless, despite being omnipotent. He looks terrified.

Looking at the picture, Jacob starts to feel an old hunger coming back. When it hits, there's nothing that makes it go away. He can eat and eat, and never get his fill. No matter who he fucks, he isn't satisfied. He's lived years bouncing from job to job, woman to woman, city to city, running from it, and now it's back. It didn't take long this time, not at all, for it to return.

In a daze, Jacob stumbles out of the museum. He feels drunk, but that's not possible. He feels sick, which is possible but not likely. He makes the trip back to his hotel carefully, unsure if he really remembers the way. Several times he blacks out, and finally he knows he can't make it any further without resting. He slumps into an alley, and passes out against a wall. When he wakes up again, it's pitch black and cold outside. In his lap is a dead pigeon.

THE LANDLORD
Paolo

THERE'S A RED LIGHT BLINKING ON AND OFF and Paolo's landlord is standing over his bed dripping cigarette ashes. It's eleven o'clock. Paolo rubs the sleep and the nicotine out of his eyes and asks the obvious question:

"Did you bring one of those for me?"

Right about then he sees his bags are packed, which is new. He hasn't even done his laundry since... well, it's not important. He sits up.

"We going somewhere, Franco?"

"You are."

"Where am I going?"

The old man shrugs, which is a perfectly reasonable answer. Before today Paolo would have described his landlord as a nice guy, but even nice guys need money for something eventually, the bastards.

"I don't suppose you'd give me a month to find a job?"

"No."

Alright, then. Looks like it's time to get dressed.

Franco's left him shorts and a t-shirt, neatly folded on the dresser, which would be great if it wasn't raining. Franco doesn't leave the house much. Paolo puts them on without fanfare or complaint. It's a testament to how little he's achieved in his adulthood that Franco was able to pack for him in the space of a morning without him even knowing it had happened. He isn't the owner of anything in the apartment except his clothes, a couple of posters, and some books.

So he's standing there, Paolo, in shorts and a t-shirt and a leather trench coat dug out of one bag or another, when he remembers the girl in his bed. She's dead to the world and Franco is still hovering over her, dripping ashes. There's surely a headache coming her way but she's got to wake up eventually. Paolo starts by throwing a shoe.

"Oy! What is your problem?"

Which is such an innocent question that Paolo almost regrets what happens next. She's yawning, stretching, and rubbing her eyes when a series of realizations strike her.

1) I am naked.
2) I have no idea where my clothes are.
3) There is an old man inches from my face.

She screams, and covers herself with the bedsheet. Paolo wonders how long Franco had let himself look before waking them up, but he puts the thought aside for now. Paolo looks around the room, but he doesn't see her clothes anywhere. Were they packed? Did Franco throw them out? Did he hide them in the front room so she'd have to walk past him to get to them? Maybe he's not such a nice guy after all.

"Franco has informed me that it's time for us to go. Well time for me, mostly. I don't think he knew you were here."

It would be nicer if he knew her name. It would probably be more comforting for her to hear it. Unfortunately, that isn't information he's bothered to acquire, and asking now would just be tasteless. A joke, really.

"Do you remember where you put your clothes?" He asks her, hopeful.

Numbly, she gestures to the bathroom. Paolo gives Franco a look, and leaves the room to fetch them. They're in a pile in front of his vanity. He imagines her 'changing into something more comfortable' here, and stopping to check her figure in the mirror. Did she think she looked good? Was she confident? She hadn't been a bad lay, all things considered, but he hadn't been planning on a repeat performance. Paolo grabs her clothes and, despite his guilt at leaving her alone with Franco, takes a moment to rummage through the cabinets to be sure they were cleared out. He might not get another chance.

When he gets back Paolo tells her to get dressed, and tosses her the clothes without too much pomp and circumstance. She casts a pointed look at Franco.

"Let's take a walk," Paolo says to his landlord.

In his living room, Paolo realizes there's one thing Franco forgot to pack. He's got a handful of books on one of the shelves, old crime novels his mom had kept around the house when he was a kid and she was alive. They're ridiculous little things with titles like "A Dame to Die For" and "Black Angels of Anaheim". They've got sentimental value, though, so he shoves them in his suitcase. It's been ages since I've read these, Paolo thinks. He ought to fix that.

"I hate to do this to you, Paolo, you know that."

Franco's trying to regain his nice guy status after ogling the twenty year old in his tenant's bed. Paolo figures he can play along.

"So don't," he says, knowing that it's too late now.

"You don't have any money, kid. The rent here's twelve hundred a month, and you haven't paid in five. That means I'm out six thousand already, and I can't be out more than that. You understand."

He does. Paolo'd gotten a neat little sum from his father when he'd passed a year or so ago, and he'd let that carry him further than it ought to have. He'll have to get a job, now. The question is who would hire him.

"I only took you in in the first place as a favor to your pa, you know that?"

He does. Franco and his dad had been fast friends, though he'd never understood the friendship. His father had been a musician, a street player whose cheap clothes belied the considerable depths of his success in that field. He'd seen his father pick arpeggios that would give studio musicians blisters trying and failing to master, and do it like he was strumming a G chord. Paolo could barely do that much. They hadn't been close.

"When's this girl gonna be done, kid?" Franco asks.

It's a fair question. That's when Paolo hears some slamming in the bedroom, and that's when he realizes she's been in there way too long to just be changing. Son of a bitch.

The windows cracked open, and she's gone out. Paolo lives on the second story. It's not a great landing, but it wouldn't kill her. It's an embarrassing way to escape from an embarrassing situation, and Paolo feels a twang of guilt that she'd felt the need to stoop to that level.

"That's one way to go," says Franco.

Paolo looks out the window. She lost a shoe, or someone did. Considering it's a five inch stiletto, though, it's probably hers.

"You gonna call her back?" His landlord asks.

Paolo doesn't even have her number. He doesn't even know her name. Even if he wanted to, which he doesn't, he could as soon get her on the phone as his mother or father.

"Wasn't planning on it," he says, and his landlord chuckles.

"It's not my place to tell you what to do, Paolo. But if you don't call her you should call somebody. You can't go through life with a different person in your bed every night, it's no way to live."

Paolo thinks about that for a second. He'd never introduced Franco to Kitsune, not once in the handful of months she'd stayed here. He wonders what he would have thought of her. He wonders what she would have done if it had been her in the bed this morning. One thing's for damn sure; she wouldn't have crawled out the window.

"Anyway, you'll need a place to sleep. I'm sorry to make you, but I do hope you've got someone to call, at least for that. Maybe not her, but somebody."

There's any number of numbers in his phone. Most of them wouldn't pick up if he called them, but there's one or two that might. He thinks about calling Kitsune, and then he remembers the sound of her voice. What a fucking waste, she'd said. That's not an option. As Franco pushes him out the door, though, he realizes there is somebody he can call. Under other circumstances, he never would, but it doesn't look like there's another choice. Alone on a street corner, he pulls up the number in his phone and dials. The name flashes across his phone's screen like a silent alarm: The Girl with the Egyptian Eyeliner.

THE COUGH
Kitsune

KITTY'S LYING ON HER COUCH WHEN the cough comes back, but this time it's different. This time it's deeper, longer. It's not that scratchy little allergy cough she gets at the start of each summer, and it's not the barking cough she gets anytime she gets a cold. It's something else altogether. With the cough comes this feeling of cold settling over her body, and she feels a strange sense of relief. A fever, she thinks, I've got a fever. Fever's good. Fever isn't cancer, and it isn't the black lung, and it isn't a lot of the things that have been bouncing around in her head since the cough started. She moves to her medicine cabinet to find a thermometer, just to confirm her hypothesis. There's just one problem. When it beeps, the little screen reads ninety-eight point six. That's exactly what it ought to read, scientifically speaking. Shit, it's rare for it to be that precisely perfect. It'd be fantastic news if it didn't mean the cough was coming from something else. She needs a distraction. Something to take her mind off of it. Luckily, the phone rings. She answers, pretending easily that she's being inconvenienced.

"What's up, Tony?" She tries to keep the scratch from her voice, but she's sure he'll hear it. He's perceptive when it comes to things like that, or maybe he just cares. Not everyone does these days.

"Hey Kitty," says his voice. He sounds like a child over the phone, but she's never told him that. These kinds of things aren't kind to say, no matter how true they are. He keeps on. "You remember I told you I had that writer guy I was supposed to be helping, right?"

She rolls her eyes. Obviously she remembers. Tony's been talking about it non-stop since he found out, and he always acts like it's the first time.

"Yeah," she says. "I think I remember something like that."

"Anyway he saw you at the *scoppio del caro* and he told me about you."

She'd gone on a whim. Actually, it was her first time watching it. They'd never gone as a family when she was young, and as an adult she'd always assumed it was just a tourist trap. She couldn't say why she'd gone this year. It was just an impulse.

"He told you about me how, exactly?"

She knows the answer to this, or she's fairly certain she does. There's only a handful of ways most men talk to each other about women, and she hadn't exchanged words with the writer yet so it certainly wasn't going to be about her warm personality and caring demeanor.

"Just that he'd seen you. I guess he could tell when he described you that I knew who he meant, and he asked for an introduction."

She's actually surprised Tony's following through on that. A couple weeks before she started seeing Paolo, Tony had gotten up the courage to ask her out. Little red rose and everything. He could barely make it through the sentence, he was stuttering so badly. It was honestly sort of cute, but not in a way that made her want to go through with dating him. She'd turned him down and he was back two days later, at her band's next show, acting like nothing had happened. He probably hoped she'd forgotten. She hoped so too, but that didn't mean she had.

"So should I consider myself introduced?"

"If you want to be."

Well she is newly single, after all. Tony knows, though he made no comment about it. He'd never spoken to Paolo, but expressed nothing kind about him. There wasn't much he could have said without meeting him. He had no job, he had no talents, he had nothing except himself. It wasn't a bad self, not really. It just wasn't enough.

"Are you setting me up on a date, Tony?"

"I don't know," he says, "Am I?"

He might be. She's dated writers before, and they're usually too self-absorbed to make good partners. Still, there are worse things than going on a bad date, and it's not like she's got anything better to do.

"Well what kind of person is he? Can you at least tell me that much before you throw me into the lion's den?"

Tony pauses. He's collecting words looking for something positive, but not too positive. It's obvious to her, but he's going to do it anyway, she supposes.

"Honestly, I think he's kind of a freak. Not necessarily in a bad way, but just… he's always zagging when you think he's gonna zig, and when you think he's gonna zag he just gets up and leaves the table. I mean literally, just walks away."

Kitty laughs at that, and she knows Tony's blushing and smiling on the other end of the line. Let him, he earned this one. It was a funny mental image.

"Anyway," says Tony, "I figured you could tell him a bit about your family."

Kitty gets a chill at that. Tony doesn't know enough about her family to know that that's not a good idea. Tony might think he does, and he might think he's being clever suggesting it, but he's wrong. She takes a deep breath and keeps the anger out of her voice.

"Why's that?"

"Well he's writing about the Roma," Tony says, "and I know your dad probably ran into them a bunch since he was working in the restaurant business."

"Yeah," she says, relieved that's all he'd meant, "yeah, we had to kick them out pretty much every other evening."

"So there's at least that to talk about, if you want to."

"Ok, Tony, you can give him my number."

"Oh," he says, "I thought you could just call him."

Kitty's about to say that's just not how it works, at least not with her, but then she feels the cough coming back. It surges out of her at gale force, leaving what feels like deep gashes on the inside of her throat. The fit lasts seconds.

"Hello?" Says Tony. "Did we drop the call?"

Can he not hear it? Jesus, it sounded like a crash of rhinos stampeding from the pit of her stomach. There's no way he could have missed it, but he wouldn't have ignored it unless he had. Tony's a lot of things, but he's not insensitive. Maybe the line really did cut out.

"Just give him my number, Tony, he can call me if he wants to."

Tony's about to say something, which would amount to nothing, so she cuts him off before nothing happens.

"I've got to go now, Tony. Thanks for the call. I'll let you know what comes out of it."

With that she hangs up. She can still feel the echoes of the cough sitting heavy at the back of her throat, like a fresh coat of paint on the wall, heavy and dripping down into her gullet.

"It's the first sign of the apocalypse," she whispers to herself, her voice hoarse from that last burst. Tony hadn't noticed that either. He must be off his game – his new toy's distracting him.

In her whole apartment, which spans five rooms not counting the bathroom or the little apse from the stairs coming in, there's only one picture of her father. She's not in it. It's an old picture, from the years before her parents had made it out of North Korea. It must have been taken by a professional. Her father's in front of one of those smoky backgrounds they use for portraits, like for school or work or something. It's just him and her sister.

Most of the time she tries not to think about her sister. Kita died before they had made it to Italy. She'd never seen Florence, or the restaurant her parents had built there. She'd never seen her father's heart soften and her mother's sense of propriety shift, begrudgingly, from the values of the old country to those of the new. She'd never known her parents, not the way Kitty did. It was hard, thinking about that, not to wonder if Kita had even liked their parents. She'd been old enough to have opinions when she died. She was eight. By the time Kitty was eight, she knew exactly what she thought of her parents. She knew what they'd sacrificed for the life they'd made in Italy. She didn't know exactly what had happened to Kita, but from what she remembered she knew that if they'd stayed in North Korea her sister would still be alive. This is exactly why she tries not to think about it. The cough's sitting in her throat like a horror movie monster waiting on another chance to peek its head out for a jump scare. There's no other choice. She's got to see a doctor.

THE PIGEON
Tony

TONY'S MOTHER CALLS HIM FOR THE FIRST TIME in two years, just to say 'Hi'. At least that's what she tells him. He dodges the bulk of the conversation, of course, he always does, but the little that makes it his way still manages to drain him. He knows he ought to tell her about the dog. That's what a normal person would do, tell their mother about a weird thing going on in their life. The thing is though, Tony isn't normal, and his mother certainly isn't. Their history reads like bad melodrama, and he usually avoids it and her as much as possible. So instead of engaging, he deflects. He tells her what he's doing for a living these days, and he tells her about Jacob, and he tells her about Florence, and when it's over he wants to sleep for about fifty years. Instead he takes a nap for maybe ten minutes, and wakes up on the couch with a sore back and a wet face. The dog's been licking him. Tony rumples his dreadlocks and says, "I really ought to give you a name."

It doesn't disagree – instead, it offers a terse half bark, and plods off to lie in the little bit of sunlight put off by the window. It's really a graceful walk, perfectly silent. If it hadn't been born a dog it would have made an excellent ballerina. Tony follows close behind. He doesn't have a great view from this window, but it looks out over the street and makes for halfway decent people-watching at the little *trattoria* across the way. Tony likes to sit and read on the bench in front of the window from time to time, and that's what he decides to do now. He plops himself down and reaches for his book – a massive text on the Florentine flood of nineteen sixty-six that would most likely bore just about anyone other than him. That's when he notices the dead bird.

"Holy fucking shit!" He screams to no one in particular.

It's another pigeon, just like the one the dog had been carrying when they'd first met. There is no blood, and there are no bite marks anywhere on its little grey and white and black body. Honestly, not a single feather looks out of place, aside from around the neck, which is broken cleanly. It's just like the one before, to the point that if the coloring of the feathers hadn't been different he would have thought it really was the same bird.

"How do you do that? You don't even have opposable thumbs."

It cocks its head quizzically, responding to the intonation of his voice but not recognizing any of the words. It's a shame that he doesn't, because Tony would really like for that question to get answered. Instead, he grabs some rubber gloves out of the cabinet beneath his kitchen sink and picks up the bird carefully, probably making one hell of a face. Historically speaking, this bird is one of the last remaining relics of the time of the dinosaurs. Once its ancestors ruled mindlessly over a kingdom of pure unadulterated Darwinism, but here it is. Neck snapped, body stiffening. It can't even beg for breadcrumbs anymore. Fucking tragic. Tony drops it in the garbage, and it lands with a surprisingly heavy thud. The sound carries a lot with it. It's a philosophical sound, burdened with questions of mortality, evolution, and what the hell 'survival of the fittest' really means. Tony tries to put his mind on something else. He goes back to his book, but it can't hold his attention. He's still thinking about the bird.

A couple of questions flash through his mind in rapid succession:

1) How did it snap the bird's neck so cleanly?
2) How did it get the bird into the house?
3) How did it get out to find the bird in the first place?

None of these questions have an easy answer. He must have left the window open, or the door ajar. The bird probably flew in of its own volition and got a nasty surprise when it landed. There is just no other explanation. The dog probably snapped its neck trying to play with it, shake it around like a chew toy. It was probably an accident. Of course, there'd been no other possible explanation for the first one, too.

Some music, he thinks, I'll put some music on.

He puts a record on the record-player. On the Beach again. It's an absolute rarity since they stopped pressing it to vinyl in the 80s, but he's held on to this old copy for years. The opening chords of "Walk On" come out oddly cheerily. He's always liked this song but felt it stood at odds with the rest of the album. Much brighter than "Revolution Blues" and much more direct than "Ambulance Blues." Still, it's the only number from the album that can manage to cheer him up, and that's exactly what he needs right now. He lets the music wash over him and tries to distract himself with other thoughts. Against his better judgment, they turn back to his phone call.

Tony's not sure to feel about hearing from his mother. They've never exactly gotten along, and he's not sure to broach the subject of his new friend with her. The dog stretches out on the hardwood. It seems happy, the dog, so that's good at least. Its weird little nub of a tail swings back and forth slowly, but deliberately. The chorus kicks in and Tony taps his foot. We're moving in unison, he realizes. The song has a great beat. He's always thought rhythm was Young's weakest point, but not here. His songs generally had unique, often thrilling guitar parts, and mystifying lyrics, but the rhythms were spotty. "Walk On" isn't like that at all. If anything, it's more like an old CSNY tune in that sense.

"That's what I'll call you. I'll call you Crosby."

The dog cocks its head. How many times do you normally have to repeat a dog's name before it recognizes it? It's got to be more than one. A hundred? Fifty?

"Would you rather be Stills? Or Nash?"

Nash isn't bad either, but he likes the sound of Crosby. He pictures the dog's dreadlocks flopping around to the tune of "Almost Cut My Hair." He smiles, and then remembers the dead bird in his trash can. The smile's gone as quickly as it came.

"Come here, Crosby."

The dog obliges. Tony had already run through the basics with the dog after he got back from the vet. It could sit on command, and would stay infinitely if asked. It's really the picture of perfect dog-hood, aside from its more murderous tendencies. It – Crosby – plods over and lies down beside his chair. He looks good there, Tony realizes.

"Good boy," he says. "Don't kill any more birds, alright?"

Crosby yawns.

"I guess we'll see how obedient you are."

THE SUITCASE
Paolo

PAOLO WAS CERTAIN THE GIRL WOULD SAY NO. He was certain she would laugh at him after he said his piece. He was certain she'd say "who?" when he said his name. The call hadn't played out the way he'd expected. In fact, she seemed genuinely surprised he hadn't called earlier. Truth be told, he'd thought about it. He'd thought about the night they'd met a lot. They'd fucked no less than three times in her room that night with her hands pressed tight over his mouth to keep him quiet. She didn't struggle with that much, herself. In general, she was the least emotive woman he'd ever been in bed with. Every motion was executed perfectly, like she'd read it out of a textbook and recreated it from memory. It was like nothing he'd ever experienced, but she acted like the whole thing was a science project. It was jarring, to say the least. Still, he'd been thinking about it. That must count for something.

He's standing outside her building, now. The last time they'd been here he was fiddling with that V neck dress and planning out exactly what he wanted to do with what she had underneath it, and now he's here with a suitcase. It's not how he expected things to go. It's not what he expected at all. The Girl with the Egyptian Eyeliner opens the door, and smiles at him with what on any other woman's face he would have called warmth.

"Paolo," she says. "You're here."

He is. He's not sure what to do in this situation, so he takes a gamble and grabs a handful of her hair. He pulls her in for a kiss, and she melts into it just enough to let him know it was the right move.

"I didn't think you were going to call," she says.

"I didn't think I was either," he replies. Usually Paolo has no trouble dissembling, but something about her makes it hard to lie to her. He doesn't waste time trying. "Honestly, I'm desperate. I'm on the street without you."

"That's so sweet," she says sardonically. "Still, I'd be lying if I said I wasn't glad to see you again. You look better by daylight."

She did too, but he resolved not to acknowledge that. There was something about her that pulled him in, inexorably, once he got close enough. He felt like a ship being sucked into a whirlpool, and he was worried his fate would be more or less the same.

"Before we go up, I need to talk to you about something."

Paolo gets a serious case of déjà vu, which is only confusing until he remembers why.

"Is this about your roommates?" He asks.

"Yes," she says. "Listen, they're sweet girls. They'll take to you, and they'll be nice, and there won't be any problems."

Paolo waits for the other shoe to drop. 'They're nice' hardly constitutes a warning.

"The thing is," she continues, "the girls kind of... well, it's hard to explain."

What was the word she had used that first night? Paolo had filed it away, but it was buried under better memories. That's right.

"Sycophants," he says. "Isn't that what you called them?"

She grimaces. The expression shifts her face into something new, entirely. It's the first time he's looked at her and not been immediately attracted, which is maybe progress.

"They mean well, but they sort of worship me. I know that sounds narcissistic to say, but it's the truth."

It did sound narcissistic. Not for the first time, Paolo gets the feeling he's making a mistake, but it's far too late to back out. I've got to find a job, he thinks. Really, this time. He does. He can't stay here.

"I guess I'll see what you mean soon enough," he says. And lo and behold, he does.

The Girl with the Egyptian Eyeliner's roommates don't all look the same, exactly. It's more like a machine assembled some basic model and an artist had customized each, ever so slightly, at the end of an assembly line. Some things were the same across the board. They all wear black, almost entirely. They all have the same small amount of jewelry, either gold or silver, no stones. There's a ring, always on the left hand, a choker or necklace, and stud earrings. They all have the same high fashion sensibility when it comes to their faces, but Paolo's quick to notice the Girl's the only one sporting her signature winged eyeliner. They introduce themselves in a flutter of giggles that almost sounds sincere. They can tell by looking at him that he's slept with her, he realizes. How many men has she brought to them to meet? Is he the first, or the most recent link in a long chain?

"This is Paolo," she tells them, and they respond in a chorus of names Paolo knows it'll take him weeks to remember.

"Paolo," she says when they're done, "why don't you unpack. I'll keep the girls entertained while you do, ok?"

Paolo nods, more than a touch overwhelmed. In the room, there's a brand new dresser with the drawers pulled out in invitation for him. Obviously this is where he's meant to put his things. He hadn't given any thought to how long he'd be staying until this moment, but as he takes his clothes out, folds them, and slides them into the dresser he realizes it might be a very long time. He's not sure when he's going to be able to work. It'd be easy for him to get a job, but to get the kind of job that would get him the kind of money he'd need for rent is another question. Unpacking doesn't take long. It must have been easy for Franco after all. He stacks his mother's books on top of the dresser, and that's it, that's the lot. From the other side of the door he can hear voices. The girl's giving a speech.

"Anyway," she says, "this is the sort of thing I call an opportunity, girls. I know I've said our time here's about adventure, and that adventure's about the new, and the spontaneous, but... well they always say, don't look a gift horse in the mouth, don't they? I guess this is going to have to be an example of do as I say, not as I do. Unless you get lucky."

The girls laugh. They fan around her like students at a lecture. One of them is literally taking notes. Sycophants, Paolo thinks. They really are a bunch of sycophants.

THE NUMBER
Tony

JACOB USED TO BE A HUMAN SPELLCHECK. He had his own little cubicle, his own little ergonomic egg chair just to sit and check over other people's work for split infinitives. He wore plaid. He spoke in a businessman's monotone. He drank his coffee with one cream and two sugars, and complained about the company e-mail client. He was just like anybody else, really. Then he got his big break.

"It was a politician," says Jacob, "A woman."

The story always starts this way; two staccato phrases staring each other down from opposite ends of the linguistic equivalent of an old saloon. Jacob scans the crowd for anticipation. Tony has already heard this story what feels like thirty times, but this time he knows he has something to top it, so he lets it go on a little longer.

"She was a beautiful woman," Jacob continues, "and insanely popular in her bullshit country. A real reformer, a real Joan of Arc kind of woman. But of course, Joan of Arc burned, and this particular reformer got shot."

One of life's great mysteries is that Joan of Arc is ashes while Tony's mother and her little dog live on, collectively seventy-three years of age. He almost says something to this effect, but he loses his window as soon as he sees it. He couldn't get the words together fast enough, and anyway Jacob is unstoppable with this story. He is a panzer tank rolling over Poland. Tony checks the sky, waiting for an air-raid siren. The only thing up there is a handful of birds.

"It was some nut job with ties to every sinister sub-sect of international terrorism on the short list. He got her with a forty-five and did himself in right after, one-two-three, boom."

He makes a right angle with his fingers in lieu of proper punctuation. It's meant to resemble a gun, Tony knows that, but it's not the way a normal person would make the gesture. Of course Jacob does few things the way a normal person would, so why should that surprise him?.

"And they put the story on my desk," says Jacob. "That was my moment. That was my lucky break. My chance to make something big out myself."

"Why?" Tony asks.

Jacob looks at him like he's committed some sort of crime. For a moment Tony thinks of Laszlo Toth swinging a sledgehammer at a polished stone Christ in far-off Rome, removing his Virgin mother's nose. The sin of his interruption will stand forever in the pantheon of great betrayals, next to Judas Iscariot and Benedict Arnold. Jacob is waiting for Tony, now, to proceed with the story.

"Why did you get the job?" He obliges, "wasn't there somebody else?"

"I was right for it."

"You were a copy editor."

"Yes, I was a copy editor. And then I did crime, and then I did arts, and now I do travel. Those are the breaks, Tony."

Tony waits for the rest of the story, but Jacob's wearing his version of a pout instead. It's a sour face that looks less like a child and more like a lion that came an inch short of its gazelle.

"You're not going to finish?"

"What for? I've told you this story before."

It's moments like these Tony wishes he still smoked cigarettes. It'd be great to have something to do with his hands to fill the silence. He shoves a piece of bread in his mouth instead and waits for his… friend?… to finish sulking

"I went to that museum," Jacob says, finally, "the one you told me about."

"And?" He asks. All Tony can think about is how Jacob can be so dramatic when he's talking. How he never gets to the point, he always needs this seemingly infinite crescendo. It would be fascinating to meet his parents, Tony decides. Fascinating and quite possibly dangerous.

"It was interesting," Jacob admits, somewhat begrudgingly, "I mean not in a way that's going to help me with the article, which is fine. But it was very interesting."

"Goya was a great painter," says Tony, "and an interesting man."

Jacob nods. There's something he's not saying about the whole experience, Tony's sure of it, but he's just as sure he doesn't care.

"Listen," Tony says, "I talked to Kitty."

Honest to god, Jacob's ears perk up. Like a fox, or a wolf. He leans forward in his seat and he makes very rare genuine eye contact. It makes Tony uncomfortable, and he wants to look away, but he manages to hold it.

"What did she say?"

"She said she wants to meet you. I told her about the article. Her father used to run a restaurant on the Oltrarno, the south side of the city, so she knows a bit about the Roma. He used to have to fend off beggars from their outdoor seating all the time, she said. Anyway, you guys can talk about that or you can talk about something else, that's up to you."

Tony's playing it cool, but he's got a plan in motion. Jacob, he's decided, is not Kitsune's type. He's too brash, too demanding. He thinks he's an Alpha, not just an Alpha male but an Alpha anything. Kitty doesn't go for being told what to do, and Jacob won't be the exception to prove that rule. They won't last a week, he's sure of it. Satisfied with his logic, he passes Jacob a little slip of paper with her phone number on it.

"I thought you said she'd call me," Jacob says.

"I told her to."

"And?"

Jacob's got a smirk on his face like he thinks he's pulled the wool over Tony's eyes somehow. There's no harm in letting him think that. Tony takes a page out of Jacob's playbook and lets the question hang in the air for a bit, building suspense. It's fun, Tony realizes. It's actually fun to be dramatic for a change. No wonder Jacob bothers with it. Tony matches Jacob's smirk, and wipes his mouth with his napkin on an internal count of five, just for show. He had planned this sentence word for word on the walk over, and he wants it to land.

"She told me she never makes the first move."

It's exactly what Jacob wants to hear.

THE DATE
Kitsune

"I HAD THIS IDEA," SHE TELLS HIM, "I had this idea for wireless headphones. No one would know you had them on. You could be anywhere – you could be at a funeral listening to a book on tape. They'd have to be flesh-tone of course, like earplugs or a hearing aid. Good idea, right? Of course someone else got there first."

He nods, but he isn't agreeing with her. He's agreeing with her body. With her form, rather than her function. That's just the reality of any relationship, at least for the first few weeks. It's human nature.

"Anyway I made myself a pair, and they almost worked, so I figure I'm not bad with a pair of tweezers."

The laughter seems real, but there's no time to test the theory. The food comes in all its glory – *prosciutto e melone*; slivers of cantaloupe sweating sugar under blankets of thin-sliced meat. The dish reminds her of summer. Grass. Ozone. Stars. She's never understood the connection but it comes to mind every time she orders it. The male – Jacob, his name is Jacob – digs in with reckless abandon. She's never seen anyone eat like that.

"So you're some kind of foodie, right?" She asks.

"Yea, I'm –" he swallows, "I write columns for a culture magazine. This time it's on gypsies but usually it's just fluff pieces. Food and art and who lived and died in this city or that city. Boring stuff."

There's something appealing about the fact that he'll be gone in a month. It's easy. No need to think long term, no need to put on an act. She doesn't mention it, but she stores the thought for a later date.

"And you do music, right?"

She doesn't answer his question right away. She does this at least once on every first date. You can learn a lot about someone by seeing how they respond to silence. Most people fill it with inane chatter. Some people get angry, and repeat their question until they get a response. Some people pout. Jacob doesn't do anything. He just eats, and periodically looks at her to make sure she's still breathing.

"I don't want to talk about music." She says at last.

"Alright." He nods.

"I talk about music all the time."

"Alright."

"Because it's what I do for a living."

He doesn't say it a third time. The wine arrives, a tall bottle of *Vernaccia di San Gimignano*, white and sweet and full of citrus. Or at least, that's how she's heard it described. She's never had any opinions about wine. He takes a swallow and smiles. She wonders if he's tasting lemon, or if he's just smiling for effect.

"So," he says. "What do you want to talk about?"

"We could talk about the food."

"Food is what I do for a living."

"That's a fair point."

She smiles. Not a thought of citrus in her mind.

"So," she says. "Tony tells me you're a bit of a freak."

He doesn't blink, but he doesn't smile either. Maybe she shouldn't play with fire, but she's come too far now to stop.

"What does that mean?"

"That you're into freaky things, he said. He didn't tell me

everything, I mean, but it's fine. I don't judge. Everyone's a bit of a freak, anyway."

"You too?"

"Oh, definitely. Bigger than you, I'd imagine."

"I guess you'd know."

The banter is interrupted by food, as it always is. As it should be. She'd ordered pasta and he'd ordered *osso bucco*. I like the bones, he'd said. He certainly seems to. He sucks the marrow down with a practiced flourish that's almost charming.

Jacob never speaks while there's food in front of him. They are silent through the entrees into the dessert, but it's a pleasant silence. It's simple. It's easy. Dessert is honey and fried dough, a Sardinian dish. *Sebadas*, says the waiter, but Jacob insists the B is supposed to be silent. She pushes sweet ricotta around with her spoon.

"So," she says.

"So," he says.

"What I want to know is what's the matter with you?"

This is a question everyone should be asked at some point in their life. She believes this firmly, but this is the first time she's ever done anything about it. Jacob gives it some thought. The question doesn't offend him, doesn't throw him off, but he doesn't have a canned answer for it either.

"Why do I have to have something wrong with me?"

"In general, guys don't set their friends up with girls."

"Don't they? I seem to remember being set up before."

"You've been told you were set up, but that's not the whole story. Guys don't set their friends up unless they're with someone."

"Tony's alone, and he set me up."

"Which means he must think there's something wrong with you."

He gives that some thought. He's cleaned every last bit of

caramel off his plate at this point, but he's still staring at it longingly. She pushes her melted ricotta his way.

"So what is it?"

"I don't know. Honestly, I don't even know Tony that well. I don't know what he'd think my problem is, though I do think I might know why he thinks I'm a freak."

"So what do you think?"

There's a pause. He's deciding whether or not to lie. It's an expression she recognizes well.

"I think... I think I don't care about people enough. I think that's my problem."

"That's a very honest answer."

"It is."

"How much is enough?"

"Enough is at all."

Now this is interesting. Most people you meet pretend to care about everyone to some degree or another, whether they do or not. Most people probably do care about everyone to some degree or another. Despite all of that when the shit hits the fan most people do nothing to help anyone else. Most people are assholes.

"So," he says. "How much is enough for you?"

For a moment she is drowning in red linen. She's completely swallowed in the cool fabric, smooth to the touch and clean as marble. Air, air – he gasps for breath and she is everywhere, surrounding him, pinning him to the mattress. Sweat shines on her collarbone like a layer of gauze and he swats at it, pulls at it.

It refuses to budge. His teeth linger lightly on the meat of her neck. She moans.

For a moment skin is an obstacle, a nuisance, another layer of nuanced lace to peel aside – and muscles, tendons, organs, bone – so nothing might remain but her bleach-blond hair and the warmth of his breath on her shoulder – harsh, harsh, heavy with words and incoherent whispering. Everything flies away. Clothing on the tile floor, lonely and cold and crumpled in piles. His tie in her hands like a silk noose.

For a moment she is gone, hovering in the air above him, pink-white and panting. The next she is binding his wrists to the bedposts.

"It's a little late," she says.

"Late for what?"

"It's a little late to ask if you trust me."

Close, close. Impossibly close. Like making love to the ocean. Smelling it on his skin, the taste of its kiss lingering on her tongue. Sweet and salty and with just a hint of citrusy wine. Scratch marks hot and red and salt-sweet on his chest. She ties the knot around his wrists. A shiver runs through her.

"Ohmygod," she says. "Ohmygod, ohmygod, ohmygod."

And with that, it's over. The waves crash one final time and roll away, low tide. In the distance, she hears the wailing of an ambulance. She lays back, stares at him. He looks like Cary Grant on an off day, she realizes. In lieu of sleep, she decides to speak.

"I'm people, you know."

He looks at her in return. It isn't a simple look, or an easy look, but somehow that doesn't bother her right now.

"No," he says. "You're a person."

THE MARKET
Paolo

PAOLO'S LONG KNOWN THAT THE BEST CURE for a hangover is a straight shot of whiskey, but there's none to be had. He settles for a lemon, squeezed directly down the throat, but it's not the same. In walks his new landlady into their kitchen, naked down to the waist.

"Where'd you learn English, Paolo?"

"School." He says, which is half true.

He'd learned the basics at school, but he got fluent on the job. He used to be a tour guide, but one drunk and disorderly morning he told the wrong Frenchman to take a flying fuck at a frog. Needless to say he found a new line of work after that.

The Girl with the Egyptian Eyeliner kisses his neck and it stings like a tattoo needle. She pulls him back into their room. One thing leads to another. The sex is an exercise in inevitability: she doesn't open her eyes anywhere from start to finish. When it's over, she throws the condom into the trash bin.

"We're going shopping," she says.

Paolo shrugs his shoulders and slides into some wrinkled jeans and a Nirvana t-shirt. He's past the point of asking questions or protesting. The moment that was possible passed away when he decided to stay here. There's nothing to do but go.

At the bottom of the stairs, they meet a few stragglers from her little cult. The girls dress so similarly you'd think they'd been prescribed a uniform. For all he knew, they may have been at some point. The Girl with the Egyptian Eyeliner is always quick to express her opinions about her cohort's choices.

"Are you all ready?" She asks them.

They nod. Their eyes are all locked on her, watching her. Subconsciously – or maybe consciously – they seem to be modeling their posture off of hers.

"Let's get on with it," he grumbles.

Giggles echo from the choir. This particular crowd contains some of his favorite specimens. There's Jessica, a lanky blonde with a bit of a lisp. Paolo finds it annoying, but the Girl insists it's cute. Cara: another blonde who most likely achieved that state of being through the use of harsh chemicals. Catrina, the group's lone redhead who seems to take pride in having just slightly lower standards than anyone else in the house. And last, there's Patience. Paolo's got a soft spot for Patience. She doesn't really fit with the rest of the Girl's little coterie. She's too soft, too innocent. She's a step behind on every joke and she has trouble falling in line with the groupthink, so she writes everything she hears down. She works so hard to be accepted. For all that work Paolo sometimes wonders if anyone other than him really likes her. There isn't time to think about it. The gang is on the move.

They arrive at the *Mercato Centrale* at peak hours. When they head out into what passes for the real world in Florence, Paolo is stuck in the role of guide and guardian. Though the Girl herself is nearly fluent, her followers can speak about a sentence of

Italian between them. They are perpetually beset by explicit offers from older Italian men that they only half understand. It's not so different from when he was a tour guide, really. This time, at least, he isn't legally culpable for any of them. Only ethically.

On the produce floor they fan out in little clusters. It's a move they almost seem to have practiced, because they operate on a kind of buddy system. Catrina pairs off with Cara, and Jessica pairs off with Sonya, and Patience... well Patience follows Paolo and the Girl with the Egyptian Eyeliner around like a dog they found on the street and fed. It makes him sad, so he calls the group back together and brings the girls to his favorite vendor in the market: a short, fat pile of a man named Claudio who sells almost exclusively citrus.

"I have *arancia rossa* today, Paolo. Blood Orange to you ladies. It's like an orange but sweeter, and red. Like if you mated an orange and strawberry together. Try it."

The Girl takes one and breaks it into segments, which she shares among the others fairly. Anyone watching would think she was their mother, even if she is their same age. The others watch the Girl's face as she bites into the blood orange. Paolo tries a bit, too. It's a good batch. Claudio's always got the good stuff, imported from Amalfi and Capri and sometimes as far as Malta. How he keeps his prices down, Paolo doesn't ask. He's guessing he wouldn't want to know.

"It's good!" Says the girl, and she drops down a few Euro. The others follow suit. At this rate, they might as well have pooled their money and given it to her directly, rather than all going together. It would have had the same effect. After finishing with Claudio, they break back into pairs again.

"I told you," she says to him.

"I know," he says, "but you don't have to encourage it."

"I don't encourage it," she says, and Paolo realizes she may actually believe this. He doesn't argue the point.

Little by little he takes the girls through his favorite vendors. After Claudio is Marcella and Giulia, a couple who run the best little bakery in the city out of a stand on the market's lower floor. Then Bruno, his butcher. Then Maurizio, who may be the one man in the world with the greatest quantity of unnecessary information about cheese. The girls are, to a woman, won over by his expertise. It's a successful trip.

"The thing you have to look for," Paolo tells the Girl with the Egyptian Eyeliner, "is their eyes. A good grocer or butcher or whatever is going to have sharp eyes. They're going to have smile lines around them, because they never have problems with their customers."

The Girl laughs at that, and Patience puts it down in her notebook. Paolo feels a weird feeling to see it, to see the ripple effect of his advice spreading through the groupthink in seconds, but it's kind of powerful at the same time. He's not sure if it's good or bad for him.

"Give us a minute, girls," she says, and they disperse to check out a wine stall. Paolo looks at her for a second, then kisses her. She tastes like blood orange and sweat and it's not as bad a combination as it sounds.

"Do you think," he asks her, his voice dropping to a conspiratorial whisper, "they'd notice if we left them here?"

The Girl smiles a cruel smile, but it's a smile nonetheless.

"I'd say we'd have fifteen minutes."

That's more than enough time. Paolo drags her to an alley behind the apartment, just barely out of view of the crowds. It's dirty, but it's quiet, and no one will bother them. At least that's what he assumes. When he gets there, it's already occupied. There's a little white cat standing in front of a circle of dead pigeons. It's eyes are gold and piercing, like the bullets in that Bond movie with Roger Moore. When it sees the girl, it hisses and arches its back. She grabs him, but it's not in the fun way.

She's going, going, gone. Fainted in his arms.

"I don't think fifteen minutes will be enough," he says to the cat. It doesn't respond.

Paolo carries the Girl back to the apartment, and he tries not to think about how light she feels. She's slim, of course, but this is different. It's like carrying a burlap sack filled with air. It isn't physically possible, but the good news is it makes it easy to get her up the stairs. Inside, he lays her flat on their kitchen table and puts her purse under her head as a cushion. He's so focused on waiting for her to wake up that he doesn't realize until then that the rest of her little cult are forming a ring around them. He panics and ducks out under the arms of the girls as they close tighter around their unconscious leader.

"She's ok," Paolo says, "she just fainted but her pulse is fine. I'm sure she just got too hot."

They don't hear him. One by one, they move to her side and plant a slow, delicate kiss on each of her eyes. The kiss stains their lips squid ink black, but her makeup doesn't seem to change. Thus marked each girl steps back, wobbles on her feet, and collapses. Patience is the last to go, and when she hits the floor, the Girl with the Egyptian Eyeliner wakes with a gasp. Wordlessly, she looks around, sees her fallen coterie, and heads toward the bedroom.

"We weren't finished," she calls as the door closes behind her.

Paolo's too weak not to follow her, but he isn't a total asshole either. He checks each girl's pulse before he gives into his baser instincts. Thankfully, everyone's alive.

THE APARTMENT
Jacob

JACOB WAKES UP IN A STRANGE ROOM under ruby sheets dotted with purple fleur-de-lis and heavy with sweat. His system's shocked and even though the rational part of his brain knows it's cold air from the ceiling fan he's staring at, the lion's share of him sincerely believes in his impending death by drowning, at least for a few seconds. He's alone in the bed, which doesn't help matters. The Korean woman – Kitty, or Kitsune, or whatever – is showering already, and Jacob knows this is the best chance he's going to get to figure her out. If he can get a handful of clues, he can string together enough of a fiction to stay a part of her life. He can have her whenever he wants her which, after last night, is likely to be often.

Her bookshelf is sparse. It's mostly poetry, the likes of Allen Ginsburg and Ezra Pound and T.S Eliot interspersed with names he's not familiar with at all. Some of the books are old, with cracked, decaying spines that speak of regular handling. Some of them barely look touched at all. This isn't information, then: these are heirlooms, not purchases. He reaches one of the Eliot books – Four Quartets. The only thing he can remember from Eliot is the first few lines of The Wasteland, and this doesn't strike him as much different. There's notes in the margins, but they're in what he supposes is Korean. There's no way to know if it's her handwriting or someone else's, at least not yet. Jacob moves on.

There's art on the walls. It's mostly black and white photos of the city, with a few sketchy architectural drawings of buildings thrown in. If he had to guess, he'd say she did them herself. She's not bad, if that's the case. She's better than some of his peers at the paper, and they get paid for it. Moving on, he can see color themes throughout the décor – she likes red – and style themes – she's clearly into punk – but nothing concrete. There's a record player, though. That's not a bad start. Her collection ranges wide, with everything from Television to the Pixies to Can to the Clash to Eric Clapton. Tears In fucking Heaven, with a little note scrawled on it in silver sharpie that says 'hot garbage.' He laughs. This is something he can use, but it's not enough.

He's about to give up, when he strikes the motherlode. It's buried under a stack of records he's sifting through. A single picture. It's old, old enough to be black and white, and old enough to start to fade. It's an older man and a young girl, both Korean. He picks it up. This has to be her, and this has to be her father. Li and Kita, it says on the back, and it marks the year as 1982. If that's right, she's lying about her age, which doesn't matter to him. She'd be about his age if he's reading it right. Kita, though, that's something. That's a name. If Tony's to be believed, she's gone by her stage name with everyone other than her mother for years. Knowing that would give him something to hold on to. Knowing that would put him in an inner circle. He puts the picture back. He can't reveal that he knows, at least not right away. When she's ready, she'll tell him. He'll get it out of her. Now that he knows it's there, he knows he can.

There's a squeak from the bathroom, and Jacob knows that means she's done. The water stops with a loud clang, and Jacob jumps to attention. Time for him to set a scene. He takes a record out of its sheathe at random and sets it on the player. The name of the artist is John Cale, and though he has absolutely zero idea who that is, he knows how to fake it. Mostly, the secret is lots of preparation. If the description on the back of the album is to believed, the song is called "Barracuda".

"Holy shit!" She calls from the bathroom, cracks open the door, and peers out with a shit-eating grin. "I haven't heard this song in like five years."

She recognizes it from the first few seconds of the guitar part, which is a pretty decent indicator he's made an acceptable choice. It's a rumbling, bouncing lead line that sounds almost danceable, but it's a bit too low and distorted for that. A synth rolls on top of it and makes the whole thing sound like a ride at a carnival. Honestly it's not something he would listen to on his own, but she obviously loves it. Then comes the voice, growling and angry and dripping with sarcasm:

> *Dark woman in the water drowning*
> *Sinking in a funny way*
> *Black footing full of faces floating*
> *Mimicking our final days*
> *The ocean will have us all*
> *The ocean will have us all*

They're dark lyrics, but the voice sings them with the cavalier pride and joy of a love ballad. That must be John Cale. Jacob's beginning to change his mind about him, after all. She's out of the shower, dry, but not dressed. Jacob's got an eye for details, and this one's definitely on his radar.

"What made you pick that one?" She asks, walking closer.

In the light of day he can see that the fox tail isn't her only tattoo. On her back is a pair of wings, and on the inside of her right arm is text, reading 'Number 13 Baby.' Another Pixies allusion, he's pretty sure.

"I like the chorus," he says, guessing. It's a pretty good guess.

Most of the time you like a song for the chorus, right?

"Me too," she says, and he waits to hear what he's planted his flag on.

Barracuda, barracuda
Won't you lay down your life to me
Won't you love me barracuda
Cause you always did bring out the worst in me

It's decided then. Jacob fucking loves this song. He's sitting in a little torn up leather chair she's got by her record player, and she climbs into his lap. She's all muscle, a little lion or cougar or something in his hands. He can't tell if he wants to fuck her or fight her or both. He can feel bones and sinew and heat rising from her and he wants it all.

Just like the night before, she produces a pair of cuffs from seemingly out of nowhere. To be honest, these he could do without. He wants his hands around her. He wants to grab great greedy handfuls of her skin, he wants to pull her and push her and move her into whatever position comes into his mind. Still, he sticks out his hands, and accepts the cuffs. Sometimes, you make sacrifices to get what you want. One of these days, she'll trust him enough to leave the cuffs off, or maybe she'll want his hands on her the way he does. He can wait for that.

THE ANGEL
Tony

TONY IS A HISTORIAN AND AS SUCH he knows his history. He knows that no matter how well preserved and despite what any number of Hollywood productions will tell you, a full set of plate armor cannot stop a bullet. It will, however, stop most blades very well, which is the only benefit one receives for wearing something that weighs about as much as the horse that carries the knight wearing it.

The woman in Tony's apartment does not move like she's carrying a horse. He's standing in the doorway with the dog, looking into her... blue, the eyes are blue. She seems to be looking through him into the hallway beyond. There's nothing there. Tony turns around to confirm that, shudders, and returns to the problem at hand. It's about then that she starts to sing.

Well it's not singing, exactly, or at least it's nothing pleasant. She moves back and forth between two notes, seemingly affected with a sort of sonic motion sickness. It's more of a whine, really. The dog hates it, and it's making Tony dizzy. It doesn't last long. When it ends she's looking straight into Tony's eyes and smiling with genuine warmth.

"You will have to forgive me," she says, "but I am quite blind."

Tony's not sure how to take that, but the dog seems satisfied. That makes it two against one.

"Please," she coos, "come in."

They comply. Tony grabs a seat on the ottoman across the table from the giant woman and helps himself to a cup of the tea she's apparently brewed for the occasion. It's stone cold. The woman clears her throat.

"Seraphim, like all species, have evolved a great deal over the years. Echolocation is one of a few gifts exchanged for others lost along the way."

She states this matter-of-factly, as though it were a remark about the weather. The woman is six feet tall, sporting a tightly woven braid of blond hair that trails from her head nearly to the back of her knees. The sword at her side is the kind of broad cleaver that a sufficiently strong knight could have used to cut a horse cleanly into two pieces. He tries not to think about this. Let's focus on the important questions first. It's probably a prop, right? Right. Anyway.

"What are you doing in my house?"

She takes a sip of her tea and smiles. Tony's thinking maybe this woman is crazy. Did the landlady let her in?

"Actually, Mr. Ducati, I am here about your dog."

So she'd seen the ad and decided to come calling. No way was he giving the dog up to some crazy person, owner or no. But wait, thinks Tony, I didn't post any ad.

"As for my intentions," she continues, "rest assured that I am not interested in confiscating him. On the contrary, that dog and I cannot co-exist in the same space for more than a few minutes at a time."

Tony points to the dog, cocking an inquisitive eyebrow. She nods.

"You may already have noticed that the dog has what you might call a violent fixation."

So she knows about the pigeon. Wait.

"How do you know about the pigeon?"

"Oh, I am afraid it is far more than a single pigeon."

There's a real problem with Tony's stomach. Someone seems to have absconded with it altogether.

"Your dog, Mr. Ducati, is entirely unholy. It is, in fact, an abomination before God." She takes a swallow and continues. "Which is why I am here, and why I cannot stay long."

Tony takes stock of his situation. The woman is limber but not muscular. She has the sword, but she'll have to draw it from its scabbard. They're standing around his couch now, but she's closer to the kitchen. In a dead sprint, she'd probably beat him to the cutlery unless she tripped over the carpet. Tony's got these Japanese kitchen knives that'd cut him open in a second if she went nuts. Shun, that's the brand. He'd sliced his finger with the bread knife once, and the skin hadn't grown back right afterwards. Better to go along with what she's saying, at least for now. There's no way he'd be able to tangle with her.

"You think my dog is a demon."

"No, I think that your dog is a dog. It is, however, possessed by a malevolent spirit."

He tries not to laugh.

"I am entirely serious, Mr. Ducati."

"Call me Tony, please."

"Tony, are you familiar with the gospel of Thomas?"

Remarkably, he is. He'd done a unit on the gnostic gospels in his graduate program. They were bizarre texts, understandably excised from the formal Christian Canon, but they had a feeling of power to them at the same time. He's amazed that what appears to be a crazy person wearing a suit of armor and claiming his dog is possessed knows anything about them. She's waiting for him to respond, he realizes. He nods.

"'There is nothing hidden that will not be revealed, and nothing buried that will not be raised.' Do you remember this?"

It's a quote that had stuck with him, that he had pulled for his thesis on the evolution of Madonna and Child art as it connected to the broader context of European History.

"Those who seek should not stop seeking until they find. When they find, they will be disturbed. When they are disturbed, they will marvel, and will reign over all." Tony says.

"And after they have reigned, they will rest." She finishes. "Very good. Do you know what it means?"

On any other day he would have said yes, but this conversation has slipped completely out of his control and he's wishing he'd installed the security system his new landlady had tried to sell him on. No one will call the cops if this woman attacks him. It would take maybe a week for anyone to even notice he was gone. He shakes his head.

"It means that there is more to this world than your senses can absorb. I cannot stay much longer, Tony, I must reach my point now."

"By all means," he says.

She gestures to his kitchen table, where the newspaper he'd bought maybe a week earlier lays collecting dust. Tony doesn't buy the paper to read it. He buys it because the man who sells it sells nothing else, and he can't handle the guilt of letting him starve. Tony remembers this one, though. The cover image had haunted him: a line of nuns wailing silently, or at least silent on paper, at some off-screen tragedy. The headline read something to the effect of 'Carrera Collision Brings Bishop to Brink'. It wasn't in the best taste.

"That man, that bishop. Do you know who him?"

"Generally speaking I don't make it my business to know bishops," Tony says. "At least not personally. Should I have?"

"You may not have met him before his accident, Tony, but you have met him since. His spirit rests within your dog. What have you named it again? Crosby?"

In this moment, Tony knows that she is not a crazy person

off the street. That option should have been taken off the table when she'd snuck into his home to begin with, or at the least when she'd known about the pigeon. It's not exactly like he's shared that story with anyone, but he hasn't told anyone about the dog either, and certainly not its name. The only other people who know are the people at the groomer's and Jacob. Of those, Jacob's the only one capable of finding someone this nuts, but Tony's pretty sure he's got other things on his mind at the moment.

"How do you know what I named my dog? I haven't got tags or anything like that on him. How did you know?"

"That is not important, Tony."

"It's important to me."

"Then we can discuss it later, but for now you must listen. I will leave soon. Carrera was not a kind man, Tony. He was a killer and a torturer, and this truth of his life will come to the world soon. In the meantime, his unkindness has come to rest in your dog, and in others throughout Florence. It will only get worse if nothing is done."

If nothing is done? What does that mean?

"What does that mean?"

But she's already leaving. As she walks to the window, Crosby looks at her and growls, a deep growl that resonates from the plaster walls of his apartment with genuine menace. It's different from the way he growled at Jacob. He's growling like he's afraid. She moves to the window, which is somehow open. Tony is maybe seventy-five percent certain that was not open when he got back, but he can't be completely sure of anything right now. She looks out the window. Her eyes linger on the Duomo for just a second, with what looks like longing.

"It means we must finish what the accident put into motion, Tony. It means we must kill him. That you must."

Tony's jaw more or less hits the floor at that, and Crosby

barks. It's the first time he's heard the sound, at least a real bark. It's higher pitch than he would have expected. He waits for her to elaborate, but she's done speaking. Tony knows this because she turns her back on him. From between the folds in the shoulder plates of her armor, Tony sees a handful of white feathers poking through. At first it's only one or two, and then it's a dozen, and then it's more. Then it's a full set of goddamn wings. They're huge, so big that they nearly scrape their tips against the ceiling. If they weren't so absolutely improbable, they'd be beautiful. She would be beautiful. She moves them slowly at first, an even, heavy motion that makes a deep throbbing sound Tony can barely register. Then she's full on flapping, and the gust of wind knocks a little succulent plant he'd had on a table by the window to the floor. The pot shatters. A few seconds later she's gone.

"Holy shit," says Tony, and heads to the window. Crosby joins him, and almost immediately Tony realizes he's got to be careful.

"Watch your feet," he says, shaking, "that broken ceramic might be sharp."

As he says that, he realizes that the succulent is back on the table. There's no question he saw it fall. There's no question he heard the pot break as it hit the floor, that he saw the soil spill out and the little cactus roll into a corner in a neat bundle with its roots.

"Motherfucker," says Tony, because there are only two explanations for this. And neither of them is anything he wants to think about.

TONY'S DREAM:
The Wall

THERE IS A MONSTER AT THE CENTER of the maze. Tony knows this with complete certainty, but he has no evidence. Some things are just facts. Absolute truth is rare and precious, but when it is found it is utterly immovable. There is a monster at the center of the maze. Tony knows this, but knowledge of the truth does not protect you from it. It only lets you see the bullet as it speeds towards you.

Tony stands in an apse at the corner of the maze. Before him is an altar, adorned with the image of the Madonna and Child. Her eyes are blacked out, hidden under a veil of spray paint. The infant looks as though it wants to escape her grasp, but there's nowhere for it to go. It's a decent piece, sculpted competently but without the subtlety and vision of the great craftsmen. He imagines the black eyes were not part of the original vision, but there is no time to inspect it further. There is a monster at the center of the maze.

When Tony was younger, his mother had taken him to a hedge maze in Provence and left him there while she went off to taste wine. He had wandered for an hour before he sat down in a corner and began to weep. Eventually, an older man had found him. Tony asked him for help, asked the man to take him out of the maze. I cannot do that, he had said. It is the rule of the maze that every man must meander through on his own. I cannot guide you. Instead, he had taught Tony how to do it himself. A simple method Tony had later understood as an absolute truth of mathematics. He had called it 'the right-hand rule'.

Now, as he had done then, Tony places his right hand against the surface of the wall. Beneath his fingers, the wall pulses rhythmically. It moves as though it has veins and capillaries, as though it serves not to divide space but to carry blood to some distant heart. The right-hand rule is simple. Keep your hand against the wall, do not take it off. Keep moving, hand to the wall, and you will eventually reach an exit. This rule assumes that space follows certain geometric laws which in theory are absolute. This, though, is not an ordinary maze. Tony knows this without knowing it. He feels it. He hopes the old man's rule will still apply.

Tony approaches a large, open area. As he comes closer, the wall's pulse quickens. It's afraid, he realizes. What is it afraid of? This is the obvious question, but the answer is not so certain. Is it afraid of the monster, or afraid of me?

At the center of the space – of the clearing – is a well. Tony recognizes it as the well from the monk's quarters at the Santa Croce in Florence. It does not surprise him to see it here. He is struck with an immense curiosity. An itch. What is in there? He wonders. But he can't go over. He can't look. The right-hand rule is an absolute truth, but to violate it would render it useless. He cannot remove his hand. The well must be left alone. There is no room for error. The wall's pulse quickens. He heads deeper in.

A thought occurs to Tony. The rule will get me out of this maze, but where will it take me first? He had seen maps of mazes solved by the right-hand rule. The paths were winding, scattered. They led all over the maze before finding the exit. They were rarely the shortest way through. As these thoughts pass, Tony realizes he knows exactly where the rule will lead him. It will take him through the center of the maze. To the room where the monster sleeps and beyond if he survived. The knowledge fills him with dread, but it is the truth. Tony knows this because the wall knows this, he thinks. It doesn't matter. He has to keep moving.

Tony comes to a door. Traditionally mazes do not have doors, but this is not a traditional maze. There is something familiar about the door. It is massive, mahogany. The brass knocker holds the face of a demon. Tony knows him as Azazel; the goat demon, the fallen Angel. This is not shared knowledge from the wall. Tony knows this because once, this door had been his door. He had lived in an apartment in Porto with his mother for three years looking at this door. It had terrified him. He was five (and then six and then seven), and the face of the demon had haunted his dreams for years even after they had moved.

Is this the monster? Is this what I will find on the other side of this door, at the center of the maze? Azazel?

His mother had told him stories of the demon to put him to bed. To hear her tell it, Azazel had taught men to work with metal. Azazel had taught men to fashion swords, and spears. Azazel had taught women to craft jewelry, to decorate their faces with eye shadow. As a child he did not understand the consequences of these actions. As an adult, he knew all too well. Azazel was a corruptor of souls, and for that he was cast out of the light of heaven. Is this his prison? Is it going to be mine? These are questions lacking answers. Tony opens the door.

The room on the other side is a child's room, but it isn't his.

He doesn't recognize the place at all. It is oddly Spartan, sterile; decorated without affection or sentimentality. He does not infer the room's owner is a child because of an abundance of toys, or the juvenile nature of the bedding. It is a small bed, folded neatly and tightly. One might think it belonged to a lonely man with an obsessive clean streak. One might think it was Tony's. Tony knows it is a child's room because this is the truth. He sits on the edge of the bed. There are no pictures to identify the room's owner, no belongings to give a clue as to their whereabouts. Most importantly, there is no Azazel. And yet, he thinks, there is a monster at the center of this maze.

This is not the first time Tony has had this dream. As a child it was frantic and scattered, but as he grew older it evolved. It developed a very real clarity. He had never seen Azazel, never seen the monster at the maze's heart. He did not even know for certain it was really there. The dream always ended shortly after he made it to this room, and sat down on this bed. He never had the chance to escape; never followed the right-hand rule to its logical conclusion. There is one other thing I have never done, Tony realizes.

As a child, Tony had been terrified of the beast that lived in his closet. There was no such creature, and he knew it even then, but the fear was real. His room was nothing like this one. He had never kept it clean. He left his toys scattered over the floor because he enjoyed walking through them. He pretended his room contained a minefield, because he was a child and he did not understand what that meant. The only thing his room had had in common with this one was the size and shape. It was like an alternate reality version of his room in Porto with his mother. Their closets were even in the same corner.

Tony goes over to the door. Unlike the mahogany door with the demon knocker, the closet door is completely innocent. There is nothing malicious or frightening about it, which is why he had never thought to open it. But there is nothing left, nothing but this to do. The dream cannot evolve in any other direction. It has become static. This is the only way. Tony takes a breath. He opens the door. Inside is not Azazel; not a fallen Angel, nor a goat-headed beast. Inside is a child: a girl. Young, could be twelve or thirteen. Korean, or Japanese, Tony's not sure which. Her right arm is missing.

"Azazel?" Tony asks. "Are you Azazel?"

The girl does not speak. She just shakes her head.

"Do you know where he is? Is he here?"

The girl opens her mouth, but the sound that emerges is not any language. It is a keening wail – almost like a song, but utterly atonal, utterly inhuman. It is the sound the Angel made the first night he found it in his apartment. Tony slams the closet door shut.

There is a monster at the center of the maze, Tony has always known this. This has always been the truth. So the question is: am I the Monster, or is she?

Part 2

Well, you heard about
the Great Pretender?
I went to see him
and he's not the same.
Down by the club
on the parking lot cinders
I was to meet him
and play his game.
Yonder stands the sinner
He calls my name
without a sound.

I saw his face in
the attic window
Yellin' down
through the broken pane
Sinner man!
What you got to run for?
Church bells rang
when he said that name.
Yonder stands the sinner
He calls my name
without a sound.

from "Yonder Stands the Sinner" by Neil Young

THE CONFRONTATION
Tony

LISTEN TO ME, HE SAYS. Never stop listening to me. Here he's just nattering on about articles and assignments and all Tony can hear is the tinny squawking of Jacob's ego. Listen to me, it says. Pay attention – this is all very important.

Today Jacob is telling Tony about the walking dead: a living human corpse. His teeth tap out a secondary speech in Morse code as he prattles on. Out loud, he's talking about the elderly, and nerves, and brain function. The old man's tumor, he explains, was the size of a nectarine.

"I'm eating," Tony says. Jacob keeps going, his mouth an engine and his endless monologue a jet of black smoke fucking up the ozone layer.

"The thing got lodged in the language center, or some medical jargon like that."

"Occipital lobe?" Tony offers.

"Could be. Point is he went nuts. Loopy. Bonkers. Very unfortunate."

Jacob is deliberately dragging the conversation to a topic he knows they will disagree on. Tony believes that people with disabilities mental or otherwise should be politely ignored, just like he would do with anyone else. Jacob, apparently, thinks they should be put down.

"So what was he doing?" Tony asks.

"Rattling off nonsense in Spanish. The family couldn't understand a word of it, of course."

"What's wrong with that? It's tragic, but it's not exactly hurting anyone."

"Ah," says Jacob, "But you didn't let me finish."

This, Jacob's ego announces, is where the pace picks up. He cracks his knuckles. Adjusts his collar. In the distance, Tony swears he hears the squeak of a first chair violin rosining his bow. They commence.

"So he's going on in Spanish, at home in hospice. Nurse steps out for a smoke or some shit, I have no idea. That's what she said, but she was probably lying. Anyway she's gone for five minutes, and what happens?"

"I don't know," says Tony.

"The man's nearly beaten his own daughter to death with a baseball bat."

"Jesus Christ!" Says Tony.

"Jesus Christ," says Jacob.

Now when a shark senses something that might be food they give it a test bite, just a nibble really, just to ascertain its edibility. At this point, the fish or the fowl, or the bleach-blonde surfer begins to bleed slow, pink clouds into the briny water. Sharks catch the scent, and the frenzy begins. This, as the television hosts like to say, is the good part.

"This doesn't disturb you?" Asks Jacob.

"It does."

"This man is a menace."

"Was," Tony clarifies, "was a menace.

"Was," Jacob accedes, "Was. Whatever. If they'd put him to sleep when they had the chance – "

"Or just confined him to a hospital bed like any other terminal patient."

"What good would that do?"

"He'd have been taken care of."

"No. A bullet and he'd be taken care of. A hospital bed and he'd attack the orderlies. What value is it to keep him going? Who does it really benefit?"

When Jacob gets going like this his face narrows to a sharp point and drives forward into the body of his enemy. He is a battering ram at the gates of logic and decency, and he is the blistering hordes of rage behind it. He can be distracted, but never deterred.

"Our species has this cloying habit," he continues, "of elevating the afflicted, you know? The sick, the helpless, the unproductive. No society can function that way."

"What should we do then?" Asks Tony.

At this point, he's learned that he's only here to serve as devil's advocate. Anything else is an unwanted intrusion.

"We let them fail," he says. "What else is there to do?"

Tony gestures for the check.

THE WALLET
Jacob

JACOB'S BEEN SCOPING THE SAME WOMAN out for a week, and he knows she's the one. She's got deep wrinkles in her face that make it look like the surface of Mars or something, and her skin is almost the right color for it. She's old, and graying, but she covers for that with the incredibly colorful dress and scarves her people are known for. She's a Roma, one of a handful that begs in the corridor between the *Santa Maria dei Fiori* and the *Piazza della Signoria*. Jacob is waiting for a chance to get her alone, for her friends to be otherwise engaged. He hasn't gotten it yet, but he knows he will, soon enough.

He keeps watching. Kitsune sometimes performs in this square, she's told him. He's yet to see one of her shows, but it's on his to do list. She's talented enough in other areas he can only imagine what she can do with a guitar. His mind drifts, but a flash of movement brings him back to the real world. It's not his chance, not yet, but it's something worth watching anyway.

The woman gets up to approach a man in a thick wool suit it's entirely too warm for him to be wearing. It's the kind of high-fashion Italian bullshit he's come to expect from the Florentines, and which she's probably learned to take advantage of. She's got that same little tiny gelato cup she always uses to beg for change in hand, and she's shaking it his way. Maybe one in every thirty people she sees will give her anything, and usually it's just the finger. But she keeps asking. She has to know this guy won't do it. She has to know he'd rather lay her out on the cobblestone with the back of his hand than give her a cent. Wait, Jacob realizes. She does know.

She keeps pace with him, getting his nerves up as she follows him through the square. She's got his whole focus. It's taking everything he's got for him to keep from raising his hand to her, and the focus is distracting him. He doesn't see the younger girl walking by him. He doesn't see her hand dart into his pocket, remove his wallet and signal the older woman. Jacob's attention shifts to the other gypsy as the old lady maintains her ruse just long enough to avoid attracting suspicion. The girl's maybe sixteen, pretty but not remarkable. There's nothing about her that would mark her as a Roma. Maybe Jacob's been waiting for the wrong person. He gets up from his seat and follows her as she walks out of the square. She's turning through the alleyways so fast he almost loses her, but he tracks her down in a deserted little square. Or he thinks he does, but she's onto him. As soon as they're alone, she rounds on him knife in hand and pins him to the wall with the blade against his throat.

"Don't you try it, *testa di cazzo*!" She spits in his face on the last syllable, which she probably views as a happy accident. Jacob doesn't know what these words mean exactly, but he can read between the lines. "I'm not so stupid, I know what you want."

"Actually, you don't." He says, "I'm a journalist, I just want to talk."

"*Vaffanculo*, get out. I'm not talking to you."

She spits at his feet, deliberately this time, and turns to walk away.

"Wait," he says, "I saw you. I saw what you took from that man."

She turns back to him. She's still got that knife out. Maybe Jacob is making a mistake here.

"I'm not going to say anything."

"You had better not, dog." This is, as far as he can tell, the nicest thing she's called him thus far. Maybe he's making progress. He offers his most charming smile.

"All I want is to ask you a few questions." He says, "I know this is hard to believe, but I'm on your side here. I'm American, I'm not Italian."

"*Porca vacca*, obviously you're American. An Italian would have just grabbed my ass and been done with it."

"I don't want to grab your ass," he says.

"Liar." She fires back, "Anyway, you talk like a schoolboy. What do you want to ask me?"

Jacob lets a little relief show on his face, just enough to help her not be so guarded.

"I want to ask you if you think your people can change. If they want to change. If they should?"

She spits, but this time on the ground. They're practically friends.

"You want me to talk, I want money. You have Euro?"

Jacob nods.

"I want ten for each question. I get to ten questions, I want another fifty. *Capisce*?"

Jacob nods again. This word he knows, if only from The Godfather.

"I answer that one for free. My people will not change, because my people are change. That is why they use this word, gypsy. To them it's a bad word, like what I called you that first time."

"What did that mean?" He asks, "Off the record, of course. I'm not paying you for that."

She laughs. "Head of a dick," she says. "But in this I am serious. To be Roma is to be change. We cannot stay the same. We are like a reflection in water. The only thing that remains the same is how people see us. Crooks. Liars. Villains."

"I did see you rob a man." Jacob reminds her.

"I did that today, yes." She says, "tomorrow I will wear a nice dress and go to a school and borrow a book from my library, and I will be a Roma then, too. The next question you pay me for."

"How much of the money you use to eat comes from things like what I saw?" He asks.

"Half," she says, "maybe less. My father runs a shop where he repairs cars. He will also buy stolen, and sell the parts."

She sticks out her hand, and Jacob places a ten Euro note in it. Her skin is rough, and calloused.

"Has anyone in your family ever experienced violence at the hand of an Italian citizen?"

She laughs, but this time it's not a light laugh. It's dark, and heavy, and it pulls her shoulders down instead of lifting them up.

"You think I carry a knife because I'm crazy?" She asks, and Jacob considers the implications of that question. "You are not the first man to corner me in an alley, you're just the first who only wants to talk."

"I'm sorry," Jacob says.

She spits. She knows he's lying, but she takes his money anyway. They go back and forth on a few more questions. He learns that her family has been in Florence for three generations, and they have never been registered or legal, despite their best efforts. He learns that her grandmother was hung for the crime of poisoning an Italian woman's children, despite the fact she had never been anywhere near their home in her life. He learns that she has seen people spit on her parents, throw stones at her parents, and that more than one drunken group of Italians has tried to burn her father's store to the ground. When it's all said and done, he's asked nine questions.

"That's it then?" She asks. She's flipping idly through the man's wallet, trying to give Jacob the sense that the things she's revealed to him aren't sources of pain – deep pain, the kind you spend your whole life trying to heal. He thinks again about that knife, and wonders how many times she's had to use it. This question, he decides, you should not ask. He nods. She starts to walk away, dropping the wallet on the ground but taking the money and a couple of cards.

"Wait," says Jacob.

She turns back. Really, she's very pretty. It's hard to tell because it's been a long time since she's been able to do the things normal teenage girls do to make themselves look good, but the signs are there. The whole thing is a goddamn shame.

"What's your name," he asks her.

She shakes her head.

"I won't print it," he says. "I just want to know."

"Maria," she says. "My father named me after the Virgin Mary."

Jacob nods, and pulls out sixty euro from his wallet. It's the last of his cash. She looks at him like she's trying to decide if this is a trick, but she knows she has to take it. This is a week of food, if she plays her cards right. This is two wallets she doesn't have to steal.

"Thank you," she says, and she disappears into the alleys.

It's about then that it sinks in how close he came to being gutted. Jacob breathes deep, and his phone rings. It's Tony. He answers, but he's not happy about it.

"This isn't the best time, Tony." And really, it isn't.

"Right," Tony says. "Sure. I just had something you might want to look at. For your article."

Jacob's already writing down as much as he can remember from what Maria told him, but he blocks out a little room for Tony's contribution on the page.

"Ok," he says. "Shoot."

"Well," says Tony, "it's about that bishop, the one that got run over by the taxi a few weeks back."

Jacob knows who he's talking about. It was all over the news the week he landed in the city.

"Carrera?" He says.

"Yea, that's him. Listen, I – well it doesn't matter how, I just kind of learned some stuff. You should look into his record on the gypsies. Apparently it's dark, dark shit."

Jacob nods. He's filling up his spiral nicely, and it's looking like he's going to have more than enough to make an article out of this. The problem is, after seeing the problem first hand, he's not sure an article is enough.

"Thanks, Tony," he says, and for the second time he means it. He almost regrets calling him an idiot, even if he did keep the thought to himself. As he hangs up, Jacob sees a shadow out of the corner of his eye. He's on his guard in an instant, wary of Maria coming back with that knife, but it's too small a shadow, too low to the ground.

"Who's there?"

There's no answer, but he can make out the shape well enough to see why. It's not a person, lurking on the far side of the alley. It's a dog – it's Tony's dog, and in its mouth is a dead pigeon.

THE RAZOR
Paolo

IT'S ONE P.M. AND PAOLO FIGURES now's as good a time as any to get up and shave. The bathroom here is a defeated mess of decidedly feminine garbage; hairs clutter the shower drain, and unwanted tampons scatter over the rusty tile like shells from an automatic rifle. He's already cut himself. The day's off to a great start already.

Meanwhile and adjacent, the kitchen walls reverberate with impromptu sermonizing. The Girl with the Egyptian Eyeliner is fond of making grand statements about the male gender to be interjected at will into her limitless monologue. Her friends, or more to the point disciples, repeat these amongst themselves in hushed tones, eyes wide and heads bobbing. Always in total, perfect unison, like the chorus of a musical or something.

Some keep entire notebooks filled with scribbled witticisms:

Tues. Mar. 3: "A man without a belt is not to be trusted."

Fri. May 11: "A man's worth is the sum of his best fictions."

And, her personal favorite: "Some men are sharks, and the rest are pilot fish."

Paolo looks at himself in the mirror. The bags under his eyes are deep enough to tell time; a ring for each week of his life lost living with this cult leader in Gucci. How long has it been, Paolo? How long have I been living here?

They've gone, now, the women. The girls.

Paolo can recall, from the not so distant past, a time when such a gathering would have held a certain sense of mystery for him. Now even the sight of them, half dressed and headed for the door, does nothing for him. They've become fixtures in his life of no more of interest than the smudged faucets, or the bidet. Her voice comes through the wall, lilting and almost musical. It's always like that when she wants something.

"Paolo? What the fuck are you doing in there?"

"I'm shaving."

"You've been in there for like half an hour."

"I'm being extra careful."

Had it really been so long? He'd barely even begun the left side of his face.

"Are you almost done?"

Her body appears in the doorway. It's not so bad, really. It'd be perfectly palatable if she didn't use it so matter-of-factly, as though it were a band saw, or a nail gun. A pile of silk drops to her ankles – really, the whole thing is quite nice. They have fucked almost constantly since he moved in, to the point that it's almost lost its charm. Almost. Paolo tries his best to generate enthusiasm, but all that comes out is stony silence.

She's on her knees, now, planting dry kisses on the insides of his hips. Paolo begins to think about pilot fish. The Girl's movements have no sense of ceremony, no style. She could be cleaning for parasites, or just checking off another item on her to-do list. Against his better judgment, Paolo begins to laugh.

"Something funny, Paolo?"

"No, I just – it tickles, that's all."

That must satisfy her curiosity, because she doesn't stop. He takes a handful of her hair. She keeps her hair immaculate – shiny and smooth and as jet black as the rings around her eyes. Holding it reminds him of, of all things, the sheets on Kitsune's bed. Paolo stares at the razor by the sink. His father had taught him how to use a straight razor the day he turned fifteen. He had always liked the ritual, even then.

"It's a strange thing, a razor," his father had told him, "Held at one angle, it performs a simple service. It keeps the body clean."

Paolo could remember the way his father had twisted the razor in his hands. He could remember how the blade caught the light and sent it shooting away into the ether.

"Held another way," he had said, turning it to demonstrate, "it cuts. Held another way, it could even kill."

His father kicked him out of the house less than a year after dropping that pearl of wisdom. Paolo had taken the razor with him.

Now that their business on the bathroom floor has concluded, the Girl with the Egyptian Eyeliner lies back on the tile with her head on a bathmat and smokes a cigarette. Her chest rises and falls with each puff of smoke. Paolo watches her breathe, but his mind is on the razor. On how strange it is for an object to change its function without changing its form.

"What are you looking at, Paolo?"

She's making a 'my eyes are up here' face, but he knows she likes when he looks at her. It's such an obvious question he doesn't even bother to answer. Or, rather, he decides to change the subject.

"So," he says, "which am I?"

"What do you mean?"

"Which am I, a shark or a pilot fish?"

She sits up abruptly. Ash from her cigarette floats down and lands in her lap.

"You're a shark, Paolo. Of course you're a shark. I wouldn't be with you if you weren't."

"But what does that mean? What's the difference, really? Either way I'm breathing salt water."

The girl smiles, and puts her cigarette out in a puddle of water from the shower.

"It means you make things happen, Paolo. That's what sharks do. They make things happen, while pilot fish watch and try to look useful."

Paolo's not sure that's true. If he could make things happen, he wouldn't be there in that bathroom having his shark skin cleaned by an American grad student with winged eyeliner. If he could make things happen, maybe he'd still be with Kitsune. Maybe it wouldn't have all been a waste. Still, it's nice of her to say.

"Thanks," he says. And for once, he means it.

THE BISHOP
Tony

JACOB DOES HIS JOB WELL, AND TONY reaps the rewards. He tells the story in hushed, excited whispers over the phone, and he's struck gold. For both of them, and for very different reasons. It's a simple enough story. As a bishop, Carrera was well liked. He was progressive in ways that could be forgiven but that made him seem kind. He insisted on living language in churches under his control. In the cathedrals, he extended the warm hand of the Lord to any American expatriate or hungover study abroad student willing to listen to him talk with entire services in English. He built shelters for abused women and other victims of violence, and he visited them regularly. In most respects he cultivated an illusion of holy radiance they served him well. Beneath the surface, though, his agenda was darker. Carrera saw the gypsies, the Roma, as an ever-growing blight on all of Europe. He was similarly antagonistic to the influx of North African immigrants, but as he was fond of saying: only one crusade can march at a time.

Behind closed doors, Carrera actively worked against charitable outreach to Roma communities throughout Italy. He passed it off as re-organizing the flow of cash to different charities, more valuable work – the work he was running himself, naturally. Of course it's much harder to argue against the funding of a battered woman's shelter than it is to argue against the defunding of outreach to an unwanted community. And regardless of the bishop's personal feelings on the matter, they really were, increasingly unwanted. It's unclear how far the reach of his influence went in solidifying the politicization of anti-gypsy sentiment in Italy. He was, for a time, the chief theological advisor for Berlusconi, who had adopted the harshest policies against the Roma the country had yet seen. When Rome built the camps to hide them outside of the city, Carrera's hand was in it. When Florence began banning them from certain public spaces, he was there too. But there was something juicier than even that. Something you wouldn't find in the local papers, something you'd only hear in whispers.

Among the Roma, it had been known for years that a certain number of those arrested never returned. Of course it was hoped they were merely deported or sent elsewhere, but it was only a hope. The reality was there was no way to know if they had been sent away, locked up, or simply killed. Some of the whisperers seemed to know for sure though. Some say they went to Carrera, personally. According to the rumors, there was a car that ran from the office of the local *polizia* directly to the bishop's manor on the outskirts of the city from time to time, in the days before his accident. At first it was rare. Once every other month, then twice a month. By the time he was hit by that taxi, it was running once a week, like clockwork.

The story goes that bishop Carrera had a theory. The bishop believed the Roma were more than just thieves and vultures, as popular anti-gypsy sentiment portrayed them, fairly or unfairly. The bishop believed they were creatures of genuine, absolute evil. He believed they were demons, and that it was his right and duty before God to exorcise the spirits that afflicted them. Barring his success in that endeavor, he would destroy them completely. Of course, these exorcisms were never documented. They may simply have been taken to a torture chamber for

Carrera to act out his inexplicable hatred in privacy. Or it may have been just that, a rumor. There would have been no way to verify it before the accident other than to ask him, and it would be even harder to learn the truth now.

"I can't print this part of the story, Tony," Jacob says apologetically, "but I can print a lot of the rest of it. This is great stuff. You've really set me up here. Thanks."

It's a real thank you, and Tony almost wants to share his source. It'd bring him some comfort if he could introduce her to anyone else. She had come by again, and again, and again. It had been four times now, in total, and he never knew when to expect her. If Jacob could see her too, then he he'd at least know that he wasn't crazy. But if he wasn't crazy, then he might have to think about doing what she said.

As if summoned by his musings on the subject, the Angel appears only moments after Jacob's hung up the phone.

"I suppose you heard that?" He asks her. She nods. "Is any of what he said true?"

"I can only tell you what is given to me to know, Tony. Bishop Carrera's soul casts a black shadow over the city. Its influence grows, daily. I do not know what caused him to hold such malevolence in his heart. Perhaps it was always there. Perhaps there is something greater at work."

"Greater?" He asks. She doesn't answer. By now he knows that if she hasn't already told him, she's not going to. He changes tactics, going with the proverbial carrot for a bit.

"I'm not saying I've agreed to anything," he says, "because I haven't. But if I were to accept that what you're saying isn't absolute horseshit…"

"I am not lying to you."

"If I were to accept that, what would I have to do? Sneak into his hospital room with a pillow? Just up and kill the man?"

Tony doesn't want to think about it too much, but it's

important to test the Angel's limits. Either she's his own mind finally collapsing under the weight of – well, really, of nothing – or she's the genuine article. Either way, it's bad news if she wants him to kill someone.

"I am afraid that it is not that simple, Tony." Of course it isn't. Why would it be?

"Why isn't it that simple? Kill the man, kill the spirit. Right?"

"I am afraid not. The motion of the spirit is complex. Destroying the body is not enough, at least not immediately. The spirit may survive for a number of seconds without it."

"What does that mean?" He asks.

"It means that if you were to do as you suggest and suffocate the bishop, then only the bishop's body would die. His spirit would simply migrate to another body, and there would be no way to know whose body he had taken."

This is insane. This is genuinely insane. She talks like she's watched too many horror movies, and amalgamated some pseudo-spiritual threatening hoax out of their skeletons. In fact, Tony's pretty sure he remembers this exact 'fact' from a Denzel Washington movie about a demon who loved the Rolling Stones. Actually, he's pretty sure he's got that lying around somewhere on VHS. That's definitely a vote for the 'I'm Crazy' party.

"If that's the case, there's nothing to be done. Even if I do what you want, which I'm not saying I will, he'll just possess another body. Right?"

"Yes, Tony. Which is why I did not only ask you to kill the bishop: I asked you to take care of it."

"What's the difference?"

Tony's pretty sure he can read between the lines on this one, but he wants to hear her say it. He wants her to ask him, or him to ask himself, or whatever the fuck is going on.

"You cannot solve this problem by killing the bishop alone, Tony. You have to destroy the building that holds his body. You have to burn the hospital to the ground."

"That's hundreds of people."

"Yes."

"You want me to kill hundreds of people."

"Yes."

"Yeah, I'm not going to do that."

She nods in understanding, which is good, but he can't get the request out of his head. I mean why would she even ask him that? Why would anyone? She begins to head for the window. She's been here for her allotted time, and she's said her piece, so it's time for her grand exit. Again. As per usual, she pauses to get the last word in.

"The choice is yours to make, Tony. It must always be yours to make. But you must know that your dog's proclivities will only worsen with time. Today it was two birds, tomorrow it may be three. Soon it will be more. Eventually you will understand that something must be done."

With that, she's gone. He doesn't even bother asking how she knows about the birds he cleaned up that morning, because there's no point. She's not wrong, not completely. Something has to be done. Something, maybe. But not this.

THE DOCTOR
Kitsune

KITTY LIES ON A COLD WHITE TABLE wearing only a paper sheet that feels for all the world like a larger-than-average cocktail napkin. A distant memory resurfaces of a poem her father made her memorize when she was very young. Let us go then, you and I, where the evening meets the sky like a patient etherized upon a table. They haven't bothered to dope her up yet, but otherwise the shoe fits.

"We're going to need you to take all of that out, dear," the nurse says, gesturing to her hair.

Gingerly, Kitty removes the ornaments in her braid. A bronze bead her mother had brought home from a trip to the Museum of Antiquities in London. A strand of copper filament she stripped from the instrument cable on her first guitar. The feather of what her father had insisted was a golden eagle, but that she knew as an adult belonged to the comparatively common red-tailed hawk. She places each on the tray the nurse extends to her, and studies her reflection in its warped steel surface. Without these things she barely recognizes herself. Without these things, she could be anyone.

"Thank you," says the Nurse, and Kitty grabs her arm.

"How long do I have to be in here?" She asks.

An hour is the answer. She knows that already. The doctor had explained everything in sterile, unadorned detail when they had set the date for the procedure. Still, every time the room falls silent she repeats the question hoping for a different answer. The Nurse flips the switch and the MRI starts with a harsh, throbbing hum. Kitty follows the protocol and lies down as flat as she can go. As the machine pulls her into its electric blue cocoon, the little cloth nearly blows away. In the dark, she does her best to sleep, but the cough is there waiting. It comes out only when she's alone. It ambushes her like a thief waiting in the alley, beating her before taking what it wants. It isn't pleasant.

"I need you to lay still, miss." Says the nurse.

"I'll do my best," she wheezes, "Sorry."

It's not easy when she's racked with hacking like that, which the nurse ought to know full well. But she holds her tongue. It's in her best interests to keep any medical professionals analyzing her on their best behavior. Seeing no better alternative, Kitty looks for a distraction. She starts to think about Jacob. At first it was just sex, which was both what she expected and what she wanted, but more recently it had felt different. Sure, they'd fucked, but he'd lingered after. He'd told her more about what he was writing, even asked for opinions. They'd set a date for him to come to one of her shows. It's nice, but it's also a subject of concern. He's attaching to her in ways she didn't expect someone to attach when they knew they were leaving, and she's starting to feel attached to him, too. She's not sure how she'll feel when he leaves. Shit, she's not sure how she feels now.

"You're doing great," says the nurse. She probably says this to all the girls.

It couldn't have been fifteen minutes. Barely a dent in the time. Kitty needs a better distraction. She can feel whatever it is that's making her cough scraping at her insides, waiting for another chance to scrape its way out. Lately, she's started to think of it as a living thing. Like a little creature, living inside of her. Maybe it doesn't mean to harm her, but that's exactly what it's doing. It's nice to think that it's just an accident, but she's not so certain.

"It's the first sign of the apocalypse," she says again, and for the first time she considers the broader implications of that.

One of her father's favorite poems, and he had many, was

"The Second Coming" by W.B Yeats. She remembers the final lines well: "and what rough beast, its hour come round at last, slouches towards Bethlehem to be born." She's never exactly been a Christian, but she knows that part of the idea of the apocalypse is the beast. What was the line in The Omen? From the eternal sea, he rises? That's another thing it's best not to think about, but it's exactly how she feels. Like something is stirring inside her, getting ready to be born. And not in the way you'd expect.

"Miss Lingo?" That's a new voice. Her doctor's. Kitty hates her last name, always has. They'd had a different one, close but not the same, before her parents came here, but they had changed it in an effort to fit in that bore exactly zero fruit.

"Yes?" She calls weakly.

"I've seen enough," he says. "You can get out."

How long had it been? Surely not an hour. The machine starts to pull her out, and she becomes conscious of the little scrap of cloth again. The doctor must sense her thoughts somehow, because he says he'll let her get dressed, and meet her in five minutes.

"I'm going to be honest with you," says the doctor. When most men say they're going to be honest it's usually a sign they're going to tell a particularly big lie, but doctors are usually a little bit different. "I don't see anything in these scans to be a point of concern."

"Ok," she says. "That's good, though, right?"

"Of course," says the doctor. And he smiles so wide she believes it, just for a second. "And we'll have the nurse do some bloodwork to rule out a few other things, just to be safe. But I want to ask you, first. What exactly made you think you needed this procedure?"

He's asking the question nicely, but he doesn't mean it that way. The look on his face says he thinks she's wasting his time. That she's looking for attention, or that she's overreacted to some minor thing that shouldn't have warranted his interference. Frankly, even if he's right he ought to be grateful for the money her insurance is shoveling into his bank account.

"I've had a cough for a few weeks now," she says, truthfully, "and I was starting to get concerned about it. There's a family history of lung cancer, so I thought I'd rule it out."

"Of course," he says, smiling that same fucking fake smile. She hates this doctor, but it's not his fault. She hates most doctors.

"The thing is, Ms. Lingo – "

"Kitty," she corrects him. "Kitty is fine."

"Charming," he says wryly, and she wants to punch the smirk off his face. "Kitty, are you still experiencing that cough? You haven't presented it in the time you've been here."

That simply wasn't true. She'd hacked and coughed so hard while she was in the MRI she was afraid she might have gotten blood on it. The nurse must have heard her.

"Yes, I have," she says, and the doctor spreads his hands in a 'well I don't know about that' gesture.

There's one way to settle this. Kitty calls on the beast. It's just waiting for its chance, after all. Just waiting to come running out, to sprint towards Bethlehem. The cough comes bursting out so violently she's afraid she'll burst. It hurts like a metal bat slammed against her spine. It shakes her whole body. If she saw a stranger coughing like this, she's not sure if she'd run to help them or run for the hills. If it was contagious, she sure as shit wouldn't want it. It comes and it goes, but the doctor's unimpressed.

"Is there anything else?" He asks, and she shakes her head.

There's two options here. Either her doctor is an actual honest to god asshole with no intention of treating her or, like Tony, he didn't even realize she was coughing. Unlike Tony, though, this couldn't be explained away as a fluke of the phone, a bad connection. He'd been staring right at her. He'd been watching her, probably looking for signs of sickness real or falsified. And he'd missed it. Maybe it's not real, says a little voice in the back of her head. Maybe it's just your imagination. If she's imagining it, she's imagining it vividly. She feels weak, and broken. Her throat feels like she swallowed a roll of razor wire. The nurse comes in to check her blood, but Kitty's not sure she should bother. Something tells her they won't see anything there, either.

THE VET
Tony

TONY'S NEVER BEEN TO THIS VET'S OFFICE before, but then he's never had a dog before, either. He's not sure how long you're supposed to wait for a doctor to show up in this context before it becomes rude. He's guessing the vet's pushing it, because he's been sitting here in silence with Crosby for almost a half an hour. A nurse had been by, of course. They'd weighed the dog at forty-four pounds, which wasn't bad for a dog his size, and determined he was flea and tick-free, which gave Tony no small amount of relief.

"Well, Crosby, I guess you can sleep on the big bed now, if you want to." He'd said. The dog wagged its tail.

Then they'd taken some blood and checked eyesight, teeth cleanliness, ear cleanliness, et cetera. So far, the dog seems to have a cleaner bill of health than Tony's ever gotten. Finally, the door opens.

"Mr. Ducati?" This is the vet. He's a big man, bigger than you'd expect a vet to be. He looks like he could bench press Tony a dozen times over and not even start to break a sweat.

"Remind me of your dog's name, sir?"

"Crosby," Tony says. "And I'm Tony."

"Crosby," the vet repeats. "Mr. Ducati, your dog is perfectly healthy. I'm glad you stopped by, but medically it wasn't really necessary. We're going to give him some vaccinations just for the usual things, but that's mostly got to do with licensing."

"Licensing?" Tony asks.

"Yes. If you want to be able to take him out in the open, he has to be licensed, and he has to be current on rabies and parvo vaccinations. There are strict rules about this. It matters less if he's home alone, but a dog really needs to meet other dogs from time to time, don't you think?"

Tony nods, dumbly. He hadn't thought about that. To be honest, though, when he thinks about taking Crosby to a dog park all he can think about is that little bird, lying on his couch with its neck snapped. All he can think about is the Angel, or the figment of his imagination, or whatever she is. We will have to finish what the accident started, she had said. It gave him a chill, thinking about it.

"There's something else, Mr. Ducati. You're aware that your dog was microchipped?"

"Microchipped?" Tony does not know what this means.

"Yes, microchipped. Typically a dog that has had an owner will at some point have this done. We surgically implant a small chip that carries some information about the owner, so that if it's lost the owner can be contacted."

Tony swallows heavily. Maybe this is for the best. Maybe he ought to follow up on this, and get the dog out of his life now. Crosby looks up at him with big, wet eyes and he knows he can't. He can't let this go, not now. There may have been a window where he could have, but it's long since passed.

"So you found them then?" Tony asks, "the people who owned him before, I mean?"

"We got an address, and some contact information, yes. I'll write it down for you."

An awkward look comes over the vet's face then, and he begins to speak in a whisper, as though he's confiding in Tony some great and terrible secret.

"Mr. Ducati, if you have the means and it is feasible for you, I would advise you to keep the dog rather than returning it."

"And why is that?" Tony is honestly looking for any excuse.

"Well, Mr. Ducati, I'm sure you'll understand when you look at the address. Suffice it to say, it's a miracle he's in such fine health. Some places are just not meant to be homes for animals."

With that the meeting's basically over. The vet shares his qualifications with Tony in an effort to ensure his repeated business, but he needn't bother. To Tony's knowledge this is the only vet in town that speaks English. His Italian is good, but not good enough for something like this. On his way out, he looks at the address. It's not, strictly speaking, a Florentine address. It's from just outside of the city, in an area that Tony knows is a Roma camp – he knows because of Jacob. He doesn't strictly speaking share the vet's obvious opinions about keeping a dog at the gypsy camp, but one thing's for certain. He's not going to be the one to take it out there.

There's one other piece of information of value in the microchip sheet that Tony files away: the dog's real name. Draca. It's an odd name, with a vaguely sinister ring to it. Tony keeps it to himself. The dog's got enough problems without it.

"That settles it, kid," he says to Crosby. "You're staying with me."

And with that taken care of, they head home.

The phone's already ringing when Tony makes it back to the apartment. It's his mother for the second time in as many months, which is a clear sign that something's amiss.

"You don't sound happy," she says.

"Most people say hello first, mother."

She doesn't laugh, but he didn't expect her to. Tony has heard his mother laugh twice since the night of his sixteenth birthday. The first was when he had called her to come and help him patch a flat tire. The second was when he told her he was moving to Florence. That had only stopped being funny to her when the plane landed.

"I'm just tired," he corrects himself. "Has something happened?"

There is a long pause. Tony imagines the little dog in her free hand, tongue wagging happily between its crooked, bratty teeth. He glances, longingly, into his bedroom and the unmade bed within.

"It is bad news, yes." She says.

"How bad?"

"Honestly, Tony, you probably won't even care."

She knows her audience. Tony's stepfather died three years ago. He has no siblings. The last time they spoke, she had pocket dialed him. It was the truest apology he had ever received from her.

"You'll have to pretend to care, unfortunately, because there's no one else for me to tell."

She's being dramatic intentionally, and Tony knows it. Still, he feels a moment's guilt.

"It's fine, mom. Really. Tell me."

"Well there's no easy way for me to say it, so I'll say it quickly. Magritte is dead."

Tony feels a chill, and sits down on his couch hard enough to knock a cushion off.

"Your dog?" He speaks more calmly than he looks.

"Yes, my dog. She died a few days ago, I didn't know if I should tell you."

Magritte had always been his mother's favored child, and Tony hated it with every fickle fiber of his unreasonable being. This is a dangerous conversation, he thinks.

"What happened?" He asks, "Was she sick?"

"No, not at all. That's the worst of it."

"Well what happened?"

"She was killed, Tony. One of the neighbor's kids."

Tony all but slams the phone into the receiver but catches it before he drops the call.

"You're lying to me," he says. His voice sounds like fists pounding on a windshield.

"I swear to God it's true, you bastard."

Tony can hear tears scattered between the bigger pearls in his mother's string of curses. It's the only way he knows she's telling the truth.

"You know, I knew I shouldn't have called you."

"Look," says Tony, "I'm sorry, alright? It's just we haven't ever –"

"This is not about you, dammit! This is about my dog."

"I'm sorry," Tony says after a long silence, "Was it an accident?"

He waits for the shoe to fall. He waits for the inevitable avalanche of guilt; for the expected outpouring of unkind remembrances.

"It wasn't," she says. "It was on purpose."

"Jesus Christ."

"Will you watch your mouth for two minutes while I speak with you? I had her in the backyard for a while because I had a few women over from church for drinks and one of them is allergic. Magritte was out in the back with a bowl of water and some dry food. So the kid, the little shit, he hopped the fence and swapped the water out for antifreeze."

"You're kidding."

"I'm not, I'm not. By the time I realized it, it was an hour too late to pump her stomach. She died at the vet."

Tony takes a long, hard look at Crosby. His left hand has formed a fist without thinking about it, and the dog stares at it with what could almost be called fascination.

"Why did you call me," he asks eventually. "Why are you telling me this?"

"I want you to come home."

"Excuse me?"

"For the funeral."

The funeral. Of course. The long driveway, the stepping stones across the mulch to the dull red door hot from the sun. The backyard, she'd bury it there. Tony knows he should go.

"When is it?"

"It's next Monday."

"Isn't that really quick? Couldn't you give people more time if you want them to come?"

"I didn't want to wait," she says. "I wanted to have you home on your birthday."

Of course, thinks Tony, and hangs up the phone. Everything happens for a reason.

THE STAIRS
Paolo

FOR THE FOURTH DAY IN A ROW, PAOLO spends hours on end pounding the pavement to no avail. He walks into restaurants, retailers, museums, offices; some of them even have Help Wanted signs out, but none of them will talk to him. It's demoralizing, but he shakes it off before he comes back inside the Girl's apartment. Something tells him carrying that weakness around would get him eaten alive in there. He's developed a little ritual to keep his head clear. He stops just inside the foyer, before he opens door to the stairs, and he works his way through their names. There's too many of them, and they're too similar. If he doesn't do this, he'll never remember, and it's a good way to keep his mind sharp. He stops at the base of the stairs and starts to go through the list.

"Cara, Catrina, Sonya, Jessica, Sara, Nadia, Allison, Patience."

He repeats it like a mantra, doing his best to assign each girl to a detail. Sonya's the one the Girl told to drop her boyfriend back home because he called her too much. Cara's the one bleaching her hair to pass as a blond. Sara's the one who dumped her whole wardrobe in the trash. Patience is the one with the notebook. But there's more to that story, because Patience is also the one at the bottom of the stairs. Well, thinks Paolo. This is new. Patience is alone, per usual, and while she's fine now it seems like she's been crying. There's red in little rings around her eyes that make her look ill, and there's no sign of a notebook in sight.

"Everything ok?" He asks.

She's going to lie and say yes. Paolo knows this because it's what he would do. It's why he's down here in the stairwell counting names. It's why he tells the Girl he just hangs out at a café during the day rather than cop to looking for work. No one likes to look like an idiot in front of their friends. Even if the people they'd like to call their friends wouldn't think of them the same way.

"I'm fine," she says. "I just wanted a minute to myself, that's all."

Paolo takes a moment to be pleased with his observational skills, but just a moment. He feels a sense of duty to Patience. In a way he had thrown off the balance by showing up on the Girl's doorstep. If he hadn't, maybe Patience would have been fine. Maybe her girl-next-door vibe would have been the project the Girl needed to keep herself busy. Of course, maybe she'd have just been shark bait. There's no point in wondering. Better to focus on the task at hand.

"You sure?" He asks her. "Cause it seems like maybe you're getting more of those than you bargained for."

She looks at him like he's slapped her in the face and for a second he thinks he's gone too far. It's the truth, but some people don't want the truth. He might have misjudged her on that count. After a few seconds, though, her expression softens. He can see it settling into her head, the words stratifying and settling into reality. It's like she's walking her way through the stages of grief, right before his eyes.

"I guess that's fair," she says, but she doesn't say anything else. Paolo figures they've got fifteen minutes before the Girl starts to wonder where he is. He wants to help, but he can't give her all the time in the world. Patience shifts her weight a little, and the floodgates start to open. They shouldn't have a problem at this pace.

"Do you like us, Paolo?" Patience asks, and he considers the question.

"I don't know," he says, "I haven't really had a choice about being here, so I try not to think about it."

"Don't lie to me."

She sees him the way he sees her. She knows he's full of shit. Maybe she's always known. She'd be the only one other than the Girl if she did, and he's not sure the Girl knows. Or if she knows, if it bothers her.

"Alright. Maybe I don't like all of you. Some of you I don't know well enough to say. Some of you I know well enough to know that I don't."

"Do you like her?"

From her intonation, he knows she means the Girl with the Egyptian Eyeliner. He knows she has an answer to this question.

"I don't know," he says, and this time he's telling the truth. "She's unlike anyone I've ever met, but not always in a way that I understand. I want to like her, because I'm drawn to her. I want to dislike her, I guess for the same reason."

"I don't think she wants this," Patience says. Maybe she's right. "I don't think she can stop it."

Now she's being a bit dramatic. At the end of the day, this whole little cult is harmless, isn't it? A couple of little haut couture clones running around the city isn't going to hurt anyone. Right? Paolo thinks about the way they all fell to the floor, and the way the Girl woke up, like nothing ever happened. It was like the group formed a colossal symbiotic organism with the Girl at its center. Maybe there was something to Patience's distress, but Paolo couldn't let her see that. He had to be strong if he wanted her to be.

"Maybe she can and maybe she doesn't want to. I don't

know," Paolo says. "But you don't have to go along with it if you don't like it. You know that, right?"

Patience gives a harsh little chuckle that doesn't suit her. It doesn't seem like a sound that could come from her, but here it is.

"Yes, I do. You know that I do. I mean yea, I could just go it alone, and let them say whatever they want, and act like it didn't bother me. But it would. It does now, and I'm trying."

She really is. She tries harder than any of them. For Cara, other than the hair, the transition's basically natural. It's like she was just waiting for the right excuse to make these changes to herself. Some of the others have made sacrifices, to be sure, but they've all been rewarded for it, and their differences have been a bit more tolerated.

"So maybe don't try so much," he says, and she looks at him like he's an idiot. It's the first time, without meaning to, that she's tapped into the groupthink sincerely. It's not his favorite moment. "I'm serious. Everyone's got their niche."

Paolo's just talking, but without meaning to he realizes he's stumbled onto something. Something she can use, if she'll listen to it. Something that makes his staircase mantras all worthwhile.

"You just need a thing, Patience. Catrina's the redhead. Sonya's learning Italian, and she already speaks Russian. Cara's a little more punk. If all they did was try to be the same, it would just be a competition. You've got to be a little different, but you can't take it too far."

Of course, it'll be hard for her. Patience is a farm girl at heart, and most of the things she'd want to be have nothing to do with anything the others care about. But he knows he's right. And he also knows the advice doesn't stop with her. If Paolo wants to move forward, he needs a thing too. Not in the house, he's already got a thing there. He's the Girl's arm candy. They're all obligated to halfway flirt with him, within reason of course.

They're all kind to him on the surface. They might question her judgment behind closed doors, but never to her face. But out in the world, he's just another guy. Just some little shit looking for a job. He needs something to make him stand out, and he's starting to get an idea of what that might be.

Back in the apartment Patience and Paolo play dumb to their meeting, but it's wasted effort. The girls are in rapt attention in the living room, where the Girl is unconscious on the living room floor. Did she faint again? Is she sleeping? Paolo watches the other girls for any sign of something amiss. It's definitely amiss but they don't seem to want to hurt her. One by one, they stick their fingers gently in the corner of her eyes, getting a bit of black on the tips. They smudge it on their forehead like Ash Wednesday, and sit in a circle around her. The ground is strewn with pigeon feathers, scattered haphazard like they'd been knocked out of pillows in a scene from some dopey college movie. Paolo looks at Patience. Silently, he's begging her not to, but he knows she won't listen. She walks into the room, takes a smudge, and marks herself. Paolo heads back down to the street.

THE UMBRELLA
Kitsune

IT BEGINS TO RAIN, FAT DROPS FALLING with a flat tick-tock on the gap toothed cobblestones. Kitty watches the carriage man cover his horses, his meaty hands tossing blankets over them with a magician's flourish. It's a familiar sight that takes her back to her childhood, when her father would take her on a carriage ride every year on the day of her birthday. It would be just the two of them, as her mother stayed at home working on a cake and whatever Kitty had asked to have for her birthday dinner. It ought to be a happy memory, but the rain makes it sad somehow, so she puts it aside for the time being. Jacob looks unhappy with the rain too, but he doesn't vocalize his displeasure. He just hugs his cappuccino and stares out into the distance. After a few weeks of dating Kitty's realized that they are very good at having sex and mediocre at the rest of what would normally constitute a relationship. This suits her just fine, but she wonders if it should. If maybe it ought to be different.

"Look at this asshole," Jacob says at last.

A tall African has appeared with a handful of umbrellas clutched under his arm in a discarded Armani bag. Kitty's seen enough street vendors to peg him as Tunisian by bone structure alone. He's heading straight for their café. For their table, even. It's a routine, if minor, annoyance to fend these sorts of people off, but one she's used to. She used to ready her best excuses whenever she saw one of these people, now she just says no until they leave.

"You want umbrella?" He asks.

"No thanks," says Jacob.

"But it's raining."

"No, thanks." Kitty says.

The Tunisian stays put for a few seconds, averting his eyes. He stares above their heads at the *Palazzo Vecchio*, that colossal reject from a sculptor's workshop that unfashionable façade of political power, the castle that drove off David and the trident of Neptune, the beast that beheaded the Medusa and burned Savagnarola along with a thousand gold leaf portraits of Christ and his world-weary apostles. He watches as a pigeon abandons its sconce, pressed between hefty stone blocks flush with the wall. There is never a shortage of crumbs in the *Piazza della Signoria*. In the distance, Kitty can hear the rusty ting of a bike bell, limping towards the *Ponte Vecchio*. It's a shit day for a bike ride.

"I'm sorry," she says. "I really don't want anything."

The African is already gone, and Jacob is summarizing the experience in the little spiral notebook he keeps in his hip pocket. It's a habit that's already wearing thin on her but she knows it's his job so she can't exactly complain. Instead, she tries to engage.

"What are you writing?" She asks him.

"Don't you think it's interesting," he says, "that Florentines will accept these sorts of people without question, but if a gypsy goes by and does the same thing they'll all but spit in her face?"

"I wouldn't spit in her face," Kitty says.

"Not you. Just generally."

Kitty has nothing to say to this. Unbidden, she's struck with a memory of Paolo. On what most people would call their second date, he'd taken her to a restaurant on the south side of the river,

La Trattoria del Carmine. He'd made a show of ordering in Italian, and she'd let him think she thought it was impressive. Kitty usually measures time on evenings like that in wine bottles, and it was two bottles into the date when Paolo perked up. A tiny Moroccan, couldn't have been more than five feet, walked in with a bundle of roses. People are always doing this in Florence, walking through restaurants with roses and staring at couples until the man feels guilty and drops a couple of Euro for it. She was just readying a diatribe about the inherent misogyny at play here when Paolo produced a two Euro coin, and the Moroccan produced a rose.

"I don't want a rose, Paolo," she said.

"Well," he said, "do you want me to leave it here?"

"I want you to have not bought it. Do you think I'm impressed by this?"

Paolo shook his head, and dropped the rose in his water glass. He didn't defend himself for a long time, not until they got home. She fumed all evening, sitting in silence while he tried and failed to ask her about her band and her guitar and whatever else. Finally, Paolo told her a story. He was fourteen years old when his father kicked him out of the house. He wouldn't tell her why it had happened, or where he lived after that, but he told her how he survived. Every day he would go to the church and pray, and every day the priest would give him a handful of flowers. He held onto them until the evening, and he sold them. However long it took. However many he sold, that was how much he could afford to eat.

"So," she said. "You didn't buy the flower for me."

Paolo nodded. That night she kissed him and meant it, but it didn't last. It was sweet, but sweet is never enough.

"You're mad." Jacob says.

"I'm not," she says, "I just remembered something."

"What?"

"Just sort of a déjà vu kind of thing. It's not a big deal. Are you ready to go?"

Jacob's acting strange. He's got this twitchy look to him, like a junky that's gone a little too long without a fix. She's seen it before, but not on him. She's seen it on her father, when he was on a morphine drip in the hospital. It's not something she wants to be reminded. She snaps her fingers in front of Jacob's face.

"You with me, space captain?"

He grins, sheepish.

"Sorry," he says, "Just a lot on my mind."

"Go on," she says.

"What would you think if I stayed for longer than eight weeks?" He asks her. He's serious, she realizes. He's really thinking about it.

"Well," she says, deciding to be honest, "I can't say I'm excited about you leaving, but would you be able to keep your job if you didn't?"

"No," he says. "But I'm not so sure that's a bad thing."

She considers what he's saying. If he stays, she'll have to tell him about the cough. There won't be any avoiding it. For now, though, there's no point. He doesn't seem to see it any more than anyone else does when it comes unbidden in the middle of a conversation, or any other activity. He might think she was crazy. She might actually be crazy, but she'd rather not think about that. Jacob gets up, and offers her a hand, which she takes. He means it as a polite gesture, but lately she finds she genuinely needs the hand just to get out of her chair sometimes.

"Yea," she says, "I'm ready to go."

On their way out of the square, he hands the Tunisian a couple of Euro.

"Changed my mind," he says. She's not sure how to feel about him going back on it. It feels like he picked up on her annoyance and now he wants to backpedal from it a little. She'll let him have this one. Her father always said, it's the thought that counts. She doesn't have long to parse her feelings.

On the far side of the square, she sees a crowd, and in the crowd she sees a face. It can't be the right face, because she recognizes it. It's soft, with cheekbones visible only as elevation, and eyes that gleam with warmth even at this great distance. She's twelve, maybe thirteen, and waving wildly at Kitsune with both arms. It's her sister. It can't be, as much as anything because her sister ought to be in her thirties by now, but it is.

"Kita," she whispers, "it can't be."

She doesn't have time to finish the thought before the cough takes her. It's heavy and fast and hard and it comes out of her like machineguns firing at soldiers storming the Normandy beaches. Jacob can't see it, but he did hear her voice.

"I knew you'd tell me," he says with a smile, and presses her against a wall. She's still coughing, but he stops her with a kiss. It burns like the cough, but it isn't the cough, so it's progress. After a while she leans into it, and its sting replaces the cough's. After a while it just feels good. She lets him lead her back to her apartment, looking over her shoulder the whole time. The cough's gone. Kita's gone. She feels cold.

THE PLAN
Jacob

THE MAGAZINE'S CALLED JACOB FOUR TIMES in the last three days, and he hasn't picked up yet. The truth is he's not sure he wants to. The truth is he's not sure he's going to. Over the years, he's set aside a lot of money by living sparely. He spends very little on himself, aside from entertaining, and while he travels constantly, he's paid to do it. He's got enough money aside to sustain the lifestyle he's used to for three, maybe four years if he plays it right. That's more than enough. He's making a life for himself here in Florence that feels different than what he had in the states. He's got Kitsune, and he's got the city, and he's got a story. Tony's clue on the bishop gave him most of what he needed, credit where credit was due. Jacob's got more than enough for an article, now. Jacob's got enough for a whole damn book. So he makes a plan.

Jacob decides to wait until the very end of his contract for the magazine before he tips his hand. They're paying his bills, after all, and he might as well make the most of that. As soon as that comes to an end, though, he's cutting ties altogether. He'll have to talk to Kitsune about it, but he already knows her answer. She'll let him stay — maybe she'll say it's just for a week, or a month, or however long it takes for him to find his own place, but she won't kick him out. She wants him to stay as much as he does. So that's what he'll do.

In the meantime, he's got plenty of work to keep him busy. He has contacts in publishing he knows will jump at the chance for an exposé like the one he's got, especially of another country's dirty laundry. It won't take him long. When he's on his game he can write five thousand words a day. Even if that number drops, it'll only take him a few months to finish. That's plenty of time, and once he's done he can find another job. Maybe Tony can get him a gig at the Institute. Maybe he'll teach. It doesn't matter. Jacob knows he has to stay because he's not done with Kitsune. The rest doesn't matter. As if on cue, he sees her. Today's the day, finally, he's going to see her play. The way Tony talks, she's the Korean Jimi Hendrix, but Tony's obviously head over heels. Tony obviously thinks he's got a shot, once Jacob leaves. Tony's in for a rude awakening. But that's a conversation for another day. Today's about Kitsune – or Kitty, as Tony would have him call her, like she's a child or something – and her guitar. Jacob feels a rumble of anticipation. The hunger's back, but he knows this will put it aside. At least for a time.

Kitsune – Kita, he knows her name is Kita, doesn't he? – Kita plugs her amp in, and there's a couple of pops and crackles that draw the attention of a crowd. She's something of a local legend, apparently. She's never been licensed to play, but that's never stopped her. Florentines either love her or hate her, but she makes a living. She makes a lot of it, between her street shows and the band. One thing he appreciates about her, she doesn't waste time with fanfare. There's no dramatic pause before she starts, no are you ready to rock? She takes a second to decide what to play, and then she's playing. Amazingly, Jacob recognizes the chords. It's John Cale. It's "Barracuda". Playing it, she manages to get the lead line and the synth part compressed to the work of a single guitar. It's amazing to watch. Her hands are in constant motion, and she captures two instruments' worth of song perfectly by her lonesome. But it's more than that, at least to Jacob, because he knows she didn't pick the song at random. He knows it's for him. When it's over, the crowd cheers, because of course they do. Kita doesn't care.

She runs through what he knows by now are a short list of her all-time favorites. There's the Clash with "Rudy Can't Fail", and Patti Smith with "Glitter in their Eyes". There's "Wave of Mutilation" from the Pixies, and, a bit surprising, "Southern Man" by Neil Young. That's more of a Tony choice, which gives Jacob a moment's concern. Still, she led off with Cale. She led off with Cale for him. She knows he's here, and she wanted him to see it. Anyway, "Southern Man" is a classic. Even he can admit that. As she wraps up Tony's number, Jacob notices for the first time that he's not here. Tony comes to all my shows, she'd said. Apparently not this one. Was it because he knew Jacob would be here? That's a lot to hope for. She's about to start another song when the mood shifts. She's standing still, looking like a deer in headlights. He's seen the look from her once or twice. It makes her look like someone else altogether. Someone younger, weaker, and altogether foreign. Someone who doesn't know where she is. The look's gone as soon as it comes, but the show's over. Kita rips the chord from the amp, packs in a flash, and makes a beeline for Jacob's table.

"We've got to go," she says. "I've got two minutes before the cops come."

Back at the apartment, Jacob tells the truth for what feels like the first time in his life. It feels good. Kita reacts to his plan about the way he expects. She puts on a show of caution and trepidation, but there's something different about the way they fuck once the truth's out there. For the first time, she leaves his hands loose. For the first time, he holds her hair in his hands, and counts her vertebrae with his fingers. When it's over, she starts to drift off almost immediately. She's always tired, it seems, lately. She's running herself ragged with all the shows, and the practices, and the meetings to coordinate gigs. Maybe with him living there, she'll lay off a little. Maybe she'll let him tell her to. First, though, he's got a question.

"Where was Tony?" He asks her, and she opens her eyes just barely, "I didn't see him at the show. Doesn't he always come?"

"He does," she says, and yawns, "but he's on his way out of town. Didn't he tell you? He got a call from his mother a few days ago, and he's got to go back home for something. It's a dog funeral, I guess, I don't really know."

Jacob's not hurt that Tony didn't tell him, but he is surprised. Usually, the guy can't pass up an opportunity to talk about himself. He gets them so rarely.

"Anyway, he says he wants to have dinner with both of us when he gets back. I told him we would. Is that ok? Tony never asks for anything."

Jacob nods, and Kita closes her eyes. It only takes her a minute. With her asleep, he stares out the window in silence. Fuck Tony. Jacob's got everything he wants right now. He's got her, and he's got the city, and he's got the plan. There's only one problem. The hunger isn't going away.

THE CAR
Tony

TONY'S ON A PLANE TRYING NOT TO THINK about the fact that today is his birthday. He tries every year, and every year he fails. There's too much bad blood there to forget about. Too many old memories. It's been twenty years, but they still feel fucking fresh, and the fact he's headed back home to see his mother doesn't make them feel any better. She's done this on purpose. It's not possible, but she has. I want you home for your birthday, she'd said. There's no way it's a coincidence. It's just too much.

On the evening of his sixteenth birthday, Tony went driving with his mother in the two thousand dollar Ford Pinto that had been his birthday gift. The brakes stuck, and the windows only rolled halfway down, and it was an Apple Green that dust and grime had dulled to something faded and hideous. Still, to Tony, that car was nothing short of perfect.

As such he drove it perfectly. He rode evenly between the lanes, going exactly the speed limit. As they got just outside the city limits the speed limit swung up to fifty-five and Tony floored it. Fifty-five was as fast as Tony knew how to go. They rolled the windows halfway down and the wind slashed at their faces. The radio played something like 'Summer of 69' in a rough crackle and his mother laughed as her hair devolved into a tangled bird's nest in front of her face. It got dark. The Pinto had only the one meager headlight, so they started to make their way home.

"Speed up!" His mother had said as they rolled into the neighborhood. She missed the wind.

Tony did. In that moment he would have done anything she said. In that moment he could almost have loved her.

In the dark, with the rolling of the hills, he couldn't see more than a few feet in front of him. Every fiber of him feared the inevitable toddler, the inevitable child wandering into the street at the last second. But it wasn't a toddler. It was a dog. A Labrador Retriever. It sat at the bottom of the hill stupefied by that single headlight, too dumb to move. Tony wasn't sure whether or not to change course. The car would barely brake, and he was going so fast.

"Don't swerve," said his mother. "Don't swerve, he'll dart and you'll hit him. Just go, he'll get out of the way."

Tony had enough time to think she was wrong but not to disagree. The brakes weren't working. He listened and he didn't jerk the wheel and he didn't move aside and at the bottom of the hill the Pinto made contact with the dog. His brakes kicked in a few seconds later, but by then he'd dragged it a couple of yards. It was stuck under the car, howling. That was all the noise any of the three of them could make until his mother screamed.

"You've killed it. Tony, look what you've done, you've killed it!"

Tony crawled through the halfway rolled window because he didn't think to open the door. He looked under the car. The dog was still alive. For some stupid reason that gave him hope.

"We can save it," he said. "I'll pull it out, and we can save it."

"We'd better," said his mother.

Tony pressed his body to the ground. The concrete was rough and wet and it left an imprint on his face with little tiny specks of gravel. It smelled exactly like a highway would smell, but Tony didn't know that then. The dog was still howling, and each shriek sounded like a factory assembly line with a broken gear shooting sparks into the air. Tony reached to get it out but it was scared or in pain or angry or insane and it bit him and it scratched him. He had to get it so he just let it scratch and claw and bite at his arms and his hands and once as far north as his face. He still has a little scar, just below his right eye, from the clawing.

Finally he got it by the collar, with its teeth sunk into his arm. He couldn't feel the pain, he couldn't feel anything. He was glad the dog was alive but it looked like more of it was missing than was there. Tony's shirt was soaked in a second. He got in the passenger's seat. His mother, already behind the wheel, said nothing. She didn't turn the radio off either, and The Blue Oyster Cult droned through 'Don't Fear the Reaper' for the ten thousandth time of their career to an audience of two. Tony held the dog as it went from rage to terror and back, from shivering to thrashing to growling and biting at him. It kept tossing tiny droplets of blood across his new used car. Where it hit the seats it wouldn't come out. He had that car for five years, and it never came out. Some of it got in his hair. Some of it was his. The scratch on his face and the bite on his arm would need stitches, but he would refuse anything more than bandages when his stepfather offered.

His mother sped to the vet, it must have been eighty miles per hour. In a residential area that's almost suicidal but they made it to the emergency vet. Tony kicked open the front door with the dog shivering, only shivering. Not biting anymore, which was better but not for the dog. Tony opened his mouth, but the receptionist just said GO! and pointed to a door that probably said emergency. Tony kicked open that door too, though he could have backed through it. A vet took the dog from his hands as he came to an operating room. The first thing the vet did was look at the collar and Tony felt cold in his chest because that thought had never once occurred to him.

"It's going to be ok," said the vet. "Good dog."

Tony would ask himself for years why he had not thought to say these things, or to check the collar. There wasn't an answer. When he got back to the waiting room with his shirt covered in blood and holes gouged in his shirt there was nowhere to sit so he sat on the floor. There was a little girl close by who was crying, and Tony knew that was probably his fault too. He wasn't crying, because the bites hurt too much. His mother was still sitting in the car. He could see her lips moving with her eyes closed and he knew that the radio was still on and she was singing along not because she liked the song or because she was happy, but because what else was there for her to do?

They waited for hours. They waited for what Tony would for years do the mental math to confirm as three hours, because it was midnight at least when the nurse came out and said 'she'll be ok'. Tony hadn't even known she was a she. That was probably the happiest he ever was in his life. He ran out to the car looking like a madman with the blood on his shirt. Looking like an ax murderer, probably. He smashed his hands on the car and left a dent which cost him three hundred dollars to put right, and he jumped up and down and said 'she's ok!', 'she's ok!'. His mother smiled, which was a rare thing, and she got out of the car and she hugged him tighter than she'd hugged him since he was four and she didn't say anything but she was crying and he'd never seen her cry before. Tony was crying too, but she'd seen lots of that. He got blood on her shirt, hugging her. It would be there later in the front room of their house when they came home to his worried stepfather.

They went back in and Tony's mother cracked open an issue of Good Housekeeping that was all about ways to pet-proof your house. She started to point out something she thought would help with her little orange Pomeranian but right at that moment, at that exact moment, the doctor came out. For some reason he was holding the dog. Tony knew it was a mistake. It was a joke. It was a TV show, but of course it wasn't. The doctor came up to him and gently set the dog in his bloody lap. Tony was wearing shorts and he felt the scratch of the loose stitches on his legs where he was just beginning to grow hair.

"I'm so sorry," said the vet. "There's been a mistake. She's gone. I'm sorry, I'm so, so sorry."

He repeated like that, like it would help. It didn't help Tony and it didn't help him either. Tony felt sorry for him. He'd had it made and something went wrong. Something went wrong for all of them. Tony's mother looked at the two of them.

"This isn't his dog," she said.

Back in the car she still wouldn't turn off the radio so they listened to 'Sympathy on the Devil' on the ride home. It was longer, because she was going exactly the speed limit and staying exactly between the lines. When they got home, Tony's driveway seemed like it stretched for miles. His wounds didn't even hurt anymore. Nothing hurt, and nothing mattered but walking and his eyes on the dull red door to his house. He could see his stepfather's face in the window and boy, was he confused. His mother stared at him like her eyes were magnifying glasses she was using to catch the sun and burn him to ash. Tony swore he felt his skin peeling, but it didn't hurt. Inside, his stepfather hugged his mother but he didn't want to get bloody so he left Tony alone.

"That is the last time," said his mother, "the last time I ever give you anything."

It was, actually. Tony never complained about the silence on future birthdays, and his stepfather seemed secretly pleased. He walked upstairs. His mother followed him alone, without his stepfather. They stood at the entrance to his room and the blood dripped on the carpet, which he'd spend hours getting out later after it had dried. She opened her mouth and for a second Tony could hear her say she wished it had been him, but she didn't say that. Tony could see the decision to stay silent and he felt guilty, so he said sorry. Her whole face tightened up to a single point and it was all white-hot and her left hand slashed the air. Somehow Tony caught it before it hit his face. He wanted it to have happened. He felt like he deserved it. But he knew that it would change everything, forever, in ways that could never be reversed.

For a second Tony's mother thought about overpowering him. She could have done it. She'd thrown javelin in college, and still hit the gym three times a week. Instead, she pulled away. She didn't say 'don't touch me'. That would have been beneath her. She spat at Tony's feet, where the blood was soaking through the carpet to stain the hardwood floors. They both knew that she would never hold him again, or provide comfort, or be there when he needed her. She could have reversed it if she had lied, but she realized that it didn't matter. It was ok that everything was lost, because it would have been lost somehow anyway. In that moment, she was fine with it. She met Tony's eyes for what felt like hours, but must have been seconds.

"Clean this up," she said.

When the plane lands, she's there in a Mitsubishi she probably got from her dead husband's dealership. She doesn't say much and she doesn't help him with his bags, but he didn't have to pay for a taxi which he figures is about as good as he's going to get. Once they're clear of the airport, she turns the radio on. Tony can hear the opening clatter of "Don't Fear the Reaper", almost immediately. This is more than just a coincidence.

THE DIAGNOSIS
Kitsune

KITTY'S ALONE IN THE KIND OF OFFICE normal people spend their whole lives dreaming about. The floor is that dark hardwood you see in all the magazines, and the desk's one of those things that looks ugly to you until you find out it's a one of a kind design from some guy from the fifties and it costs closer to fifty grand than fifty. There's art on the walls she recognizes from textbooks, and she's not sure they're reproductions. She knows being a doctor's good money, but this office isn't the result of one man's work. His parents had money, and their parents before them, and probably further back. For all she knows about lineage in Florence he's a goddamn Medici. It must be nice, having money like that. People pretend it isn't because suffering is hip these days, but it must be nice.

It's about fifteen minutes before he shows. It's enough time for her cough to drain the little bit of energy she had when she came in. At this point, it's never more than a few minutes away. It comes constantly, and she's learned that most people won't notice it. But some do. An old woman had stopped her in the grocery store to ask her if she was alright. You don't look well, she'd said. Are you eating enough? Kitty's not sure how to feel about the fact that a stranger could see it while Tony and Jacob let it slide without comment. But the worst is her doctor. She's not even sure why she's here. He clearly thinks she's lying, or that she's overreacting to some minor flare up of allergies he can't even see. She's not looking forward to this meeting.

"Miss Lingo," he says, pushing his door open with the confidence of a man who can replace it with the flick of his wrist. "I'm glad you're here. I trust you're well?"

What a goddamn asshole.

"I'm sorry about the way our conversation went at our last meeting," he says as he takes his seat. "You must understand I see many patients who waste my time, and at that meeting I believed you were just another one of those patients."

She waits for him to elaborate, to clarify that he doesn't think she's a lunatic or a hypochondriac. He's waiting for her to accept his apology.

"Of course," she obliges. "I understand."

"That said, Miss Lingo, there truly was nothing of concern in your MRI. That means we can rule out cancer, which I know was your chief concern."

There's a shoe that's going to fall. She can see it on his face; he's trying to find the best way to say what he wants to say without scaring her. She recognizes the expression from the meetings she attended with her father. They're the second sign, she figures. Her father had been too weak by then to complete the set.

"But there's something else that is. A concern I mean." She says.

"Yes, unfortunately," he says, donning a pair of Prada glasses and producing a stack of paperwork. "That is why I called you here. You recall we took blood the last time you were here?"

Of course she recalls it. The nurse had taken four tries to find a usable vein. Kitty looked like a junky when they were done. She nods, and he takes a deep breath. Here it comes.

"Your bloodwork shows, essentially, an elevated immune response. Considering the sparsity of symptoms you're presenting, there's limited options for what it can be."

Sparsity of symptoms, sure. A cough that splits your lungs apart like a piece of bread at a restaurant table could hardly be called a symptom. This is a waste of time.

"I don't want to be overly technical, but I don't want to alarm you unnecessarily either. I believe you may have a parasite."

A parasite? Some little bug hidden away, leeching off her every meal and moment of rest? It's a possibility, but something tells her it's not the whole story.

"Why do you think that?"

"Well, assuming the symptoms you reported are accurate, I think it's the best explanation. The sense of weakness you described, even the cough, although I haven't seen it present myself, can best be explained by something like a lung fluke."

"Wouldn't it have shown in the scan? Something like that?"

"Depending on its position, not necessarily. Such creatures are often very small, and may not be visible until they've grown. But they don't have to be large to be a problem."

There's no arguing with him. She can't explain why she thinks he's wrong, but she knows that he is. He proscribes her a heavy dose of antibiotics, which she'll take. If she's sick, antibiotics can't hurt. But increasingly, Kitty knows it's more than just a sickness. Her mother would say she was being afflicted by a spirit. She'd send her to an acupuncturist, or a medium, or god knows what. Maybe there's something to that. A disease is something anyone can see. A disease, her doctor could look at and know it was real. Her friends, the guy she's fucking, they'd see her coughing. This is something else.

"Thank you, Doctor Laurenti," she says, and he smiles.

Her father always said, never burn a bridge you might want to use to run away. Her father was usually right.

THE STREET
Paolo

PAOLO COMES FACE TO FACE WITH A PAIR of crimson oxfords, things of beauty really. Two-toned leather. Precision stitching. He donates a few minutes of his time to their cause; looking through the glass and probably salivating like a kid at a *gelateria*. He can't afford them, at least not now. They're at least a thousand Euro. Paolo can barely scrape enough together to take care of his needs at this point. He'd inherited so much from his father, and pissed it all away. But there's one good piece of news to take away from that experience. Paolo knows luxury when he sees it, but he doesn't expect it. He knows how to sell it, but he's not too good to. Paolo knows now, that's the kind of job he needs – the problem is convincing anyone else to trust him to do it.

There's a hole in Paolo's resume about five years deep. The last real job he'd worked was that gig as a tour guide, and considering that had ended with him raising his middle fingers like a white flag and his bosses telling him they never wanted to see his face again, it was hard to justify telling anyone about it. After that, he'd done a lot of things under the table. He'd worked with street vendors and black market types, and then he had his dad's money, and he did nothing. He's not proud of it, but that's not what anyone hiring wants to hear. He has no references, no experience, and nothing to show for his life up to know, as far as an employer is concerned. All he has to do, though, is show someone what he's made of. He's so busy thinking about how he's going to do that, he almost misses his chance.

There arrives upon the scene a certain destitute-looking woman, nothing unusual, at least at a glance. She's a stocky number in a crusty bathrobe and pristine ultraviolet stockings, sort of what you picture when you think 'homeless woman'. She asks him for a cigarette.

"Don't smoke ma'am." He says, a bit flip, "S'bad for you."

She seems to accept this, but she doesn't leave. She could be waiting for a new answer, or just standing around. Paolo looks at her again. He'd taken her for one of the more conversational homeless one occasionally encounters in Florence at a glance, but now he sees that's not the whole story. The bathrobe certainly gives that impression, but the jewelry she's sporting belies it. Even if she'd had the kind of big fall from grace you hear about in the news, she'd have pawned it by now. She'd get enough from the sale of the diamond on that ring by itself to give her a bed to stay in for a couple of months. Long enough to clean up, get ready, and get her shit in order. The fact she hasn't means there's only two options. She doesn't want to, or she doesn't have to. Either way, she's more than she appears, and Paolo figures he ought to give her another chance.

"Can I help you?" He asks, because she's still staring at him like she wants something.

"You don't recognize me?" She says, and he doesn't. At all. "Well you were very young, the last time you saw me. I was a good friend of your mother's, you know."

She's lying. Isn't she? What are the chances he could hang around on these streets for years and never see her, or never be seen by her. Of course, the odds are probably pretty good as large as Florence is, but still. If she really can recognize him at a glance – wait.

"If I was that young, I'm surprised you can recognize me." He says, and she grins.

"You look like your father, the year your parents met. Spitting image. I know you, Paolo. I used to babysit you."

Something's coming. A memory, unbidden. An apartment, over the Arno, and an older couple. The man was a scientist, and the woman managed their money. She had a head for properties, his mother said. She could turn a warehouse into a home people would pay thousands for.

"Claudia?" He says, and she smiles, "Claudia Misuri?"

"Do you play chess, Paolo?"

Her apartment is exactly how he remembers it, down to the Venetian glass bowl on her kitchen table, perpetually overflowing with citrus. There's a huge window above the table that drapes it in sunlight during the day. By night, it's got a perfect view of the river. Paolo remembers the reflections of the lamps in the Arno at night. He remembers the sound of the river, interspersed with his parents' conversation. He sits down.

"Would you like anything?" She asks.

"No ma'am. You don't have to feed me, I'm fine."

She laughs, and puts a plate of prosciutto and melon slices down in front of him. It's his favorite, and he gets the feeling she knows that. She didn't just pick a recipe at random. Had she known where to find him?

"Of course I'm going to feed you, Paolo, I owe your mother that much. I was asking if you needed anything else."

Paolo thinks about the Girl, and his time in her home. It

would be nice to be able to leave. To strike out on his own, and make his own choices on how to spend his time. To take her someplace he chose, rather than her. Or to take her nowhere at all.

"What are you doing these days, Paolo?"

She can see it on his face, and probably on his clothes. She knows the answer to this question.

"I'm not really doing anything. I guess I kind of took it easy for a bit, but taking it easy can be harder than it looks."

She laughs, but he's got a point. She takes out her chessboard. Paolo remembers her playing with her husband, every Sunday evening. He'd stay with them sometimes, when his father was off playing a concert somewhere and his mother had to work a late shift. He'd always been scared of the old man, but Claudia was nothing but kind to him. He can't believe he had forgotten about them.

"I know it's hard for you, Paolo," she says. "It was a terrible thing, what your father did. That's no way to grow up."

He shifts in his seat uncomfortably and looks out the window.

"Yea, it wasn't easy."

"It isn't easy now. Back then it was impossible."

She's setting up the pieces on the board. He tries to help, but he doesn't really know how. Paolo's played chess maybe four times in his life, and none of them landed him a win.

"I'm going to make you a deal," Claudia says, and makes a surprisingly serious face. "If you can beat me at chess, I'll give you a job. I'm getting old and I need someone to help me show my properties. I want to help you, Paolo, but I can't just give it away. Show me that you're hungry for it, and I'll give you the job."

It's exactly the kind of thing he needs, and she knows it. She knew his father, and she knows him, and she knows he can do it.

If she didn't she wouldn't have bothered. She just doesn't trust him yet, and maybe she shouldn't. She's not sure he's not still the little shit that burned his inheritance in a year and a half. He knows he isn't, but he's done nothing to show her or anyone else as much yet. If he can show her, though, this is all he'll need. This is freedom.

"So," he says, "you'll just give me a job if I beat you at chess."

"Call it a job interview."

Paolo hasn't been to many job interviews, but he can't remember a chess board at any of them. The whole thing's too good to be true, but maybe Claudia really is that nice. Maybe she saw him looking down and wanted to do something about it and the job is all she could come up with.

"Is this what you normally do for your job interviews?"

"No Paolo, it isn't. But showing people properties and making sure they pay their rent on time isn't something you need some special degree for. You just need to work. If you can work hard enough to beat me, you can work hard enough to do that too."

What she's saying makes sense, and honestly, he's got nothing else going for him. He makes a decision, then, to beat her. As long as it takes.

"Ok," he says, "I'll do it. But first you have to show me how the little horse moves."

THE HOUSE
Tony

MORNING BREAKS LIKE AN EGG AGAINST the asphalt and Tony's been awake for six hours. Sometime around three in the morning it went quiet because the raccoon digging through the recycling got spooked by a car engine backfiring, or maybe a gunshot, but now the street's starting to move. Tony watches the orange light spill wet and sticky over the black tar where the rain hasn't sunk in yet. They'll both dry up soon enough. There's an old lady powerwalking by with a bright green five pound weight in each hand. A teenager from the house next door sits on his porch picking cautiously at the strings of a dreadnaught guitar. His brother – Tony assumes it's his brother – watches him with his legs crossed holding a goldfish in a plastic baggie. One of those kids probably killed my mother's dog, thinks Tony, as he drinks the last of his cocoa. It's cold.

Tony watches as the younger kid gets off his porch and wanders into the street. Despite the affluence abounding in his mother's neighborhood, there's a pothole in front of their house that has lived here longer than most of the neighborhood. It's filled with water, the remaining vestiges of the half-assed nightfall that fell last night. The kid bends down in front of it, drops his goldfish into it, and returns to his brother with a chuckle. The older kid shakes his head and visibly sighs before heading back inside. Tony's taking bets that the little brother is the culprit.

The last bloom from his mother's hydrangea fell off a week or so back, and he digs his heel into its remains as he walks toward the goldfish. The kid watches him from his porch with his hand on his face, but he runs inside when Tony flips him the bird.

"Little fucker," Tony mutters to the goldfish, and sets his mug down in the road next to the pothole. He looks at the fish for a few seconds. It's solid orange like someone spray painted it, but it was probably born that way. Tony figures it'd take an hour, maybe two for the puddle to dry out and the fish to stop breathing. He scoops him into his mug with a little bit of water and heads inside.

"I got you a fish," he says to his mother. "The little shit next door dumped it in the pothole."

"Language, Tony," says his mother, but not with feeling.

Magritte's funeral is short and quiet. Tony stands together with his mother, the only family in attendance. The rest of the crowd are all strangers, at least to him; three of them, friends of his mother's most likely. That or the dog's. It had been cremated, and his mother pours the ashes from a little trash bag into the lifeless earth. It is twenty-three degrees outside, and their collective breath forms a little cloud of fog above their heads.. When it's done the friends leave Tony to make hot cocoa and watch his mother cry by himself.

They sit in the kitchen and say nothing, for hours. Steam rises from her microwaved vegetables. Slowly, the squash congeals to mush. She prods it with her fork.

When his mother got the dog it was meant to be Tony's birthday present. He was twelve at the time. His favorite movie starred a pair of talking dogs and a cat, expressing their Manifest Destiny on a rollicking adventure Westward to find their lost owners. Tony wanted a dog just like the one on the cover of that

VHS tape, down to the voice. He had to have it.

They went to the pound and walked through the cages. He waited for the voice. He waited for something to speak to him, figuratively or literally. Nothing came of it. It was all a flurry of explosive barking and snipping and clawing at the cage bars, but why wouldn't it be? His mother grew impatient. Finally, they came to the last cage and there it was. It's description called it 'rust-colored' but Tony had always thought of it as 'orange'. His mother fell in love immediately. She had to have it. Tony went back and pointed glumly at a sullen Pit Bull, but she was already completing the paperwork. Magritte, née Sparkles, came home that afternoon. Tony got a book for his birthday that year. Four years later, it was a car.

Tony gets up and chucks their paper plates and food into the garbage. Normally she'd chide him for the waste but she's basically catatonic at this point. He goes to the fridge, gets her a beer, and drops it in front of her. No reply.

Jacob calls Tony at midnight to tell him all about his new theory, which is about ants. Ants, he says, form the model of a perfect society. Tony listens through the speakers of his mother's landline telephone, an honest-to-god phone with an honest-to-god chord. Oh, he thinks, to be perfect – to be an ant!

Ants, Jacob would like him to know, will do anything for the good of their colony, to promote the growth of their species. Ants will make towers out of corpses. Ants will drown themselves to make a raft. Ants will use their own bodies for firewood. Or they would if they had chimneys. In loving detail, he describes the struggles of the soldier ant, and the sacrifices it makes for the all-powerful queen. It seems to Tony to be little different from the lives of most humans. Jacob disagrees.

"Don't give me that working class hero bullshit."

This is how Jacob talks now, or maybe nothing's changed and Tony's just getting tired of it these days. Over the phone, he reshapes Jacob's image into a caricature of the real thing from the cadence of his voice. He gives him a black cape with a red velvet liner. A grease-slicked pencil-thin moustache. Ah, he thinks, but who is this being tied to the railroad tracks? The answer to the question is obvious as soon as it's asked.

Jacob has this theory that ants, mindless as they are, represent a standard for humanity to follow. If everything falls into place, if all the planets align and all the prophets are spot on in their predictions, we may someday achieve the perfection held by ants.

"Isn't that a little dramatic?" Tony asks. He likes to ask these questions. It's good to bring the conversation down to earth every now and again.

Jacob's breath is heavy and loud and Tony wonders how much he has had to drink. He's excited, nearly to the point of self-parody. Ants, he insists, can never be destroyed as long as there are orders for them to follow. As long as there is the colony for them to protect. As long as there is the species. Tony reckons he's six drinks deep, at least, depending on the bartender. He could hear the spittle flying through the air on that last half-shouted statement.

"What you've got to realize, Tony, what you've got to realize is that we, humans, we're inferior to the insects. All our higher reasoning and we're inferior."

Tony twirls the stiff rubber chord of his mother's phone between two fingers. From underneath the pile of books by the sofa a stack of framed pictures of him as a child leer out, sheathed in a thick enough coat of dust to endure a harsh winter.

This is a waste of time.

"You're drunk," Tony says.

"You don't believe me."

"You're insane. Good night."

"I'm not trying to insult your intelligence, Tony, I'm just saying it's worth nothing to be intelligent in the grand scheme of things. The natural world doesn't give a damn if you read Nietzsche or Wittgenstein. The only advantage we have over other species is our numbers, and you know it. There are more ants than humans, and so they are the superior species."

"Yes," says Tony, "and there are more idiots and lunatics than men of true genius, but that's why we value them."

"You're just making my point for me."

Tony spends a solid six or seven seconds of silence giving him a long, baleful stare before he realizes he can't see any of it. He releases a small sigh.

"I'm going to bed," Tony says.

"You know I'm right."

"About what?"

"We will never exceed the efficiency of ants. Our species will never surpass theirs."

"Oh? Prove it. Jesus Christ. You're always talking but you never say shit. You just keep inflating your ego until it pops or you get tired of pumping in air."

Tony is finished speaking now. Jacob's teeth grind over the line and Tony knows he is looking for something to say to leave him on a sour note.

"You know, Kitty told me her real name."

He is very good at this.

"Kita," Jacob says. "Her name is Kita. She told me when we were fucking the other night."

"Bullshit," Tony says.

"You know how she likes it, Tony? She likes it from behind.

She likes it when I grab her hair, and I push her down, and I make her do it my way."

"Bullshit," he repeats.

"Sure," says Jacob. "Not that you'd know what she likes. She wouldn't fuck you to save your life. She wouldn't even blow you to save hers. The only thing you are to her is a readily available self-esteem boost, and you damn well know it. Have fun with your mother, Tony."

With that, the line's dead. Good riddance.

The next morning, Tony comes down to find his mother exactly where he left her, but with three more beer bottles next to the one he had brought her.

"Will you be alright if I leave?" He asks.

"You're leaving already?"

"I'm sorry, I can't stay longer. I've got a flight."

"You haven't even been here two days."

"I know," says Tony. "I can't leave my apartment alone for too long."

He thinks about Crosby, home alone with his pile of birds. Even if that weren't occupying every inch of his brain not buzzing at last night's argument with Jacob, he would still have to leave. He could feel his feet itching to run for the door. He'd felt it since he walked in.

"You'll be alright?" He asks.

"I'll be alright."

"You're sure?"

"I'm sure."

"Ok," says Tony, and then, "can you drive me to the bus stop? Are you ok to drive?"

He winces at the question, but she seems to miss it. She just nods. In the car the radio's down to nothing and Tony's not sure if he should turn the knob. He's on the lookout for tears. Any sign he shouldn't be leaving, ethically. His mother's expressions give nothing away.

"Mom, I'm sorry about the dog."

"It's fine, Tony. I'm fine."

She didn't know what he meant. They never communicate, even when they talk. He stays silent for the rest of the trip. The bus station comes into view.

"You know that I love you. Don't you, Tony?"

Tony knows by the look on her face that she isn't lying. He doesn't know what to do with that information, but he knows he's right about this. He ought to say it back to her, but he's not sure he can. He's not sure that he does.

"Don't, mom, it's fine. You don't need to say anything like that, really."

"Fine. Will you at least call me when you get there?"

"Of course."

But he wouldn't call. He never calls.

THE CARDS
Kitsune

"I WANT YOU TO VISUALIZE YOUR ILLNESS. Can you do that for me?"

"What do you mean?"

"Think about your illness. Think about how it makes you feel. Think about it as an object. How does it look? What is its shape? Do you understand?"

Kitty nods. Her doctor had told her it might be a parasite, that it could only be a parasite, so the illness ought to resemble some sort of bug or worm. At worst, it would be a collection of little creepy crawlies swarming around on her lungs in some mindless drove. Still, when she closes her eyes it isn't an eight-legged creature she sees. She has a clear image of her illness – of her affliction – as a predator. She sees a black shark, inky and sleek, circling her as she treads water. She sees a single fin sticking out of ice-cold waters. This is how she describes it to the fortuneteller.

"I see," says the woman across the table.

She has this nervous tic she performs every so often with her cards. She takes a card from the middle of the deck, twirls it in her hand, and puts it back on top. She does this three times as Kitty describes her imaginary shark illness, and again as punctuation for her own commentary.

"And what does your doctor say?"

She sets the deck down on the table. They have frayed edges, the cards, and any number of bent corners and dings. She's had them for a long time. They've told a lot of people their future, or they've told a lot of people lies. Most likely, they've done a little bit of both.

"He thinks it's a parasite. Says it has to be, with the symptoms I have."

"But you don't agree."

"I have no idea, I'm not a doctor. I just know the treatment hasn't done anything. I feel zero percent better. If anything, it's getting worse."

"I see," says the woman across the table.

"Are you ready to begin?" She asks.

Kitty nods.

"I have arranged the deck into the Yin Yang spread. We use this formation to weigh both sides of an argument."

"Is this an argument? What are the sides?"

"On this side," she gestures to her left, "is a shark. On the other, a parasite. The cards will show us what these creatures are made of, and how they can be tamed."

She has a strange cadence. It's most likely an affectation, but it makes her sound possessed. Like a spirit is pulling each word unbidden from her throat. As far as performances go, Kitty's got to admit it's pretty convincing so far.

"I will start with the two cards at the center."

The reader flips them over one at a time. The first shows a picture of a young boy – the Page of Pentacles, says the reader – holding a coin marked with an occult symbol. The second is an old man – the Hermit – carrying a crooked staff. She pushes the cards towards Kitty and looks at her ominously. The silence is long enough that she realizes she's supposed to react somehow.

"I don't know what this means."

"They are each symbols of ritual and stagnation. Their

presence at the center of the spread tells us that the nature of your life is contributing to your illness."

"The nature of my life?"

"Your lifestyle."

"My lifestyle hasn't changed, but I've only just gotten sick. It must be something else that's changed."

"We will see. I can only tell you what the cards tell me."

She pulls over three more cards, the right side of the circle. This is the bug, Kitty reminds herself, the doctor's side of the argument. The first is the King of Swords. As makes this reminder, she curses herself for buying into this, even for a second.

"Your doctor has made up his mind already. This is what the King indicates – he stands for a strong man in your life, with dark hair. He is strong-willed and unbroken, you cannot persuade him he has diagnosed you incorrectly."

Her doctor is a brunette, but so are most Italian men. The reader herself is entirely bald. Had she had cancer? Some women simply lose their hair, but perhaps hers had been taken. Perhaps, Kitty thinks, perhaps I'm being insensitive to come to her for advice about my health. It's too late to think about that now. The next card is up.

"The Moon indicates confusion. Your doctor's confidence is likely a façade. Beneath it he has no idea what is ailing you, or how to help."

"Well that's a comfort."

"Yes. The last is the Tower. The Tower symbolizes change. Failing to change will result in disaster. In conjunction with the Moon and the King, this is a bad sign. It seems that your doctor will be too stubborn to change, and this will lead to his downfall. Or yours. Be wary of his advice if it remains the same."

There are five cards drawn now. I feel no better, Kitty thinks. Was I expecting to? All of this had been her mother's idea, whether she knew it or not. Her mother had been telling her to come here for years. As little as her doctors had achieved, she was desperate for a second opinion. She needed someone to tell her what to do. The reader pulls three more cards.

"This is your shark," she intones.

Her voice is utterly monotonous. Dispossessed of any emotion whatsoever. So, Kitty thinks. What will it be? When she closes her eyes she sees Kita's face, rendered in the faux stained glass stylings of the Tarot Deck. 'The Sister,' the reader would announce. It means that you cannot be saved, as she could not be saved.

"Three cards. The High Priestess, the Queen of Swords, and the Lovers. The Lovers draws in reverse."

Kitty shakes herself from her reverie. "What does that mean?"

"It means your shark is an emotion. Your illness feeds off feeling, rather than your body."

Your shark is an emotion, she thinks, sounds like the name of a book of awful poetry. The sort her father would have turned his nose up at like a carton of rotten eggs as he read it. But he still would have finished the book.

"So how can I stop it? How do I hunt a shark that feeds off of feelings?"

"This is what the last cards will tell us. There are two remaining. The first is a suggestion, an idea of how you might proceed. The last card is a prediction. It tells us what will happen if nothing changes. If you stay on your current path."

The first card. The Wheel of Fortune. The image on the front reminds her of a compass rose on an antique map. The cards are arcane, but attractive. They hold weight as objects. It's all an act, she tells herself, I have to remember that. None of this is real unless I let it be that way, and I'm smarter than that.

"The Wheel indicates impending change. Do not fight it. Let

it occur. Seek this change, and you may find your cure instead."

"And the last one?"

The reader holds the card in her hand, twirling it idly. It is impossible to say if she is sincerely pensive, or simply acting with dramatic intent to increase her odds of a tip. She presents the card as if it were a citation, its face hidden from view.

"I want to warn you," she says. "I want to warn you that it may not help you to see this. This is nothing more than a warning. It is enough to know that there are consequences, you do not always need to know what the consequences are."

"I've come here to know. I want to know what happens if this shark decides to take a bite."

The reader nods. The last card turns. Its face is a raven, black as ink. It sits on a pile of bones. Something about the bird's blank snarl gives her a feeling of déjà vu, but she can't explain it.

"Death," she says. "But Death does not always mean to die."

"So what does it mean?"

"The drawing of Death does not mean the death of the body. Not always. It does mean that something will come to an end. Something will stop, or it will change so dramatically as to become unrecognizable."

"Death does not always mean to die," Kitty repeats.

"I hope that this helps you. I will need you to pay me before you leave."

Later, Kitty stands on the street alone. It is a warm day, but her body shivers and stutters with every slight flutter of wind. She searches her phone for a number, any number to call. Her mother would only worry. Jacob would only laugh. Tony, she thinks. She dials.

"How was your thing?" He asks almost immediately.

Tony's always been good about remembering things. He never forgets a birthday, always calls and leaves a nice message. Anything you mention to him, he will recall even weeks later.

"It was fine," she says. "A little eerie, maybe, but whatever."

"Well did you learn something? Do you feel better?"

She thinks about it for a moment.

"I learned a lot, if anything was real, but everything I learned was strange. Every card we pulled made things darker, and weirder."

A car glides by; a black Fiat. A chill falls over her as it passes. She could swear she saw two women standing on the corner in her reflection as the car went by. Two women around the same age, the same height, the same build. One stood sturdy and strong. It was almost a model's pose. The other was curled and huddled, shriveled almost. Sheltering herself from a cold only she could sense.

"So tell me one thing," Tony says, "one thing you learned."

She sighs, and rubs at her eyes. She can feel a headache stirring – feels like a killer.

"My shark is an emotion." She says, and coughs.

When she pulls her hand away from her mouth, a thin spray of blood lingers on her palm. She hangs up the phone.

THE DINNER
Jacob

THERE'S ONLY ONE PART OF TONY'S BIG welcome-home dinner that Jacob's looking forward to. He's looking forward to the dumb look on Tony's face when he tells him he's staying. Kita's bought a bottle of wine he recommended for her, and Jacob's made a salad. He hates making salad, but he likes what it communicates in this case. To him, this says yes, I could have put effort into your evening, but I opted not to. He hopes Tony can read between the lines.

They're greeted at the door with a hug, in Kita's case, and a firm handshake in his. It's obvious Tony wants to pretend their phone conversation while he was out of the country didn't happen, and Jacob is fine with that. Tony looks tired, and Kita acts tired, and Jacob's the only one who feels like a tiger pacing in a cage. It'll be a shitshow of an evening, he'd bet money on it. Luckily, Tony's got dinner ready almost the moment they walk in. Maybe it won't be such a long night after all.

Tony's made *caponata*, and Jacob's man enough to begrudgingly admit that it's not bad by any means. The eggplant is soft and pillowy, with none of that spongy, gummy texture you get when it's store bought or poorly cooked. Tony says the secret's in the salt. You've got to slice it thin and coat it in so much salt you'll think you've ruined it, let it draw out the moisture, rinse it off, then press out what remains. It keeps the eggplant from sucking in fat during the cooking. Jacob's also man enough to admit that he didn't know this.

After eating a few bites, Kita asks Tony about his trip. Clearly it's the opportunity he was waiting for. Jacob makes a conscious effort to not listen, but he hears enough to paint by numbers. Tony's mom is your classic ice queen who didn't hug him enough, and now he's a sad little broken man who doesn't want a free vacation back to his home country for a few days. He's said it before. If Tony were a gazelle he'd limp so far behind his herd he'd end up in the middle of the next one. He'd live forever that way, but he'd do it alone.

"Well," Jacob says, "maybe our good news will cheer you up a little bit."

He can't tell if Kita buys this strained affectation of kindness, but he can tell Tony doesn't. Either way, it's worth it.

"We didn't want to tell you while you were gone and dealing with all that, but I changed my plans, Tony. I'm going to stay in Florence for a while."

"How long is a while?"

"Honestly, I don't know. Maybe all of it. The whole damn thing. I haven't gotten far enough to decide yet."

Tony goes white as a sheet, white as the marble façade of half the churches in Florence. It's worth every minute of listening to his vapid whining about his mother to see him cringe.

"That's great," Tony says, finally, "Are you gonna keep staying at your hotel?"

"With her," he says, gesturing.

"Amazing," says Tony, but he could just as easily be saying 'toaster oven.' His mind's in another place.

"Let me help with the dishes," Kita says, and he nods glumly.

"I'll let you two do that, then," says Jacob. "Won't be enough room at the sink for three. Can you point me in the direction of your bathroom, Tony?"

From the hallway, Jacob can hear their voices from around the sink. Tony's prodding her for explanations about Jacob's decision to stay and her level of complicity in it, he's sure of it. He's looking for any sign that she's less than thrilled. Trust me brother, Jacob thinks. If I haven't found it you sure as hell won't. Next thing he knows, Tony's put a record on. It's Neil Young, because of course it is. Tony's a one trick pony. Jacob doesn't know the song but he can make out the lyrics:

I'm a vampire babe, sucking blood from the earth

Jacob rolls his eyes so far back for a second he's worried they'll get stuck back there.

"Real subtle," he mutters.

Anyway, it's a perfect opportunity to take a look around. Tony's a mystery Jacob normally wouldn't bother to solve but, honestly, anything is better than sitting and listening to them talk while Neil Young crows like a cat's orgasm. He tries the door next to the bathroom. It opens. Amazing how well people trust their friends, even the ones they don't like. There's just one problem. Tony's almost as good at keeping secrets as he is.

It's the dog from the other day, a month or so back. When he'd just landed, when Tony had given him Kita's number. The dog Tony said he was getting rid of. The dog that carved up the groomer. When did Tony decide he was going to keep it?

It's black, mostly the dog, and it looks like it's made of the sort of rope you'd use to tie a ship to a post at a dock. It's lying on Tony's bed like it belongs to him, which in a way Jacob supposes it probably does. Let's be real, Tony was never going to be Alpha, even in a pack of two. Jacob uses his best 'people talking to animal' voice and walks towards it. It's quiet, and it watches him with caution, but it seems happy to let him touch it. Until he does, at least.

The moment his fingers hit the thing's greasy dreadlocks, he feels like he's burst into flames. He feels like he's melting. He feels like his hand is fusing to it. His vision's blurring at the edges. He seems to see everything wrong. Instead of the dog he sees a snake, coiled around a black stone. Or, well, not a stone. It's like oil, or something slick, but formed into what could almost be called a solid. He only sees it for a moment, then the illusion is shattered, because the dog's barked, the dog is barking and has leapt off the bed and backed into a corner.

Kita and Tony are there in a second. He's still got yellow dish gloves on, because of course he does. He throws them aside.

"I didn't know you had a dog, Tony." Kita says, oblivious to the situation. She gets that lost look on her face for a second, and in that second Jacob's vision fucks up again. He sees the snake, and the ball of oil. He sees feathers all over, grey and motley and floating or falling like dust balls in the air. Tony's no different, he's absolutely the same. But Kita's not Kita. She's someone else. Someone taller, lankier. Someone dressed to the nines in fashion she'd never bother with. She's got a better figure, and better posture, but Jacob can't say he likes the look better overall. The energy's all wrong. He shakes the vision off, and this time it stays away. For a moment in transition, he could swear he saw both girls, together. They look so alike, he can almost combine them into one. Maybe he does, briefly.

"What did you do to my dog?" Tony asks.

"The dog looks fine, Tony," Kita says, but on cue it starts to whimper. Without realizing it, Jacob's been making his way back towards it. Tony crosses the room in an instant to get between them. The dog hides behind him like he's it's goddamn mother.

Maybe it isn't not alpha material after all.

"What's its name, Tony?" Either she really is oblivious, or Kita's making a hell of an effort at diffusing this situation.

"Crosby," Tony says, distracted, and he's checking the thing for signs of damage. He looks under the collar and behind the ears. He pokes its ribs and lifts its tail and obviously, there's nothing wrong with it. Jacob, meanwhile, feels like he got struck by lightning. No one's asking about that, but why would they?

"I think maybe it was a mistake. Having you here."

"For dinner?" Kita asks.

"Sure," Tony says. Tony's not talking about what happened with the dog now, or not just that.

"Fuck you," Jacob says.

"Jake," Kita tries, but it's too late.

"Fuck me? Where the fuck do you get off? You broke into my room!"

"I just opened the door, I was curious."

It's the truth, but not according to Tony.

"The door was locked!"

It wasn't. Was it? Jacob can pick a lock, if pressed, but he's pretty sure he would remember if he'd actually done it. He shakes his head at Kita. She shrugs.

"You can't just come in here and touch my shit. Touch my dog. Not without my permission."

"You told me you weren't keeping it! I didn't think you still had one!" Jacob yells. Why, he's not sure. He genuinely didn't care until they started yelling. Still, when he says that Kita takes notice. She's hurt Tony told him something she didn't know, by the looks of it.

"I don't fucking have to tell you! It's my house, I can keep whatever I want here."

"Shut up for a second," Jacob says, and raises his hand.

"What?"

Jacob doesn't feel right. The dog's looking at him like he's kibble, and he needs to keep an eye on that, but his vision's starting to blur. He's starting to see the woman again.

"It's the cat," he whispers, and it is. In the window, watching.

"Jesus," Tony says. "How much did you drink before you got here, anyway?"

Kita gets between them then, and drags Jacob to his feet. Now she's the one checking for bruises and bites and bumps, and the look on Tony's face tells him everything he needs to know. Jacob's the winner here, but he doesn't feel like one. He feels like he got pulled out of a house fire.

"I think maybe we should go," she says quietly.

"Yes," Tony says, "I think that would be best."

They gather their things and head to the door. Jacob can feel a headache coming that would lay a bear low. He wants to get at least a few words in before the argument ends, but he's lost his shot. Something's happening, and it's taking his full concentration to endure it.

"I also think it's best if you don't call me anymore, Jacob."

They're standing in the door now. Tony's got his arms folded and the dog behind him and Kita's just holding a little Tupperware full of *caponata* with a face like she just saw a car crash and doesn't know which body to resuscitate. She gets that lost look for a second, and she shakes it off. It's happening more and more, but Jacob doesn't have time to worry about that.

"Anyway," Tony finishes, reaching for the handle, "if you're out a job, I guess I am too." And with that he slams it shut.

Kita doesn't ask questions, she just watches carefully as he makes his way down the stairs. By the bottom he's regained his composure, and he starts to walk faster on their way home. Whatever happened, whatever that dog did, whatever he saw, Jacob knows one thing. The hunger is back. And this time, it's not going to go away.

PAOLO'S DREAM:
The Girl in the Rain

THE SUN SITS HOLDING UP ITS END of some forgotten bargain, and the wind blows cold. Florence wakes to a mediocre morning; the last drunken students pile onto their mattresses in varying shades of undress, swirling considerable clouds of stink with the force of their exhalations. Dogs bark. A shadow falls on the city in the form of a crane; massive and red, hook dangling rusted and useless from its phallic expanse. Paolo walks through the affected area with a bit of a limp, keeping to the wall. Who he's avoiding he can't recall, but he's pretty sure they want him dead. It's a messy business, always has been.

He steps into the bar. Most places would make a face if you asked them to take the whiskey bottle down before five, but not here. Rossi's a friend – the kind of friend who never gives a first name – and he never asks a question that doesn't have a one-word answer. Today's an exception to prove the rule, though. He can see it forming behind the old man's eyes, a real doozy. After all those years of holding it in, it ought to be a regular diamond.

"Why the fuck you bleedin' on my barstool, kid?"

Unexpectedly valid. Paolo can't remember if the hole in his leg is from a knife or a gunshot, but it doesn't seem to matter. He grabs a coaster from the bar and slides it under his thigh. Problem solved. Rossi hands him a glass of whiskey; Dunville's

Three Crowns, better than either of them can afford by far.

"It's on the house," says Rossi, "if you tell me what all this is about."

Paolo drains the glass. It's good, better than he deserves. He lets it settle a minute before he ruins it with speech. The barkeep's a patient man.

"It's about a woman," he says, with finality. And isn't it always.

For a moment, the bar fades away and Paolo's thrust into the events of the night before. The crane's lit up by a spotlight, working overtime and seemingly unmanned, on what Paolo can't seem to say. He's hoping he'll remember what comes next, but there's nothing for it except to start walking. It begins to rain.

Faces appear over the cobbles – one first, then a crowd. Paolo marks them in passing, but they're not who he's looking for. He's looking for her. At this point the girl's an urban legend. She can bring a room down with the flick of a wrist. She plays to sold out bars and venues across the city. Paolo's heard her described, but only in whispers. Florence believes absolutely in the watched pot rule. If you talk about something beautiful, you'll kill it.

Ahead, he sees a flash of light. Cameras. Something tells him it's her, but not the way he expects. After the white light comes red and after the red light comes blue. There's a goddamn kaleidoscope spilling out into the street. He's seen this happen before, and it doesn't end well. Not for the first time, he pushes his way through the crowd. They're congealing into a single mass, united in their efforts to obstruct him. The closer he gets, the harder they fight him. It's like swimming through cooling steel. He's got a window to break through, and it's closing. Like he always does, he makes it, and he sees her. There's just one problem. It's not her.

The girl's not dressed in much, but what little there is, it's black. Her hair's black. Her nails are black. Her eyes are black, and the trail of blood pooling from her mouth to the sidewalk, that's black too. Paolo can just barely make out wings around her eyes, and a name comes to his mind like an echo from another life – "The Girl with the Egyptian Eyeliner." But something about the eyes is different from what he expects her to look like. He tries not to examine his expectations for a stranger's corpse – because this is, after all, a stranger. Right? He wants to say he can't put his finger on what's changed, but that's just it. He can. Before his eyes, he sees the outline drawn in eyeshadow on the girl's face change. They're not just wings, they're feathers, spread wide. Ready for flight. Something about it is wrong.

"A woman?" Rossi asks.

Paolo's back in the bar. This dream bounces back and forth like an epileptic every time he dreams it, and he's fucking sick of it. He wants to glue himself to the barstool, and finish the story for a change. Especially now. Especially when the story's not the same as it was the last ten times.

"I knew her," Paolo said, "from before."

This is the old story, but he's telling it about a new girl. The Girl with the Egyptian Eyeliner. The Girl whose Eyes Took Flight. The dead girl. The corpse of his dreams.

"She dead?" Rossi asks. He's skipping to the punchline. That's new too.

Paolo hears the door to the bar open, and he reaches for his holster. There's nothing there. He's certain he's got a gun in this dream, he's fired it before. It's gone now.

"Shop's closed, pal," Rossi calls to the figure in the entryway. Paolo can make enough out to know it's a man, but not much else. He's got a bad feeling, cold along the base of his neck. The man ignores him, so Rossi repeats it.

"Get lost," he says, but the shadow crosses the room in a heartbeat. That's what it is, Paolo realizes, a shadow. It wasn't obscured by the light, that's really all that it is. Before he can warn the bartender, Rossi's throat is slashed and he's slumping to the ground.

"Jesus Christ!" Paolo shouts. The man may be a figment of his imagination, but he's a friendly one.

Never in all the times he's had this dream has he figured out who hurt his leg, but his money's on the shadow now. It takes the stool next to him, leaving bloody handprints on the bar top.

"You know me," it says, in a deep voice.

"You're wrong there," Paolo says, and finishes his drink. It's the last Rossi'll pour, so he might as well enjoy it.

"You may think you don't," it insists, "but you do."

Paolo supposes it's possible. He supposes this could be his Empire Strikes Back moment, and he'll chop off the shadow's head to find his own neck underneath. He'd like to think he's not so unoriginal that his subconscious couldn't do better than that, but he's not sure.

"Who are you then?" He asks, and he swears it grins. He's never seen darkness glint, but there's a flash of something that's not quite light from where its mouth would be. He gets that chill again, but he hasn't got an answer yet.

"Let me show you," says the shadow, and then Paolo's back on the street.

"Son of a bitch," he whispers, but something tells him he needs to run. He's got that wound in his leg already, but this time it's fresh. This time it hurts, not just that dull echoing ache of a pain you've adjusted to, but the fresh sting of a new injustice. Whoever or whatever made it is still here. Everything in his body wants him to move, but he overrules the warning. It's just a dream, he promises himself. It can't hurt me.

That may or may not be true, but either way he's got to see it for himself. He knows that. If he doesn't, it'll just keep hunting him until it gets what it wants.

The blue and red lights are flashing, and now they're casting shadows on the alley Paolo's propping himself against. He can see the outline of a pair of policemen, the ones standing by the body of the girl, whichever girl it is now. He can see a crowd, shifting and changing its size based on the rotation of the lights. For the first time, though, he can see something new. Something darker, more solid. It's a shadow, but it's not coming from the police lights. It's the reason they're here, not the other way around. It's coming towards him, closer and closer. Paolo can just barely make out the shape, and he can feel himself slipping towards consciousness.

"I have to know," he calls to it. "You have to come before I wake up, I have to know."

It follows his command and steps into the light, not that it helps. Paolo can make out the outline, but only that. It's a shadow, but it's not the shadow of a man. It's the shadow of a big, black dog.

Part 3

Lover,
there will be another one
Who'll hover
over you beneath the sun
Tomorrow
see the things
that never come
Today

When you see me
Fly away without you
Shadow on the things you know
Feathers fall around you
And show you the way to go
It's over, it's over

from "Birds" by Neil Young

THE GYPSY
Jacob

IT IS HAPPENING AGAIN. The sky over Florence shudders silently with flashes of heat lightning. Jacob watches an Englishman with an old guitar cover James Taylor in the *Piazza della Signoria*. His voice hits the notes and bounces off the old stone. He's singing "Handyman" with one foot on the spot where Savagnarola burned piles and piles of books and paintings, and the other in a puddle of bird shit. People clap and throw money at him like he's actually accomplishing something. Like he's anything other than an imitator coasting on the success of marginally greater men to carve out a lesser success for himself. On any other day, Jacob would revel in his ambivalence to this idiot and his little kingdom, but today he can't. He woke up with the hunger at the start of the week, and it hasn't left him since. He can't eat his fill. He can't fuck enough to be satisfied. There's only one choice, and he's embarrassed that it's taken him so many years to see it. Don't lie to yourself, he thinks. You saw it before; you just weren't ready to follow through. Not until tonight. He's right, of course. But tonight's different. Tonight, he's ready. Tonight, he's going to satisfy his hunger. At least for a while.

He leaves the guitarist and his throng of admirers behind. Much as he'd like to start here, there's too much attention being paid. It's too well attended. There's too much light. This isn't the place, and these aren't the people. Tony knows what he needs. He's been thinking about it since he cornered that gypsy in the alley. He's been watching her. He's been waiting for his chance. If you're going to be extreme, he thinks. It's best to take it all the way.

Jacob knows that at night, Maria and her family float around the edges of crowds like the one he just left, looking for stragglers. They're predators, picking off the weak. It's what he admires about them. They're the antithesis of what he finds so deplorable about the vast majority of the world's unwashed masses. They're the anti-Tony, in a word. Theirs is a life of survival of the fittest in action. And it's not just the way they act when they're pushed into a corner. It's the way they shop, buying only what they need. It's the way they speak – a barrage of clipped, aggressive phrases that cuts through the bullshit like a razorblade. He admires them, but admiration only gets you so far. Jacob's a predator's predator. He doesn't want to settle for some straggler, limping behind the herd. He wants the hunt. He wants the kill.

Jacob catches sight of her a few blocks away, walking away from a cloud of Italians watching a street performer butcher Sting, loaded down with a heavy pocket full of jewelry. She looks for all the world like any other kid, walking home with her head in the clouds, but he knows better. He knows her senses are heightened. He knows she's waiting for someone to notice her, or to notice what she's taken. He knows the hand hidden idly in her pocket is running over the handle of that knife. He follows from a distance. He knows she sees him in her periphery, but she hasn't decided if she's being followed yet. She'll wait for a street she knows well, and try to lose him in the jumble. He can smell the apprehension on her. It smells like the rain on the cobblestones the night he landed in Florence. It smells like the cabdriver, and his box of incense. What was it he had said? He said Jacob would come to believe him. Maybe he already does.

She's already proving him right, ducking onto a side street with a practiced flourish. She thinks she can lose him, or get the jump, but she doesn't know he's ready. That he's been walking these streets for a week, mapping them out. Studying the layout from an overhead view he found online. He figures she'll do one of two things. She'll either loop back around to get back on the main road, or wait for him in a little alcove halfway down to scare him out of whatever he's planning. He followed to far back for her to recognize him, he made sure of that. The safe thing would be to loop around, but he knows she won't take it safe. She wants to prove her strength to a universe that's called her weak her whole life. It'll be him or her. That's exactly what he wants. That's exactly what he needs. He can feel his stomach tearing itself apart in anticipation. He follows her down the alley, and checks his watch. It's ten forty-five. In fifteen minutes the street musicians will all, in unison, box up their guitars and go back to the real world, and they'll release their crowds into the street. It'll be a horde of witnesses. He doesn't have long. Luckily, he doesn't need it.

He finds her exactly where he expects to find her, leaping at him from the darkness of a little alcove halfway down the alley. Because he's expecting it, he catches her knife arm mid-swing, and uses it to pull her to the ground. She struggles, but he's stronger than she is on any day of the week, and today he's something more. Something sharper, more dangerous. He slams her hand against the concrete once, twice, and on the third try he breaks her grip.

"*Merda*," she whispers. "It's you."

She's not sure what he wants, and she's terrified. He's using his weight to keep her on the ground. She's not strong enough to lift him or push, and he's got her knife now. It's a nice knife, with a mother of pearl and cherry wood handle. When this is over, maybe he'll just keep it.

"Yea," he says after a while, "It's me."

She spits up at him, as big a wad as she can summon, and she's a good shot. It catches him right between the eyes. He admires her defiance. It's almost a shame to kill her, but he can feel every muscle in his body tensing up in anticipation, waiting for the moment that's just on the edge of arriving. He just wants to savor the feeling a little first.

"Do what you're going to do, *cazzo*, I'm not afraid of you."

She's lying, but he's not the one she's trying to convince. She's fooling herself, and that's what matters.

"You think I haven't met men like you?" She asks, her eyes starting to get glassy. "You act kind, but it's bullshit. Your kindness is a lie. You were only kind to me because you wanted something, and now that you didn't get it the kindness is gone."

He thinks about that for a moment. He had gotten what he wanted from her that day. He'd gotten the story, and anything else she'd given him was secondary.

"No," he says, "I was kind to you because you made me sad."

"Fuck you. You corner me twice in an alley and I'm the one who is supposed to be sad. You think it's sad that my family fights to survive, but you don't do shit about it. You think it's sad that I carry a knife around, that I need it, but here you are doing the exact same thing I need it for."

"That isn't what I'm doing," he says.

This isn't like what happened to her before. She's not going to walk away from this, scarred or otherwise. Jacob needs her to understand that. He needs to see it in her face.

"Liar," she says.

"You said that last time."

"Because I see how you look at me. Like I'm a goddamn *filetto di manzo* on your plate. You don't fool me. Do what you're going to do, I said."

So she'd seen it. She'd seen the hunger, even then. She saw it before he'd felt it return himself. She'd even known, somehow, that she would be its target. Maybe she didn't know how it would manifest, but she'd seen it. He'd tricked her into forgetting, that last time, but he wouldn't be so lucky again. Jacob takes her knife and lays it against her neck. She starts to shudder, and now he knows for sure that she's lying. She's afraid of him. Afraid, even though she has no idea what he really wants.

"You know," he says, "when I got here, to Florence, a man told me something. He said God was closer to him than the veins of his own neck. Do you believe that?"

She swallows, and now he's tipped his hand. Now she knows. He can see it in her face, and he feels the hunger rising. He's shaking, he realizes. His hand is twitching.

"Answer the fucking question," he tells her. "Answer and I'll make it quick."

"I don't believe in God," she says, and a handful of tears run down her face. She really is pretty. This is such a fucking shame. "God would never allow a man like you to live."

This is it. This is the moment. There's no more time to savor it, not if he wants to get away.

"You're wrong," he says, and he starts to draw the knife across her throat. "I'm not a man. I'm a goddamn shark."

Jacob watches as the blood follows the knife across her throat. She's wheezing and croaking, but she's good and she never screams. He knows she's trying to save him the satisfaction, but she's doing him a favor, too. She's letting him watch, when he ought to be running. Somehow the thought makes him sad.

"I'm sorry," he says to her, and not for the first time. "I'm sorry, but it had to be you. I don't know why. I wish it could have been different."

As soon as the words leave his mouth Jacob knows he isn't alone anymore. He looks up, ready to deal with the problem, but it isn't a person. It's that goddamn cat.

"This is three times," he says to it. "Any more than that, and I'll quit being nice."

It's almost like it hears him. Like it understands him. It must, because it hisses at him. If he had a rock he'd throw it, but all he's got is the knife. That, he needs to keep.

"You're lucky I can't stay," he mutters under his breath, and he can't. He wasn't lying when he told Maria he was a shark. Just like a shark, he's got to stay moving, or he's dead in the water.

The cat hisses as he begins to walk away. Jacob looks over his shoulder, and it's gone, but there's something in its place. It's a feather. A single, snow-white feather.

THE BOARD
Paolo

CLAUDIA'S CHESS SET IS COPPER, which serves only to exaggerate the socioeconomic commentary inherent to the game. The pawns, handled at regular intervals each game, have developed a thick, mossy patina of oxidation. Working up the ladder each strata is less green, shinier – the kings are downright gleaming. The first time he handled them, Paolo reminded her that a good polish would revert the entire set to factory settings, but she says she won't hear of it. She takes a peevish delight in the board's tacit satire. Unfortunately for Paolo, he's got what amounts to a genetic predisposition to find the whole thing off-putting at best.

Paolo tries his hand at beating her three times before he knows he needs outside help. Only problem is where to get it. The third game, she'd beat him in maybe fifteen moves. His pride can handle losing, but he needs the job and he sure as shit isn't getting it any other way. So he does the only sane thing there is to do. He buys a board, and he practices. At first, the Girl makes fun of him, but when he explains himself, she plays along. She gets excited, even.

"This is exactly what I'm talking about," she assures him. "You're making things happen."

"I'm not making anything happen unless I beat her," he says.

A few more efforts pass, and Paolo's starting to feel the

weight of the task. He gets close enough to put up a fight, once or twice, but he's pretty sure Claudia's just playing with him.

"Next time," she says, "Try and think more than one move ahead. Think about the shape of the board like a city, and the pieces like people. Think about a crowd, filling out a cathedral. Think about whatever makes it make sense to you, really, but that's what I do."

Paolo takes the advice, but try as he might he's not getting any better. Then, one day, the Girl's done.

"Listen, Paolo," she says. "You know I'm glad you're trying, but I'm sick of seeing this shit. I don't want it in here."

"I thought you wanted me to make something happen?"

"I do," she says, and she puts a hand on his shoulder, "but the things I'm interested in you making happen you're making happen less these days. You care more about that chess board."

Maybe that was fair. It had three or four days since their last session, and the Girl's used to getting her way once or twice daily at this point.

"How can I make it up to you?"

She has a couple of ideas.

After that, Paolo does as he's told and takes his chess outside. He finds a table with the chess scammers at a local park, and though they're beating him constantly he's too broke for them to get anything out of it. They'll take the practice, and as long as he acts like he's beaten them if anyone rich comes near, they get something out of the deal too. He's hanging out with them when he sees the paper.

The headline's something gruesome about the murder of an underage Roma a few alleys off from the Ponte Vecchio a night or so back. The article's not much better. She'd had her throat slit, and had lost enough blood by the time she was found she was light enough they didn't need a stretcher to get her into the car. The worst bit is no one bothered to contact her family, or they couldn't find them. There was no statement from the grieving mother. No calls for vengeance from the enraged father. Nothing. Paolo's aware of these things, and they affect him, but they're not what catches his attention. What catches his attention is the picture. They're showing the crowd gathered around the police-do-not-cross line the morning they found the body, and there's a face in the crowd he recognizes. It's Patience. No matter how much he wants to, he knows he can't let this go.

When he confronts her, she's angry, which is actually a surprise. He was expecting guilt, or at the very least a simple right-place wrong-time explanation. And actually, she was at the right place at the wrong time for the picture. Here Paolo's worried she's having a fatal attraction moment and she's closer to Sex and the City.

"I was on a walk of shame, Paolo." She says. "You told me to find a thing, so I found one. By now, I've found more than one. And you know what? It's working."

She's not wrong. The girls haven't totally accepted her, but their fearless leader's signed off on enough of her little midnight trysts that Patience has earned their respect. This isn't what he wanted to talk about, but he's not sure how to change the subject now.

"I don't care about that," he assures her.

"Good," she says, "because I'm not stopping. I'm not doing it for the others, I'm doing it for me. I like how it makes me feel."

Patience is lying to herself, but it's not in Paolo's power to tell her the truth. Not about this one.

"I'm glad, Patience." He says, "really. But honestly, that's not what I wanted to talk to you about."

She blushes the color of a San Marzano tomato, and looks to the corner of the room.

"Oh. What did you want to talk about then?"

"Your picture's in a newspaper article talking about a dead body. I just wanted to make sure you were ok."

She goes back to eye contact. She's surprised he's asking. Why, he doesn't know. Shouldn't someone have asked?

"I mean, it was horrible, seeing it. The blood spilled out of her in the strangest way. When they picked her off the street, it looked like she'd made a snow angel on the ground, but in blood."

Paolo grimaces at the description, but it sure as shit paints a picture. The paper had avoided showing the body, so it hadn't occurred to him that she would have seen it.

"She didn't look like she suffered, is the strangest thing." Patience has a wistful look on her face, like there's something admirable about this poor girl and her ruined throat. And hell, maybe there is. "If anything, she looked like she'd finally found peace. Do you think that's possible?"

Paolo honestly doesn't know. It's hard to imagine finding peace in someone cutting you open and bleeding you like a pig, but then she can't have had it easy. Paolo doesn't know much about the Roma, but he knows that everyone in the city, in the country, in the goddamn continent hates them, and that kind of hate is hard to live with.

"It might be," he says at last. "If you say that's how it looked then I'm sure she did."

"I wonder if she knew the man," Patience continues, "and whether it would be worse for her if she did or didn't. I can't imagine it either way. I don't want to imagine it at all, but honestly, I can't stop. It's all I can think about, and no matter how hard I try it just gets worse."

"Is it better to talk about it?"

"Maybe," she says. "Yes, I think so. But if you don't mind, I'd like to talk about something else, or maybe just stop."

Paolo nods. He's exceeded his daily allowance as Good Samaritan in the house already. But the invitation to keep talking does give him an idea, so he floats the question.

"You don't play chess by any chance, do you Patience?"

She smiles, and it lights her up like a match hitting a pile of dry pine needles. He'll take that as a yes. There's a knock at the door, and Patience goes to answer it. The stranger on the other side could pass as one of The Girl with the Egyptian Eyeliner's disciples, but Paolo's never seen her before. Like most of them, she's a knockout – though she can't be much older than seventeen. The crazy thing is, Patience seems to recognize her. It takes her a second, but a flash of knowing crosses her face and she pulls her into a hug.

"Maria!" Patience calls, and Cara and Catrina come fluttering in. "Maria!" They echo.

It looks like the Girl's crew has grown by one, somehow. Paolo tries not to think about it, but his odds of success are looking slim.

THE FIRE
Kitsune

KITSUNE AWAKENS TO THE SOUND of sirens. Red and blue light spills through the cracks in the shades, splintering off into flashing constellations across the bare walls of her apartment.

"That one looks like a cat," she says.

Jacob stirs at the sound of her voice. He rolls over and shoves his face into his pillow.

"That one there, by the crack from where I threw a plate at an ex. It looks just like a little kitten."

He rolls over and stares blankly, following the line of her extended finger. His eyes widen in recognition, with a little more drama than the situation requires.

"Yeah I guess it does. That one over there looks like a horse."

There's a whole goddamn zoo on her wall, apparently.

"I wonder what they're wailing about?"

He asks the question but she knows he doesn't care. He doesn't, and she doesn't. All she feels is a mild curiosity, but it's enough to get her out of bed.

"It doesn't sound like they're moving," he says.

They aren't. She can see the shadows of the emergency vehicles on the street, and a bustle of uniformed men scurrying around them. It's then that she smells it; smoke on the breeze, sneaking in wisps through her window. She shuts it.

"It's a fire," she says.

That's got his attention. He slouches up in the bed, the blanket draped over his shoulders like Eastwood's poncho in The Good, The Bad, and The Ugly. With the blinds open they can see flames alight in the windows of the building across the street. It's not a huge fire, but they can't seem to get it under control. They're running around like little tourists trying to find the best place to take a photo, but nothing's getting done.

"Look at them go," says Jacob.

He's behind her now, resting his chin on her shoulder. It's an oddly affectionate gesture, but the hands snaking around her hips tell a different story.

"Where are the hoses?"

"I don't even see a fireman, it's just police."

One hand slithers up her side, and she leans into his chest. On the street residents of the burning building watch their lives erode in slow motion, their hands pressed against their temples or tearing through their hair. It's mostly older people. They've probably lived there for years. An entire lifetime of accumulated memories, possessions, and dust is disintegrating before their eyes. Jacob's tongue takes an exploratory taste of her earlobe. She gasps.

"Wait," she says.

She can almost hear his eyebrow rise, but his hands keep moving.

"Let me get a chair."

When she was eleven years old, someone set fire to her parents' restaurant. No one had caught the arsonist – her parents insisted that no one had even looked, and she believed them. She remembered walking into the building with them days later and seeing the damage. Blackened walls, shattered glass. Charred chairs and tables and ruined pots and glasses everywhere. For years after she had dreamed of that fire. In her dreams she had set the blaze herself. It raged around her, but it did not harm her. She laughed as it destroyed everything her family had fought so hard to build. It was a strange dream, but she had never thought of it as a nightmare.

Now, Jacob sits in the chair with his back to the window. Kitsune straddles him, her eyes on the fire. Her body's in the moment, but her mind is across the street. She can feel him looking at her, trying to meet her eyes.

"Oh Christ," says Jacob.

He pulls her tighter to him and she shudders.

"'Sune," he murmurs.

She's never known a man to use her full name in bed. Her stage name. She supposes it would be a little awkward.

"'Sune." Again.

She remembers the way the place smelled. It smelled like that for over a year, even after it was clean. It's the same smell wafting through her window now, burnt glass and charcoal. It fills her nostrils, drowning Jacob's sweat-smell and dominating her senses. What do the people on the street smell in the smoke? She wonders. Can they smell their mother's paintings burning, or their best wedding china? Or does it all just smell the same?

"I want you." He says.

For a moment Kitsune tries to capture some of the warmth from the fire, to take it vicariously into herself. Much as she tries, she remains cold. Lately she is always cold. It's not external; no amount of cover resolves it or improves it. A flash of flame licks out the window of one of the apartments, shattering it. By now the firemen have arrived, and hoses fire sheets of water from the street into the air. The water dampens the flames but it can't seem to kill them.

Finally, she takes her eyes off the window and looks down at Jacob. He smiles and grabs her hair. Now the affection is gone. Now passion is all-consuming, beyond control. It's no different than the fire across the street, but it doesn't warm her either. Not at all. She tries to smile back at him, but she can feel herself failing. She tries to kiss him, but he tastes like ashes and it makes her recoil.

"Kita," says Jacob.

She stops. Her eyes widen. It's a nickname, he's trying to give me a nickname. She tells herself this but it doesn't help. That has to be it. Doesn't it?

"Kita." Again.

All of a sudden her hands are around his throat. This is not a romantic gesture, not this time. His expression changes quickly. He knows this is real. She leans in close and hisses in his ear. The venom in her surprises her, frightens her, but it also makes her feel strong, and for a moment, healthy.

"Don't you ever, ever call me that. Never again."

It's just a mistake. That's all. He doesn't know, no one does. That's what she tells herself, at least. But maybe she's wrong. She tries to relax.

She turns her eyes back to the window, her hands still clutching tight, but not as tight as before. The gesture is maybe a bit romantic now, at least in context. Out on the street, the sirens are still ringing, but the fire's out. This street is going to smell like smoke for years, she thinks. Jacob splutters. He's losing oxygen, and his face is losing color. Kitsune realizes that she could kill him, then. That it would be easy. That no one would know he was gone. Not even Tony knew where he was right now. No one but her would miss him. The thought doesn't surprise her as much as it makes her sad. She relaxes her grip. The hoses fire into the windows with renewed fervor, and a gush of smoke billows out, for a second forming the shape of a pair of wings. It's a different kind of smoke, now. A sadder kind. Jacob moans. The fire is over.

THE ROSE
Tony

TONY'S BROUGHT THE BISHOP FLOWERS, which ought to count for something. If nothing else it will explain his presence, if anything suspicious should ever come of this visit. To anyone who asked, and a few who didn't, Tony told a story of an encounter he'd had with Carrera while he was on the brink of suicide. The bishop had talked him from the ledge, Tony said, bringing a little twinkle to his eyes. He's not sure anyone buys it. Tony's got small number of talents, but lying isn't one of them. At the end, though, they let him through and they don't bat an eye. Either they buy it or they can't be bothered to care if he's telling the truth.

Alone with the bishop in his hospital room, Tony feels the weight of what the Angel asked of him more clearly. Not because he feels a sense of malevolence or power here, but because he doesn't. What he sees is not a man twisted with hate, nor a devil, nor a vessel for some hypothetical sinister spirit. What he sees is an old man on life support. Pull any of a hundred chords and you could extinguish his life. The Angel would have him believe there would be consequences for such an act. But he already knew that. There were always consequences for taking a life, there had to be. It's the sort of thing that transforms you. That makes you a different man. A lesser man.

"How about you, bishop Carrera," Tony whispers, "are you a

lesser man?"

If Jacob's source was to be believed, Carrera was a bona fide serial killer, specializing in gypsies. They were perfect victims because they wouldn't be missed. Tony's not a killer himself, but he's seen enough television shows to know that's somewhere on a serial killer's list of top priorities when choosing a target. It's hard to imagine the sort of things Jacob had told him about coming from this weak old man. Then again, considering the source, maybe it was all just a load of horseshit.

Tony's had a hard time doing anything other than mulling over the events of the other night in his head ever since it happened. He knows he locked the door before Kitty and Jacob showed up. There's no question in his mind about that. He'd walked the dog a bit before they were due to arrive, put him in the bedroom, locked the door, and stuck the key in his pocket. He went over those steps and formed a visual memory of each in his head. There was no way it hadn't happened exactly as he was remembering it. Still, Jacob had made his way into the room. So either he'd picked the lock and lied about it, or someone else had let him in. This didn't seem very likely. It couldn't have been the dog, of course: no opposable thumbs.

So Jacob had broken into his room looking for what, exactly? What did Tony have that Jacob could possibly want? What on earth made him think he'd find anything? The best Tony can figure is Jacob wanted to embarrass him, to dig up some kind of dirt he might find in a locked room. It was clear from the way he'd talked about Kitty over the phone that Jacob knew how Tony felt about her. Did Jacob see him as a threat? Is that all it boiled down to? Were they just middle schoolers throwing rocks over who got to take a girl to a dance? That was part of it, Tony could at least admit that to himself, but it wasn't the whole story. That much was made clear when Jacob touched the dog. The dog had yelped like he'd been struck, like he'd been injured.

Tony had checked and checked, but found nothing wrong. Jacob hadn't been bitten, either, as far as he could see, but he left looking like he'd been hit by a bus. Tony had accused him of drinking too much, but the bottle of wine had sat half full when they left. And Tony had handled most of that himself. Jacob had arrived sober, and left the same way.

Whatever happened, it isn't a mystery he cares to solve. Now that Jacob's here for good, Tony has to decide if it's worth his time to apologize. It doesn't matter which of them is right, that's the only way forward. He doesn't give a shit if he sees that prick even once more in either of their lifetimes, but if he loses him he might lose Kitty. That, he isn't ready for. He'll have to rein it in.

"I've got to go," he says to the bishop.

It feels somehow comforting to talk to Carrera as though he's alive. A real, breathing monster would be easier than a vegetable, somehow. It would be an enemy to fight against instead of just a life he was being asked to take. He sets his flowers beside the bishop's bed, and heads out. The nurse waves to him, but studiously avoids hearing another round of his awful storytelling. Tony figures that means his little ruse worked.

When he returns home, his constant houseguest has returned. This time, she greets him with a newspaper, instead of a cup of tea. The headline is more bad news. A gypsy, dead in the streets in a ring of blood that looks like a chalk outline gone wrong. The article keeps dropping the words 'hate crime' and 'act of terror' but something tells him they don't have the full story.

"It is very important you are truthful with me, Tony," says the Angel, her eyes letting him know exactly what mistake he made, and what it will take to fix it. "I need to know if anyone other than you or I have been in the presence of your dog."

Tony nods, dumbfounded. The Angel doesn't break eye contact.

"Jacob," Tony says at last. "It was Jacob."

THE KITCHEN
Paolo

THE MORNING AFTER MARIA SHOWED UP, Patience comes back from the market with no less than three potted plants. She sets one on an elevated ledge by the window in the kitchen to catch the sun, and another in a corner in the living room. The little sign sticking out of the soil in the first one tells Paolo it's an African Violet, and the purple blooms confirm the diagnosis. She grew up on a farm, she says, and she's sick of not having plants around. She's sick of having to walk a mile to see something green. There's very little plant life in the city center, that's true. Regardless, Paolo's expecting the Girl with the Egyptian Eyeliner to turn around and throw them out the window, but she surprises him.

"Cara," she says. "Do me a favor and see if you can find a calla lily next time you're out? A really dark one, black even, if you can manage it."

Cara leaves without finishing her coffee.

A day later the apartment is flooded with foliage, and Patience is the de facto second in command, at least for the time being. The position has wavered between Catrina and Jessica and Sonya before, but Patience and her plants have thrown such a complete coup that it will take them at least a week to get the balance of power sorted. The black calla lily stays in the Girl with the Egyptian Eyeliner's room. Paolo actually likes it, or likes the way she treats it at least. She's gentle with it, and takes the same thorough care of it that she takes of everything else. Though their apartment looks at any given time as though it had been hit by a whirlwind, the Girl and her personal space are nothing less than the picture of cleanliness. The other girls have flowers too, of course. Cara buys a rose because she's brainless and doesn't know what else to buy. Sonya buys a stargazer lily because she wants something similar to the Girl's, but different enough to be safe. Catrina, with brass balls as usual, buys a cactus.

Most of the girls plants only live because they fear the consequences of their death, but Patience is the definition of a green thumb. She keeps herbs in the kitchen: basil, and mint, and sage, and chives. In the living room a peace lily filters the air and rids them of the stench of the socks no one's bothered to pick up since long before he moved in. Her African violet She adds a new one every so often, and no matter how many she juggles, they all live. It's a feat, but Paolo's more interested in the other new talent of hers he's discovered recently. Patience is the best chess player, other than Claudia, that he's ever seen.

With her in the Girl's good graces, Paolo feels comfortable breaking out the board again as long as he's meeting his mistress's needs, and he's playing with Patience. They practice as often as possible, Patience walking him through openings and aggressive stances, defenses and ploys. She explains the key terms to him. *En Passant* is the right a pawn has to take another pawn that has moved to its side in an effort to pass it by. A fork is when one piece threatens two enemy pieces simultaneously. Check and mate he already knows, but he lets her explain the subtleties to him anyway. She'll make an excellent teacher someday, if that's what she wants to do. Whatever she wants to teach. She lives up to her name, and has a gift for simplifying the game's biggest ideas and concepts without sounding condescending. Finally, after a few days of practice, and running over a plan of attack with her, Paolo thinks he's ready. He sets a date to go back to Claudia's place, and agrees to rise to the challenge one more time.

Claudia's kitchen is flooded with the smell of pumpkin. She's been making ravioli all day in preparation for his arrival. Paolo doesn't just come as an excuse to eat, but he'll readily admit he's come to savor her meals as much as he does her company and the opportunity it might afford him.

The key to pumpkin ravioli, she confides, it to use very little actual pumpkin. Pumpkin itself tastes like globs of wet nothing. If you stuff your ravioli with pumpkin only you had better make a hell of a sauce. The actual recipe is quite complex. The flavor is simulated with a number of ingredients, including the same brand of jarred pickled vegetables his father used to keep in bulk, and crumbs from *amaretti* cookies. Paolo can't taste them without thinking of his parents. Every December, without fail, they'd snuggle up on the couch to ring in the New Year. They didn't bother with TV or radio, they just looked at the clock. As soon as their kiss had ended, which was often quite a long time coming, they would have one drink: Amaretto, with a splash of sour mix. You'd need a dozen to get you drunk, but that never seemed to stop them.

The food, of course, is part of the distraction. It's part of the game. Paolo realized that when Patience was walking him through the defenses. Chess is sixty percent in the eyes, she'd told him. You can win a chess match simply by never breaking eye contact. If you can go longer than your opponent without blinking, even better. The food was Claudia's way of making him feel comfortable, and comfort was exactly his problem. She knew that. He'd been nothing but comfortable, ever since his father died. Even when Franco threw him to the curb, he'd found a way to make himself comfortable again only what, two hours later? He'd eat her food, of course, but he now saw through the ruse behind the meal. Let her think she had him fooled, and he'd prove her wrong. This time, he would win.

It takes exactly thirteen moves for Claudia to realize something is different, that he's changed. Just like Patience taught him, he's been counting them.

"You've been practicing," she says, frowning in studied concentration.

"Is that cheating?" Paolo says, sliding his bishop forward to make a fork of a knight and rook.

"Actually," she says with a smile, "it's exactly the point."

She favors the rook and lets the knight go. Taking her knight puts his bishop at risk, and they both know it. The question is if she sees what happens if she takes it. She'll have to move her queen to do it, and Paolo's got a rook two moves away from sacrificing itself for that prize. She's smart enough to catch him at it, so he asks himself what Patience would do. Distract, distract, distract – that was her motto. He meets Claudia's eyes and asks her a question.

"Do you remember that old love song my father wrote for my mother?"

"Of course", she says, smiling warmly as she takes his bishop. Paolo doesn't tip his hand as he moves through his next steps.

"It was called Four Quartets," he says. "My father tried to read Eliot because my mother did and though he said he couldn't understand a word of it, he loved the title."

"I remember," she says. "Gianni told him he should have called it 'The Hanged Men' instead."

"Did dad think that was funny?"

"What do you think?"

His father wouldn't have laughed at that, but he would laugh at the sight shaping up on Mrs. Misuri's kitchen table. Paolo's got her in check, with mate just around the corner depending on how she wiggles out.

"I think," Paolo says, fiddling with the bishop she had taken earlier idly, "that my father wouldn't have recognized a joke if one of them took the guitar right out of his hands and made a run for it."

Claudia smiles sadly, and moves her king diagonally towards his side of the board, taking his last bishop. It's exactly what he needed. He moves a pawn forward, and replaces it with a shiny new Queen. A promotion for a promotion. Claudia looks at the board and, smiling, claps her hands. For a second, he wonders if she'd seen it coming and let it happen anyway, just happy that he'd worked to improve. At the end of the day, it doesn't matter.

"When can you start?" She asks him.

THE EYE
Jacob

JACOB DOES AN HONEST TO GOD double-take – the kind you'd expect to come with a little cartoon sound effect. It shouldn't be her, it just isn't possible. It can't be her, but it is. It's Maria, the gypsy whose wrists he'd slashed to ribbons only a week before. It's her, but she's different. The girl's decked head to toe in clothing brands there's no way she can afford and she wouldn't have bothered with stealing: Gucci, Armani, that kind of thing. There's a silver bangle on her wrist that would attract far too much attention for her to even think about, not to mention the fact that the skin beneath it appears to be intact. A flurry of possibilities rush through his head all at once, most of them verging on the Soap Operatic. Maybe she has a twin sister. Maybe she faked her death. He shakes his head, because nothing like that is an option. This is like the cat, and it's like Tony's dog, and it's like the hunger. It's something bigger than him that wants to play him like a fiddle, and he's not going to let that happen. Jacob keeps a safe distance because he can't know for sure if she still has her uncanny knack for catching a tail, but he knows he can't let her go without following. He doesn't have a choice. Something is going on here, and he needs to get to the bottom of it.

At a distance, he watches her work her way through what has got to be the most – what's the word the college girls use? –

basic, it's basic — the most basic day he could possibly imagine. First, she grabs an Americano of all things from one of the cafés lining the *Via del Calzaiuoli*. It's one of those kitschy tourist catchers that charge at least a Euro more for each drink than a place a block away would have the balls for, and make it with a Nespresso. She takes a picture of herself with it and flirts with the barista and spends too much money for a croissant filled with apricot jelly. He knows this because she's letting him get close, much closer than the real Maria ever would have. She laughs like an airhead from a sitcom, and she touches the barista's arm, and he looks like he wants to squirm out of his skin but deep down he probably likes it. Jacob rolls his eyes. After she's done, she hits the street and heads in search of gelato. She walks straight past what Jacob knows to be the best place in town for it, which is hardly a secret, to one of those dumps with the artificially neon mounds of under-frozen gelato pressed against their show window and buys a massive cone laden heavy with chocolate. More pictures.

Jacob's just beginning to think the 'evil twin' theory held some water after all when the sea change comes. She swallows the last of her gelato like an anaconda finishing off a rat and suddenly, the smile is gone. She stops winking at younger Italian men in leather jackets, stops pressing her face against the glass at the perfume stores, and starts to get serious. Jacob isn't sure whether to be relieved or apprehensive, but he doesn't have time to choose. She's picking up the pace now, heading south towards the river. She maintains a perfectly straight line and people either get out of her way or they get pushed aside. It's getting hard to follow her. In the middle of the Ponte Vecchio she stops and stares at another girl who looks remarkably like her. She's taller, the other girl, and has red hair that looks like it was dyed in sheep's blood, but in every other respect they are the same. They have the same cobbled-together black ensemble of high end clothes and sparkling silver jewelry. They have the same sharply-lined makeup, heavy and again, black. They have the same expression on their face: dead and empty and searching. As Jacob watches, they reach their hands to each other's faces, brush their fingers over each other's eyes, and move on. The red-head nearly bowls him over as she strides past him, but Jacob has his eyes on Maria, if that's still who she is. She's still heading south.

Now she's weaving further and further into the quieter side of town. It's an area Tony told him that artists and intellectuals tend to flock to, apartments that look rundown from the outside but host the opulent dens of violin restorers and master sculptors. It's dead silent here. You can't hear the flood of tourist footsteps or the chatter of street vendors, just whatever noise you bring with you. For Maria, that's nothing. Her own footsteps are silent, like a tiger stalking in snow. Jacob tries to match her but he probably needn't bother. She's laser-focused on whatever her task is now, he could scream her name out and she wouldn't respond. Probably. He's just contemplating testing that theory when she stops, so suddenly he almost bumps into her. He's right behind her, close enough to grab her and end this now, but he doesn't. He wants to watch.

She's stopped in front of one of the idol windows that line so many of Florence's streets. Behind the glass is a small yellowing marble bust of the Madonna, staring out with an expression that's probably meant to be pious but to Jacob just looks constipated. It's a lesser work, to be sure. Some of these windows are beautifully crafted, featuring both Mary and her sacred spawn, but this is not one of them. Still, it's intact, and that counts for something in a city aging faster than its fleet of art restorers can keep up with. In silence, Maria reaches her hand out to the glass. It rests against the pane for a moment, and the glass starts to change. Jacob wants to believe his eyes are tricking him, but they're not. The glass is darkening, and becoming opaque. Like it's burning, or being painted, or just turning to charcoal. It spreads from her hand like ink in water, until a huge circle of the glass is blackened. And then it shatters. It breaks like safety glass, into tiny little even bricks that tumble to the cobblestone, somehow, without a sound. Maria moves closer to the Madonna, inspecting it closely. The hole she made is a perfect circle, which to his chagrin makes Jacob think about Tony, and a story he'd told him about Giotto. This isn't the time for that. Maria reaches her hand out, in the same gesture she'd made to the redhead on the Ponte Vecchio. It's almost a tender gesture, borderline romantic, but that's not the intent. She brushes her hands over the statues eyes, and leaves them blackened. They look like someone took a can of spray-paint to them, and Jacob is again reminded of Tony, bitching about cleaning up after this exact act of vandalism over and over again. He thinks about telling him only for a second, before knowing he never would have, even if they had been speaking.

The whole thing is over almost instantly, as though her hands were drenched in paint, but they're clean, Jacob can see that. As she walks away he presses his finger against the Madonna's sockets. They're perfectly dry. Maria repeats this process three times across the Oltrarno before she comes to a stop in a little alley. For the first time since he'd started following her, since he'd seen her from across the piazza and almost had a heart attack, she turns to face him. There's a familiar expression there, but there's no alarm or panic, just recognition. He comes closer, again, close enough to jump her and drive her to the street and finish what he'd started, but he doesn't. He can't, and he's not sure why anymore.

"Hello, Jacob," she says, and reaches her hands out to him. He knows he ought to stop her. He knows he ought to take his knife and gouge out her eyes before she paints him black, but his arms feel like lead. He can't move them, he can't even cry out.

He knows this should frighten him, but for some reason it doesn't. She touches his face and her hands are cold, so cold. They don't feel like human hands, they feel like marble. She draws herself closer to him and there is no heat coming from her at all. Nothing that makes her feel alive, and maybe she isn't. She runs her fingers over his eyes, and his nose, and his cheeks, and his lips. She traces her hands across his body in a way that is at once clinical and sensual, but he feels nothing. She settles them on the small of his back, and pulls him close for a kiss. He doesn't respond at first, but he can taste her as her tongue moves into his mouth. She tastes like a candle smells when you blow it out. He closes his eyes and accepts the kiss, starting to reach for her, but as soon as he touches her, she's gone. There's a faint black mist in the air that settles to the ground slowly. Jacob's first thought is ashes, but when he puts some on his finger and takes a taste he knows that's not what it is. It's black mascara.

THE MIRROR
Kitsune

IT'S HARD TO TELL IF THERE'S SOMETHING wrong
with her or something wrong with her reflection, but one thing's
for certain: they're not the same. It could be her eyesight, she
tries to assure herself. It's been fading in and out since the cough
moved in. She's been getting less sleep, less rest. The cough's a
shit roommate. It holds loud parties at all hours, and takes
whatever it wants from the fridge. She'd evict it, but she's not
sure she holds the deed. The jokes aren't helping, though. She
knows it's not her eyes, not this time. There's something wrong
with her reflection, and it's not going away.

Kitty runs some tests. First things first, she closes her left eye,
and then her right. Generally speaking, reflections reflect, but
hers is inverting. It's treating her every action like script written
out on paper it's trying to read backwards. When she winks left,
it winks right. When she winks right, it winks left. This, she's
pretty sure, is not her imagination. Next she opens her mouth.
The difference here is a bit harder to pick up on. When she does
it, she opens wide and sticks out her tongue, like she's going to
take her temperature. To be honest, she probably should, she's
got to be running a fever. The reflection just pulls its lips back
over its teeth. Its growling, she realizes. Silently, but that's what
the gesture signifies. Its teeth are bared, and it wants her to see
them. She closes her mouth, and thankfully it follows suit. There

was something unnerving about the growl. It was an expression she'd never made, never in her life. It didn't feel human.

Upon closer inspection, there's subtler differences at play. She knows from how she feels that her reflection should be drawn, wan, pale – at the least, she should have bags the size of suitcases underneath her eyes, but the reflection looks like it's ready for the runway. Kitty hasn't even put her makeup on, but that hasn't prevented it from applying its own. They aren't colors she'd have chosen. The lip color's bolder and brighter than she likes, and she's added length to her lashes. And there's – Kitty assumed it was glitter, but on closer inspection, they look like freckles. That's not possible. She's never had freckles anywhere but her shoulders, all earned one summer when she ignored her mother's advice and leapt into the ocean without sunblock. Her mother had never let her forget to wear sunblock again.

"Who are you?" Kitty asks the mirror, and it mouths it back a second later, in silence. She looks familiar, but it isn't her. It's someone who looks like her, someone who could be her cousin. Or her sister.

Just as she's thinking that, she hears the door fly open. Jacob's been a fluttering blur of kinetic energy for the last couple of days, and she can't keep up. He's going on and on about the gypsy problem, and his book, and honestly it's more than a little draining to be around. He's a miserable room-mate too, but he's got nowhere to go and she doesn't have the energy to kick him to the curb. Something dark, deep down, makes her wonder if he'd even leave if she asked him to. She doesn't have time to follow that lead now, but she puts it aside for later.

"You here?" His voice calls. Her reflection shakes its head.

Kitty has maybe thirty seconds to try and interpret this information before Jacob's put two and two together and made his way into the bathroom. The reflection looks nervous, and this unease only increases when Jacob opens the door.

"You changed your perfume," he says, taking a deep whiff of the air. In a way, he's right. She hasn't bothered to wear any in days. How had he not noticed that?

"What does it smell like," she asks, eyes on her reflection. Its eyes are pleading with her, but they're watching him, too. He looks exactly the same, and she's not sure if that should reassure her or not.

"It smells like..." he takes another whiff, "French Lavender. Maybe a little sweeter, like there's some other stuff thrown in. I like it. It's new?"

Her reflection points to a bottle on the bathroom counter, next to the sink on her side of the mirror. Kitty looks down. On her side, it's her same old bottle. Cautiously, she lifts it up to take a look. Different bottle, different label. Both half full. She sprays it into the air. To her, it smells the same, but Jacob's got a scent. His nose at least is reaching the other side of the mirror.

"I guess I've had it a little while now," she says, lost. "I just don't normally use it."

"You should," he says, crossing the span of the bathroom to put his hands on her hips. She can barely feel his hands, but she can see them moving her closer to him.

Her reflection looks terrified, the instant he touches her. It looks like a child, lost in the woods. If Kitty's ever made this face, she can't remember what scared her like this. She hears Jacob's zipper, and the sound of denim dropping to tile. She knows she's always cold now, but his skin feels hot against hers. Not just hot – scalding. She almost flinches, but she wants the heat. More than that, she needs it.

"Closer," she whispers, and he obliges. Her reflection looks like it wants to run, but he's behind it, too. They can't escape. Kitty coughs, and blood sprays on the mirror. Jacob can't see it, but the girl in the mirror can. She's started to cry, now. They both have.

THE CLUB
Paolo

ON NIGHTS WHEN PAOLO COMES to La Grotta alone, he'll have to slip the men at the door anywhere from ten to twenty Euro just to get in. With the Girl and her crew trailing behind him they barely even pause to stamp hands before opening the gates. Dry ice mist pours out into the streets, and the girls start in. It's that easy. The bouncers are buzz cut toughs with biceps the size of the Statue of David's, with matching military tattoos and the clear imprints of brass knuckles in their pockets. Paolo's heard of undressing someone with your eyes – hell, he's even done it himself on occasion – but these guys aren't stopping at ocular foreplay, and they're not being gentle with it either. They let most of the coterie through undisturbed, but as Patience glides by with her blond hair and her V-cut neckline, the man on the right sticks out a hand and palms her ass like he's checking an apple for bruises in the market. She turns the color of a spring tulip, but she says nothing. Paolo gives him a dirty look and gets a dirtier one back. They both know he can't take it any further. If he gets tossed on his ass back to the cobblestones, there's worse than that waiting to happen to the girls inside the club. With a sardonic half-smile, he steps through the door.

All the Girl with the Egyptian Eyeliner has to do is stare at them with that look she uses to get Catrina to stop talking and a cluster of younger study abroad kids clear out from their table, freeing it up for her and her cronies. They fan out in a half moon with the Girl at its center, looking for all the world like The Last Supper restaged by a gaggle of Prada models. Paolo takes the empty patch of booth offered to him, stepping into the role of Mary Magdelene to the Girl's Jesus Christ. As soon as he's situated, she settles into his lap in a decidedly un-Christian manner. With everyone in their places and maybe an hour until the band comes on, the girl begins to hold court. Men appear seemingly out of the ether to chat up the others. Like clockwork, they lay their best lines down. The girls' only response, to a woman, is a brief burst of hollow laughter that sounds like birds mourning a broken nest. They make eye contact with the Girl with the Egyptian Eyeliner, and she either raises her eyebrows or shrugs her shoulders. A shrug, evidently, passes for a yes, and a few of the crew allow themselves to be led out onto the dance floor. Paolo watches them dance, but he knows there's a limit to what he can do. He's not their bodyguard, no matter how much they might need him to be.

"Let's dance," the Girl says, and Paolo follows her out onto the floor. Closer to the speakers, he feels like he's having one of those pads they use in hospitals to restart hearts tested on his ears. The base is distorted and crunchy and, in short, not to his taste. At this point he knows enough to know it's not to the Girl's, either, but she doesn't let it stop her from dancing. She rubs up against him like she wants him to smell like her, and it's working. He's too busy breathing in her perfume to get the ball-sweat and Dracar Noir scent of the club in his nose. She's taken a break from the Thyme and Verbena she usually wears for something citrusy, and he's deep in the cloud. Pulling her close is like taking a deep breath of the market – of the city. He inhales her, and for the first time she smells like home. It's an illusion, he knows, but it's working.

Paolo puts his hands on her waist. When he was young, his

father told him that dancing with a woman was like playing a musical instrument. There's a right and a wrong way to do it, but as long as you're not doing it wrong the difference between good and great lies in the little details. For a guitar, it's the vibrato on the high E as you switch chords, or the scrape of the pick just right against the string to make that squealing sound most people associate with passionate play. For a woman, it can be anything. It can be laying the flat of your palm against their bare skin, or counting their vertebrae one by one. He knew a girl once that more than anything loved it when he would kiss the tips of each finger. For the Girl with the Egyptian Eyeliner, he knows it all comes down to just one move. He pulls her hair off to one shoulder and lays his hand heavy on the crook of her neck. Right against the jugular. He squeezes just a little, and pulls her tighter into him. He knows it works because her pupils dilate and her eyelids widen, just for a moment, before she shuts her eyes and presses her lips to his ear.

"We've got forty minutes before the band starts," she says. She's speaking in a whisper but he can hear what she's saying loud and clear, even over the bass. He grins a sharp, wolfish grin. It's exactly what he wants to hear.

After she spits him out and he slides his jeans up, she's back to business. Aside from the muted chatter of the unimpressed club girls, the bathroom's damn near silent compared to the dance floor, and she takes advantage.

"The band's on in fifteen minutes," she says, and pulls out a compact mirror to check her makeup. The black around the eyes has run a little, so she touches it up. She manages to do this without breaking eye contact.

"Have you seen them before?" She asks him.

"I'm not sure," he says, "who are they?"

"They're The Foxcatchers," she says, and he feels a chill creep up his spine, "I saw them the first week I was here, at a dive in the Oltrarno."

She keeps talking. Paolo knows it's happening because he can see her lips moving, but her voice is fading under the dull roar building in his ears. She's going on about the front-woman, some badass punk rock chick with a hawk feather in her bleach blond hair. Paolo nods, and offers the obligatory 'cool' and 'awesome' she's looking for, but he already knows this story, because he was probably there, somewhere, when it happened. The Foxcatchers are Kitsune's band. She's the badass punk rock chick. The Girl with the Egyptian eyeliner slides her dress over her shoulders and gives him a look. He zips her up mechanically, silently. They head back out.

By now, each member of the crew has a guy in tow, and there's barely any room left at the table. Most of the men are Italian, which is the Girl and her crew's norm, but the ever cutting-edge Catrina's pulled a Moroccan with an orange and black pashmina. Paolo focuses on these little details. The more of them he logs, the less he thinks about the Foxcatchers. The less he hears that voice in his ear. How long have I lived here, Paolo? The music stops. There's a brief boo before people pick up on the implication. The moshers and punk heads replace the club kids on the dance floor like the changing of the royal guard.

"This is gonna be good!" Yells Patience. The other girls roll their eyes. She's drunk enough that Paolo would normally worry about her, but he can't concentrate on that right now. One of the army dropout bouncers, the one who grabbed Patience's ass earlier, is calling the band to the stage. The lights dim.

He hears the twanging of a guitar. It's just a D chord, with a bit of sustain, and she's got the capo on the fifth fret. The lights come up, and she's center stage.

"Holy shit," Paolo says, just quiet enough that the girls can't hear him. She looks terrible. There's pits in her eyes deep enough for someone to drown in, and they're almost black they're so dark. She was thin to begin with but she's lost weight. Too much weight. She looks like you'd need to tie a string to her to keep her on the ground. Her hands are shaking, but she's not missing a note. At least not yet.

They're playing an electrified cover of "Eleanor Rigby" he's heard a hundred times if he's heard it once, but there's something wrong. The lead vocals come from an Armenian Architect Kitsune met on a trip to Prague, but Paolo can hear her on the backup line. Her voice is hoarse, and she keeps backing away from the mic to cough into a white cloth speckled with blood.

"Holy shit, she's dying."

The girl gives him a look like he's lost his mind. Apparently no one else can see she's sick. Not the Girl with the Egyptian Eyeliner, not the crowd, not Catrina or her Moroccan, and not Patience. Wait.

"Where did Patience go?" He asks.

The Girl shrugs. The Italian who tried to pick her up shrugs too and that's when Paolo realizes she left alone. This presents a conundrum, because he knows he ought to try and find her, or at least convince one of the girls to check the bathroom. But he can't leave Kitsune like this. The song ends. She's wiping sweat from her brow while the rest of the band high fives. He's never seen her so wiped out at a show, especially not from just one song.

"What do you keep looking at," the Girl asks. He knows he needs to be more subtle, less obvious, but it's too late. Kitsune sways, stumbles, and falls. He's out of his seat before he can think better of it. The Girl grabs him, and he shakes the hand off. He wants to get up on the stage, but she's already being led away. The Girl grabs him again, and this time he lets her.

"We need to go, Paolo," she says. He doesn't argue.

"Where's Patience?" He asks, and she shrugs harshly.

"She probably left with that bouncer," says Cara.

"Yeah," echoes Catrina. "Girlfriend's turned into a big 'ole skank lately."

That produces a laugh that makes him want to run, so he does. He makes a beeline for the door, and the Girl with the Egyptian Eyeliner catches him just outside the awning.

"You're embarrassing me, Paolo," she says in a harsh whisper. She's genuinely flushed, which is a sight he's never seen from her with her clothes on. She expects him to come to heel, go back inside, and blame it on the drink. She expects him to kiss her ass and be her arm candy for another night, the next in a chain stretching all the way until she's gone, leaving the town in a flutter of foundation powder and false lashes. But she's forgotten – Paolo's not a pilot fish. He's a fucking shark.

"No," he says, and he has never seen the face she makes at that before. "No, you're embarrassing yourself."

He walks away on that one, knowing it won't get any better for him if he continues. It was a hell of a line to end on, but there'll be hell to pay for it in the morning.

THE PHONE
Tony

THE HEAD ON TONY'S BEER IS too damn big – it's the only thing he can think about. It's the only thing he wants to think about. If anyone at the bar were to ask, he would probably tell them everything. There must have been a hundred of them, he'd sob, all with their little necks broken. And the dog... he just looked so sad. All this he'd say and more, but no one's asking him the right questions.

Tony had come home that morning to find Crosby placing the pigeons neatly into rows. Or he'd thought they were rows. He'd never caught the dog making his little arrangements before. They usually weren't complex. It was usually a line, or a pyramid. Sometimes a circle. One time, a pentagram, which was decidedly more alarming. This time, there were too many for a simple shape. This time he was spelling something. It was too late for the birds, so Tony let him do it. It took an hour; Crosby had only been halfway through when Tony got home. Tony watched the letters form one at a time. By the time it was almost over, Tony knew what he was spelling, but he still let him finish. He had to be sure. Azazel, read the pile of dead birds. Tony swept them all into five garbage bags, and took them down one at a time over a couple of hours. When he was done, the dog was snoring peacefully on the couch.

The thing is that murderous psychopath or no, Crosby is just about the only friend Tony's got these days. He's always there, ready with a goofy grin or a soggy kiss. He's incapable of borrowing and not returning money. He never gets too drunk, never leaves the refrigerator open. He doesn't lie, and he loves unconditionally, or at least he seems to love Tony. Best of all, he isn't even human. He's the perfect roommate.

Tony's eying his phone with a nauseous suspicion. There's just shy of seven numbers in the thing, one of which is most likely a figment of his imagination. Another's a college student he picked up at least four years ago, too drunk to notice he wasn't a real Italian. The rest are mostly worthless.

That hellish freak of a beer just sits there, taunting him. He almost drinks it out of defiance, but something stops him. He slides open the phone and dials an emphatic three. His speed dial is only four people deep, and one of those is a shrink he hasn't been to in nearly a year. The phone rings. Again. Crossing himself, Tony shuts his eyes and downs the beer. Not bad, actually, he thinks. Number three picks up.

"Tony? What's up man?" It's Kitsune, naturally.

'What's up' is really the sort of question one should ask oneself before one picks up the phone. Tony doesn't have an answer. Her voice sounds a touch deeper over the phone. It gives her an air of constant sarcasm or disinterest, which has always made him anxious. Now, several beers deep and reeling with PTSD from the avian carnage in his apartment, the effect is somewhat magnified.

"What is up?" He fires back. Great line, A-plus.

She laughs. It's a stirring sound, all sincerity and music. Normally it would give him no shortage of cheer to hear it, but the pit in his stomach is too deep to climb out of.

"You're drunk!"

She seems sincerely pleased with her observational skills, though to be honest that was low hanging fruit.

"I'm working on it," he concedes. "So I thought I'd call and have a chat."

The mood shifts. It's all silence on the other end, but nevertheless he can hear the smile fade from her features. He closes his eyes. He can picture her face forming a small, tight, unintentional frown. He can see the dimples flattening, then shifting to wrinkles. It may have been his imagination, but she seemed to have more of them than he remembered when he saw her last.

"A chat."

Her voice is flatter now. Deeper, but with no trace of the sarcasm that was there before.

"If you have time."

"I have time," she says. "I just wonder what you want to chat with me about so badly."

Another issue he ought to have decided beforehand. He re-opens his eyes, and sees a fresh beer on the counter before him. The heads keep getting bigger and fatter. It's as though the tap dispenses foam, and beer is the unintended bi-product. He says nothing.

"Because the last time we had a chat, Tony, you and Jacob went apeshit on each other, and I just watched on the sidelines. I don't suppose you're calling to apologize for that?"

"I'm not," he says. "But I am sorry if that was weird for you."

"Weird." She repeats the word. Considers it for a moment.

"Awkward." Tony tries a different approach.

"Of course it was fucking awkward. I honestly have no idea what even had you so revved up. Either of you. You wouldn't let me get a word in edgewise."

"I'm sorry-"

"Not to mention it's now basically impossible for me to even see you. I live with him, Tony. Neither of us is working right now, really. I can't exactly step out at random hours, and you're not exactly worth keeping secrets for."

He downs the beer. What did that make, nine? He signals for one more, and the bartender raises an eyebrow. Money down. The beer arrives. This is the sort of place where no one asks questions. Where they can't afford to, because you may be their only customer for the night.

"So what is it?" She asks. "Why did you two suddenly start tearing each other's throats out?"

This is the moment, he thinks, this is the moment where you hang up the phone. She'd be furious. But she'd get over it. The truth couldn't be moved past so quickly.

"I guess we've had that coming for a few months now."

"He's only been here for a few months, Tony."

"I guess that's my point."

"So you're upset he came? You were so excited about it. You wouldn't shut up about your new pet project."

"No, it's not that."

"Well what, then?"

"It's what he's done since he's been here. It was just supposed to be a visit, just a quick tour of the city and its sights. A couple of interviews, a trip to the city records. I was supposed to give him what he needed to get a good story, and he was supposed to go when he was done. He wasn't supposed to quit. He wasn't supposed to leave his hotel and sell his shit. He wasn't supposed to-"

She sighs. She always does that when he talks too long. She hates monologues – he'd discovered that very quickly during their friendship. She would find any way to stop him in his tracks if he strung more than three sentences together. He's always wondered if she feels that way about everybody. Maybe it's just him.

"So are you mad at me then? For getting him to stay?"

"No, I couldn't be... I mean I'm not."

And there it was. Maybe she wouldn't catch it. Maybe she'd let it go. She laughs again. It's a different laugh than before. There's a touch of cruelty in it, but it retains the music. No chance, he thought. I could never be so lucky.

"So what is it, Tony," she asks, "You have a crush on me?"

"It's not like that, no. I'm not a child anymore."

"What, then?" The color drains from her voice, the fun. "You want to fuck me, is that it? Well, you and almost everyone else."

"No, that's not it."

"So you're not attracted to me at all."

Silence. The pint glass is a black hole absorbing all cogent thought. He sticks out his tongue, worthless. If he had any good ideas, this would be the time to use them, but he is unfortunately out of stock.

"Then what the fuck is wrong?" She continues. "We're friends, aren't we? You come to my gigs, I answer the phone when you call. I don't do that for everybody, you know. Shit, I even screen my mom's calls half the time."

"It's not enough. Not for me." Now he's really regained his composure. A plus.

"Are you trying to tell me that you love me right now, Tony?"

"Would you be surprised?"

"You really are drunk. I'm with someone, you know that."

"And do you love him?"

"I don't know," she says. With feeling.

A black mood comes over him then. The sort of depressive state that swallows sound and confusion: that bends the light and shifts the weather. It's the kind of funk that eliminates all options, save one.

"Why him?" Tony asks, flatly.

"How the fuck should I answer that? You set me up with

him, Tony, you tell me."

She's right about that. Tony remembers the conversation vividly; he could hear her over the line as she scribbled out the number with a drawing pencil - perfectly good graphite wasted. He should've snapped the tip right off. Jacob's a bit of a freak, he'd told her. That had been an understatement.

"He's sick. He's a sickness. He infects everything, and he'll infect you too." And there it is. He'd meant to say nothing.

"If he's so awful, why did you set me up with him? I'm your friend. You want me getting 'infected?' What does that even mean?"

Tony shuts his eyes and counts to three. You've got to rein it in, he thinks. There was still time to hang up the phone. Put it down to the booze and leave it at that. She might even believe it.

"You know what, don't answer that."

He couldn't, even if he tried. There is true anger in her voice now. He's seen her riled up, seen her yell and scream and even throw a punch in fits of rage, but nothing like this. There was a calmness to it. A stability.

"You set me up with him because I wouldn't date you. Which you know because you've asked before and I said no. You thought, ignorant shit-stain that you are, that if I hit rock bottom romantically, you could come in and pick up the pieces. Be the shoulder to cry on, and catch me on the rebound. Tell me I'm wrong."

He couldn't. He'd given it only a little bit of thought at the time, consciously, but on some level that was probably exactly what he'd wanted. She knew him too well. Better than he knew her, and definitely better than he knew himself.

"What do you want me to say?"

"Be a man, Tony. Tell me the truth."

"Fine," he says. "You're right. I didn't think about it when I set you up, but you're right. I just wish you'd see that Jacob,

Paolo, that guy with the awful fire engine tattoo, they're all the same, you know? And I'm – "

"Don't. Don't give me some speech about how you just love me so much, and how you know you'd be good for me. Don't tell me how you've watched me whore myself out to guys you just know aren't good enough for me. Don't tell me how you've always been there for me, and if I'd just think about it I'd see that I could love you, too. I'm a human being, Tony. I've seen the same damn TV shows you have, but we're not on television right now. You don't get the girl just because you're there. Being my friend doesn't entitle you to being more than that."

This is the longest he's heard her speak uninterrupted. She seems almost out of breath. A fit of coughing overtakes her. How long has she been sick? He's going to kill her, he thinks. Jacob's going to kill her. I don't know how, but I know he's going to do it.

"I'm sorry," he says, but he can hear how weak the words are.

"No," she says. Is she crying? "What you are, Tony, is sad. And now you're alone."

She hangs up the phone. After staring at it for a few slow seconds, Tony finishes his beer.

"I'm not alone," he says to the dial tone. And he isn't. He's got an Angel on speed dial.

THE NAME
Jacob

KITSUNE NEVER ASKS HIM WHERE HE GOES and why he goes there. He's been gone for hours, and when he comes back she's awake. Maybe it's better to say nothing. Maybe it's better to let her guess and hope she guesses at something harmless. After all, it's not as if he can tell her the truth. He's marked another kill for tonight, and all he needs is the victim. Still, there's something he wants from Kitsune, first. There usually is.

When he finds her, she's sprawled out on the couch, staring at the phone in her hands. She's upset, but Jacob knows it's not with him. He's not sure how he knows, but he does. He sits down, picks up her head, and sets in on his lap. He waits in silence for her to tell him, stroking her hair. Every time his hand comes to the little hawk feather, he pinches it between his fingers. A hawk flies fast enough when diving for a kill that if it misjudges and collides with something unexpected it will snap its neck. Jacob supposes they have that in common.

"What's wrong?" He asks at last. He has plans for the night, and there's no room for delay. She'll have to cut to the chase.

"Did you know Tony wanted to be with me? Back before you came to Florence?" She asks back.

Did she not? The guy stares at her the way a mediocre chef looks at a five star meal. Like she's all he wants, but she'll never be his. Jacob had seen right through it from the moment Tony gave him her number. It was obvious from the way he talked about her. It made the sex even more satisfying, to know. Not because he especially wanted to hurt Tony, but because having something that other men covet is a special feeling. It feels like power.

"Yeah," he says, "I might have picked up on that after a while, I guess."

Jacob figured Tony's plan was to use Jacob as grease to get himself through the door. Jacob was only supposed to be here for a few weeks after all. They'd have had a little fling, he'd get her all worked up, and then he'd vanish into the ether. Tony would present himself as the next best thing, and in desperation she'd take him in. It wouldn't have worked, even if Jacob hadn't thrown him for a loop by staying put. He just wasn't her type – she didn't go for jellyfish.

"Did he finally say as much to you?" He asks, and she nods.

He looks at her phone and sees the evidence. One call from an hour ago, accepted. Maybe ten minutes long. Another six calls rejected over the next forty-five minutes. Jacob tries not to laugh. Looks like Tony struck out, naturally.

"He called me," she says, as though she isn't deliberately letting him look at the screen. She leaves all of these secrets out for him to find and acts surprised when he does, like he's so thoughtful to figure them out on his own. It's almost cute. "He called me and told me. I don't think he meant to say anything about it, but he was drunk."

"What do you think he wanted to talk about?" Jacob asks.

For the first time since he came in, she sits up and makes eye contact. It's comforting to see she hasn't wasted any tears over this. If anything, she looks angry. I should tell her, Jacob thinks. Maybe she wouldn't be upset about it. Maybe she'd even learn to like it. At first, of course, she'd be terrified. She might even threaten to turn him in. But the way she looks right now, Jacob wonders if she would really do it. He can see it in her face, she wants Tony dead. Maybe he could make that happen.

"He wanted to talk about you," she says.

A cold wave sweeps over Jacob then, and his vision goes black for just long enough that she has to notice something's wrong. She doesn't comment about it, but it must be obvious. The rage has got to be radiating out of him, drawing little cartoon squiggle lines off his body into the atmosphere. He really will kill that little shit-stain. Not today, that's too obvious. But he will do it.

"What did he say," Jacob says at last. His throat's dry. It takes her a second to respond. Longer than a second. She's got that lost look on her face and he doesn't have time for it right now. He repeats the question.

"He said 'Jacob's sick. He's a sickness.'"

The irony almost makes him double over with laughter. Tony's the epitome of survival of the fittest failing in the human race. He's got no drive, no hunger, no fight. He's the gazelle with the limp at the back of the herd, and Jacob's the lion. Jacob's not the sickness, he's the goddamn cure.

"What does that even mean?" He asks. She shakes her head.

"He really fucking hates you, did you know that?" Jacob shakes his head, and that's the truth. This he did not know. "I've never heard that kind of hate from him before. From anyone, really."

"So what," Jacob says, "you're wondering what I did to deserve it?"

She shakes her head. "I am," she says, "I mean I'm wondering what you did, but I don't think you do. Deserve it. I don't think anyone does."

Jacob feels a touch of genuine sadness, because in that moment he knows that he can never tell her the truth. She would never accept it, accept him. They share a certain apathy for the crush of humanity that surrounds them, but hers comes from a sense of their failure to meet her standards. His is genuine. She's too good for this world, and he can fix that. Not her, he wouldn't dare. But the world, that he can change. Piece by piece.

"I think I know," Jacob says, "but you're not going to like it."

"I don't like any of this, Jake," she says. He likes that she shortens his name, even if she didn't ever ask for his permission. It suggests ownership, and he doesn't mind letting her think that's a two way street. At least for now.

"You remember that fight Tony and I had the other day?" Of course she does, and they both know that. It's just a rhetorical device to ask. She nods. "Well it wasn't the first one. When he was out of town last month I called him up and he was not in the mood for it. I guess I should have realized he wouldn't be, but that's not really my forte."

This is a lie. He'd known full well Tony would be damn near catatonic under the weight of all that bullshit. His relationship with his mother was a soap opera, which normally Jacob doesn't care for. But just like when you see a familiar face on the news, something about knowing the players involved made him want to tune in. And he couldn't resist a chance to shove some bamboo shoots under that fucker's fingers.

"Anyway," he says, "I was telling him about my book, and he kind of... well I guess you would say he snapped at me. Something about how all I care about is boosting my own ego."

The exact line had been 'you just keep inflating your ego until it pops or you get tired of pumping in air'. Jacob remembers because it was a better metaphor than he'd thought Tony would be capable of.

"I shouldn't have snapped back at him, but I did. I knew that the fact we were together was a sore spot for him, so I made it about you."

"About me?"

"It was some schoolyard shit about me sleeping with you, I'm not proud of it."

It's a calculated risk to tell her this, but he knows the focus of her ire is on Tony, and it won't shift to him for anything less than a true disaster. It pays off. Any anger she feels at him passes in an instant and returns to its original focus.

"I could see how that would upset him, I guess," she says, "but do you really think that's all it is?"

Jacob shrugs. It's better to let her fill in the blanks.

"I think he's just jealous of you," she says. She's found the angle, and he just has to let her reel it in. "I mean not just because of me. But you know he's lived here for years and he hasn't made the kind of connections and friends you have. I think he's really lonely."

It's close enough. He places his hand on her shoulders and starts to gently pull her closer.

"I'm sorry," he says, and they're hard words for him to say but she's worth it. "I shouldn't have pulled you in to it."

"I don't think that's what happened. I think if anything, I'm the one who got you involved."

That's all the opening he needs. At this point he's pulled her against him, and he starts to kiss gently at the nape of her neck. He knows her well enough to know what she needs to get the message, to know what he wants. This is one of a handful of gestures with a one hundred percent success rate on communication. The others are a bit harsher than this situation requires, and he saves them for another time.

"Well," he says, and walks his fingers down the front of her jeans. The big brass button on the front unclasps, louder than he'd thought was possible. It's like the gunshot that starts a dog race, or the first firework that starts the show. She lets out that little rush of breath that lets him know he's got her, and he moves to seal the deal. "It sounds like both of us owe the other person an apology. Let me give you mine, first."

Thirty minutes or so later he's inside of her on her bed, grabbing her flesh in greedy handfuls, and this is exactly what she wants. She's on top, trying to act like she's driving this car, and he's happy to let her think that. There are gashes in his back she made with her nails earlier that are deep enough to bleed, but for now she's just holding on for dear life. She's close. He knows the signs by now. He picks her up and puts her on her back, and her eyes widen.

"Kitsune," he says, as he pins her arms by her side, and he repeats it for good measure. "Kitsune." He's never met a woman who didn't love to hear her name called. It's about then that he realizes she's started to cry. He doesn't stop, but he does start to move more gently. He lets her hands go, and she wraps them around his shoulders. He kisses her and she tastes like the ocean, salty and sweet and deep and wide.

"Ana," she whispers. "My name is Ana."

He doesn't expect that to be enough, but it is. The truth is nature's aphrodisiac and he is its victim. The thing is, it's not the name he had expected. He'd seen 'Kita' on the back of that old photograph and thought it was her. She'd even said it, that day in the rain, though she'd made him promise not to use it later. So who is Kita, if it's not her? That's a question for another time. There are more urgent matters to attend to, now.

"Ana" he says, and it sounds good on his tongue. "Ana."

It's enough for her, too, and they finish in unison, eyes locked on each other and calling their names – their real names, for once – into the darkness. Jacob's one regret is that he can't share his truth with her the way she shared hers. He can't tell her that as soon as she falls asleep, he's going out into the streets to find another woman. Not to fuck, of course, he's not the kind of man who cheats. He is, however, the kind who kills. That's his truth, and for now, it has to stay hidden.

"Ana." He says it again, but this time it's different. This time it's almost kind, almost gentle. He's not sure where it comes from, but he's glad for it. "Why did you tell me? Why now?"

She kisses him. It's a long kiss, the kind movies back in the eighties used to end with. He can almost hear the guitar riff kick on in the background as he runs his hands through her hair, softly. He can almost see the credits roll in the corner of his periphery.

"I wanted you to know," she says. "I want just one person to know the truth."

As she drifts off to sleep, Jacob makes a decision. When he finally kills that bastard, he'll be sure Tony knows the truth too. The look on his face will be too good to pass up.

THE DEAL
Tony

TONY'S ALWAYS FIGURED THAT BEING SUICIDAL is a lot like being an alcoholic. Either way, once you've got the itch it's going to be with you for the rest of your life. An alcoholic can go entire months without feeling the need to drink, then suddenly catch the chorus of a familiar song and be overpowered by a craving. Once that thought slips in – I need a drink – it's a constant companion. Suicide is much the same. Once you have considered it, and considered it seriously, the thought never entirely goes away. It's an option on your table, and nothing will take it off.

The idea had first come to Tony in his late twenties. He woke up one morning, got out of bed, and poured himself a bowl of cereal. The idea appeared with no warning. It had begun with the realization that he had eaten the same cereal every day since he was six years old, without fail. He had never changed brands, and it had never occurred to him to. It was the lack of ambition that had bothered him, rather than the cereal itself. He still eats the same brand now. The thoughts spiraled on from there, one by one. He couldn't think of any particular reason why he ought to kill himself, but neither could he think of a reason not to. After finishing his breakfast, he went to the store. He bought two bottles of sleeping pills, and one bottle of wine. It had been a cheap purchase. He had spent no more than twenty dollars. In his car, on the way home, he heard "Don't Fear the Reaper" for the first time in almost ten years and almost punched a hole in his steering wheel. His hands were shaking by the end of the song. He could barely see the road for the tears.

Back at home, Tony struggled with the cork on the wine bottle for so long he thought they'd have to draft an armistice for him to get it out, but he finally got it. It was shit wine, but he had no one to blame but himself for that. For whatever reason, he paced himself, taking all of twenty minutes to kill the bottle. He reached for the pills, but thought of something first. He set out a pad of paper and went to his record cabinet. He slid a Neil Young '45 onto his player, B Side up, and dropped the needle down. He closed his eyes and tried to listen, but he couldn't help but sing along.

> *I hear the mountains*
> *are doin' fine,*
> *Mornin' glory*
> *is on the vine,*
> *And the dew is fallin',*
> *the ducks are callin'.*
> *Yes, I've got mine.*

When it had ended, the page was still blank. He couldn't think of anything to say. He didn't have any reason to go through with killing himself, but he didn't have any reason not to either. Still it seemed empty to do it without something to say, so he decided to wait. He put the pill bottles in a drawer in his bedside table, and went to sleep. To this day, Tony's certain whether he'd started with the pills he'd have gotten the job done. Right about now he's not sure if that would have been better or worse.

When he gets home, the Angel is waiting with a cup of tea. Having complained the first five times, this time she's kept it hot.

Scalding, in fact, but he appreciates the gesture nonetheless. Easier to let it cool than to make it warm again. He sits down at his dining table with Crosby next to him, and she sits across from them. Not for the first time, Tony notices there's dust on three out of the four chairs here. Not for the first time, he remembers those pills are still in that drawer.

"Are you in my head?" He asks her. She shakes her head.

"Can you prove it?" She repeats the gesture.

This would be so much easier if she left any sign of her presence. A feather, or a footprint, or a scratch on the hardwood; anything at all would be enough. It would be so much easier if he hadn't spent his whole life laughing at the very idea of Angels. Still, over her head he sees Crosby's haul for the day. He's lined up seven birds in a line on the mantle, each with their necks snapped just so. One thing he's never thought about before is that they probably don't suffer much, the birds. They don't look like they do at least.

"If I do this, I have to be sure that I don't kill someone who doesn't deserve it."

The Angel sighs, and Tony could swear it's a sigh of relief. Do Angels even feel emotions? If so, which ones and how deeply? She settles into her chair like a man in a suit and a power tie getting ready for a job interview.

"There is no way to be certain, Tony, you know that."

He's not sure if she's speaking abstractly or not. Either she means that there's no way to be sure that the people he kills would deserve it, or that there's no way to be sure that everything would go to plan regarding who does and does not die.

"I understand that," he says. "But you have to let me try."

"How do you propose to do it?" She asks.

He's been trying on plans for size all week. If he tripped the fire alarm, the nurses would most likely roll the comatose patients out first, which would defeat the purpose. If he put up signs, people would be either disinclined to take it seriously or they would take it so seriously that it would be impossible for him to go through with it.

"I'm going to cut power to the building, first."

This, he has decided, is the only way. After reading up on hospital policy – with thanks due to the local library – Tony found exactly what he needed. In the event of an outage, the generators will kick in almost immediately, but they can only last so long. If the outage is judged to be likely to exceed that time, the hospital begins to transfer its patients. First are the children and pregnant women. Second are the elderly and oncology patients. Those deemed close enough to recovery are outright dismissed. Last on the list? The coma ward.

"They'll put a skeleton crew up to keep watch over the comatose patients."

The full number on the crew is twelve souls. Six nurses, four orderlies, and two doctors. The generator's reduced to the level needed to run that floor, and they hope they don't have to proceed to the next step.

"You are aware of course," the Angel says in a voice that from anyone else he would have called kind, "that those men and women will likely be innocents. And they will likely die."

Tony nods. This is the big ask, the big caveat. Without it, he's not sure what to do. He can't imagine putting the dog on the street again for someone else to find. He can't imagine doing nothing and watching the sine curve of the dog's pigeon problem peak, fall off, and stop altogether when he runs out of prey altogether. The only other option is in his bedside table.

"That's why I need you to save them for me. All of them."

"Tony," she starts, but he raises his hand.

"If you're going to tell me you can't interfere, I'm sorry, but I have to call bullshit."

Her feathers are quite literally ruffled, which under other

circumstances would have struck him as funny.

"How is it anything other than interference for you to show up at my house five times a week and try and guilt me into doing this for you?" He asks her. "How is it anything other than interference for you to tell me any of this in the first place? Do you know what would have happened if you hadn't shown up?"

She shakes her head, and for the first time he realizes that she's not omniscient, at least not completely.

"The second time he brought home a dead bird I'd have taken him to the pound. After a week, they'd have put it down."

"That would not have resolved the problem, Tony." She says.

"Maybe that's true, but it wouldn't have had anything to do with me anymore. But you interfered, you influenced the course of human events or whatever it is you aren't supposed to do. You did that, and now I'm in this. I could die, you know? This could kill me, and it would be because you interfered. All I'm asking is that those twelve not join me."

The Angel thinks about it for a long time. This is the longest she's been in his apartment at once, Tony realizes. How much longer can she say? If she's right about her and the dog, it can't be too much longer. Finally, she stands up. She flexes her wings, and folds them behind her. For a moment he forgets she has them. For a moment he forgets she's not a person.

"Alright, Tony."

"We have a deal?" He asks.

"Yes," she replies, and with that she's gone.

Tony goes through the motions of getting ready for bed. He takes Crosby down to the street, comes back in, cuts the lights, brushes his teeth, swishes some mouthwash around, and lies in bed a little. For the first time since he bought them, he opens the drawer that holds the pills. The bottles are dusty, and he brushes it off. He opens one, and pops a single pill. For now, it's just to help him sleep.

KITSUNE'S DREAM:
The Ferryman

THE FERRYMAN'S VOICE IS BARELY AUDIBLE over the sound of the waves, but Ana can understand him perfectly.

"They will not let you pass."

He's an older man, in a faded yellow poncho and a fisherman's cap. His beard is ragged and his eyes are milky, almost glassy with cataracts. Despite his age he rows with powerful strokes. Rhythmic, perfect even.

"We have money." This is Ana's father. "It's not much, but-"

"That is not what they want. They will not let you pass."

The boat has five passengers. Ana, her mother, her father, her sister, and the man rowing.

"I assure you, we will be able to pay our way in full. We cannot suffer delays in this."

Her father is a strong man in a clean suit and his voice holds confidence. It's a nice suit. Pinstripes. He tries in vain to keep the river off of it. Her mother is quiet. She's working on her needlework, has been for the length of the trip thus far. She gives her husband a practiced smile. The boat pulls up to the dock.

"I am terribly sorry esteemed sir, but I cannot let you pass." This is the soldier.

It's the same gray man it always is. Gray beard, gray eyes, even the uniform gray. It might have been black once, or green, but a few rounds of bleaching out bloodstains sucked the color right out. There's no way past him and no way around. The river is wide, and there's only one ferry. He's got a gun in the holster on his hip – grey.

"We have money." Her father brims with confidence. "We have money if you want it."

"It is not a question of money."

"No," says the ferryman, "it is never a question of money."

"We can pay it. Whatever the price, we can pay it."

In the soldier's hand is a box. Her father nods in understanding.

"It's your decision, dear," says her mother.

"You may want to look away," says the ferryman to Ana.

Ana is seven in this dream. Her sister is with her, and her parents, all of them running, escaping from the communist North to the free South. The guard is the first obstacle, and the solution is always the same. He proffers the box; lacquered, black, and lined with red velvet. Ana's sister – Kita, her name was Kita – gives a well-practiced shrug of resignation. Their mother puts another stitch in her needlework. There's a stiff scraping, a metal on bone sound. Kita drops the better part of her right hand in the box.

"Are you hurt, child?" Asks the ferryman.

"No." This is Kita. This is Ana's sister.

"Then we should continue."

The river is wide. Kita keeps her smile on, big and white. She sits on the opposite side of the ferry from her family, the ghost of her hand a cauterized mess. There is no blood, only an absence. The quiet is the worst thing. There should be screaming at the minimum, moaning or cursing. Tiny waves ripple over the surface of the water, catching and refracting an apathetic sunrise. The only sound is the lapping of the water against the boat. Oars splitting the water in their stride – rhythmic, perfect even. An ideal stroke.

"Look Ana," says her mother, "It's almost finished."

The needlework pattern is a swallow on the wing, against a backdrop of lilies. Kita's favorite bird and Ana's favorite flower. She ignores her mother, and looks at her sister.

"Does it hurt? Your arm I mean."

Kita doesn't speak. She just smiles and shakes her head.

"We're going to send you to the nicest school when we get to Yeongcheong, Ana." Her mother does not make eye contact. "You'll just love it. All children deserve a great education, don't you think dear?"

"Of course, dear." This is Ana's father.

Her father is straightening his papers and counting his money in preparation for the next checkpoint.

"Will it grow back?" Ana asks.

"We're going to send you to an international school. For gifted girls."

"There will be another checkpoint before we go much further, sir."

Her father looks at the ferryman as if seeing him for the first time. His eyes are full of scorn.

"Yes, yes, of course. Can't do anything these days without bleeding the checkbook dry."

"Will you be withdrawing from the same account?"

He doesn't answer, just puts the money back into his pockets with the lint and dust.

"It'll be so nice to have friends from other places. Don't you think so, Ana?"

"Answer your mother when she asks you a question, Ana."

"I don't care about school." This is Ana.

Her father raises the back of his hand, but the ferryman holds it back.

"We will be there soon, sir. It would be best if you stay in your seat."

"That's preposterous, we're in the middle of nowhere."

He turns to point to the nothingness beyond, but just as he does so they make contact with another dock. The same soldier is there. The same gray man.

"I suppose they'll charge us double," says her father, "now that we're this far in."

"Now now, dear. There's no need to be cross."

Ana begins to cry.

"I am terribly sorry esteemed sir, but I cannot let you pass." This is the soldier. His voice is the same. His face is the same. Everything is the same, and he holds the same black box.

"You're joking." This is her father. "You have to be joking."

"Most definitely not, esteemed sir."

The ferryman hands the soldier their papers while her father continues to complain.

"We've already paid." He is insistent. Angry, even. "We've come too far to turn back."

"Your papers are in order. Still, you may not go further without payment. I am terribly sorry."

Ana is squeezing her sister's arm like she means to crush it, but Kita doesn't seem to notice.

"You have to let go now, Ana." This is her sister.

The ferryman separates them.

"Dad?" This is Ana. "Dad, please. You can't."

"Be quiet, Ana." He says.

"Hold my needle, won't you sweetie?" Says her mother.

Ana covers her eyes. There is a thud. Kita's other hand falls into the box. Kita does not scream. She does not cry.

"Is it done now?" Her father asks. "Are you satisfied? Can we leave?"

"The payment is sufficient. You may proceed."

"It is almost over," says the ferryman, "only one more pass remains."

"Bleeding us dry, that's what you're doing. You won't be satisfied until we're nickel and dimed to death."

It is dark now. Ana's mother works quietly on her needlework. Ana hugs her knees and rocks back and forth. Kita looks for all the world as though she never had hands to begin with. The dock is gone. It is nowhere to be seen in the water behind them, and there is nothing to be seen in the water ahead.

"This river is very strange, isn't it?" This is Ana's father.

"In what way, sir?"

"We have been out here for hours, and yet it seems we haven't moved at all. There are no landmarks on the horizon, no other ships to pass us by. I cannot even see the checkpoint we just passed."

"The river is the size that it needs to be, sir."

"Yes. Yes, I suppose it would be."

He has not given back the knife. He holds it in his left hand, inspecting the blade which still, despite its recent use, appears clean. He runs the flat of it along his palm idly, watching his reflection in the metal. Ana's mother throws her hands up in the air. She gives an odd gesture of suppressed enthusiasm, which ends before its own beginning.

"It's finished," she says, "I've finished it."

Her father gives the needlework a cursory glance and dismisses it with pleasant apathy.

"Look! Look, Ana!"

She shoves the thing into her daughter's face and she sees it clearly for the first time. The pattern is faded, and vaguely visible, but it is not stitched in. Only one stitch has been made. A single x, repeated hundreds of times over. Ana smiles weakly.

"Take it, please. I made it for you."

Ana drops the cloth into the water. It floats.

"This is getting to be ridiculous." This is Ana's father. "We're running out of resources. I can't just keep paying for our passage each time they –

"You will pay because you must," says the ferryman. "And because you cannot go back. This will be the last stop."

Her father is staring at the knife. In the distance, the outline of a dock is visible against the fog.

"But what can we give them? We can't take anything else from her."

The same gray man is there, with the same uniform and the same pistol and the same eyes. This time there is no box. This time he is alone.

"This is preposterous," says her father, "you know that. It's a scam is what it is. They'll take everything from us if this keeps up."

"You have made your decision. It is too late to turn back."

"And you, what will you take?"

The ferryman doesn't get the chance to answer the question. The boat hits the dock with a dull thud, and the gray man steps forward. Ana moves forward and reaches for her father's sleeve, but her mother grabs her. Too hard. Her grip hurts.

"Don't bother your father when he's busy, sweetheart."

"I am terribly sorry, esteemed sir, but -"

"But you can't let us pass. Yes, we know. And what is the cost this time? What will you take from us?"

"You have made your choice. You cannot pass without payment."

Ana breaks loose at that and moves to her father's side. She stretches out her left arm and rolls up the sleeve.

"It's alright, Ana." This is Kita.

Ana shakes her head.

"You'll see. It'll be alright."

Slowly and with dignity, Kita takes a step out of the boat and onto the dock. As her foot hits the wood her clothes change. They lose their color. They go gray, and so does she. The ferryman begins to row. Ana watches her sister recede into the fog without blinking. Without crying.

"Well that's it then." This is her father. "They've taken it all. We'll just have to start from scratch in the south."

"The cost was set long ago, sir," says the ferryman. "And you knew it when you paid my fare."

"I did no such thing! I've given you nothing!"

"You've given me what I require."

"And what is that, then?"

"Your choice."

Ana watches her father with contempt, having pushed herself to the far end of the boat, where Kita had been sitting.

"You're going to love it in the south, Ana," her mother says. "You'll see. We'll send you to a nice international school with nice international students. You'll make new friends from new places. You'll learn about other countries. It'll be nice, to be in a new place. To have new friends. Don't you think?"

"Yes, mother. Of course mother."

Part 4

I never knew a man
could tell so many lies
He had a different story
for every set of eyes.
How can he remember
who he's talkin' to?
'Cause I know it ain't me,
and I hope it isn't you...

I guess I'll call it
sickness gone
It's hard to say
the meaning of this song.
An ambulance can only
go so fast
It's easy to get buried
in the past
When you try to make
a good thing last.

from "Ambulance Blues" by Neil Young

THE KNIFE
Jacob

NIGHT FALLS ON THE CITY AND ONLY the dogs are silent. Jacob's got a scent. The hunger is back, and he feels like his bones are home to a trillion little termites burrowing and building condominiums in the holes that they dig. His legs feel like they want to snap underneath him, but somehow he keeps running. The sound of his sneakers slapping the cobblestone echoes against the yellowed plaster like firecrackers. As the sound bounces between the alley walls the chaos makes it feel like the whole damn city is running from him. But it's just one girl.

The blonde's in black, and it's not running attire. It's a short cut dress that isn't made to stretch and the faster she runs the more it rides up. Jacob can't help but notice the sight, but the hunger's got nothing to do with sex. He's going to kill her. Just like he killed Maria, and that young nun on the Oltrarno the week before, and a fat housewife he'd caught unawares the week before that. But this one is different. This one is special. This one thinks she can run.

There's no way she'll outpace him. Even without the dress hindering her, and the heels, Jacob's in better shape. She's quick on her feet, but she's wearing out. He can hear her breath now, hot and ragged and tearing through her throat like a stampede. She might as well stop, now. She might as well die comfortable.

It's better than dying too exhausted to really fight. As Jacob suspected, though, it's only a matter of time before her outfit catches up with her. A big gap in the cobblestone catches her by surprise, and she stumbles and falls. She's still on her back when he pounces. He pins the arms first. She seems like a scratcher, and anything under her fingernails might be enough to get him caught.

"I'll scream," she says.

"I want you to scream," Jacob replies, and he isn't lying. He'll have to rush things if she does, but he'll enjoy it much, much more. "It's better if you scream." She doesn't scream, but she doesn't spit, either. It's a shame. He liked that move.

"I'm going to tell you a story," he tells her. She looks terrified. He drinks that fear in like wine, citrusy and cold. "I'm going to tell you what happened to my father, when he was serving in Vietnam. Do you want to hear that story?"

She nods.

"Liar," Jacob says, and she starts to cry. This is so perfect, the hunger's already starting to subside. But he's taken it too far, much too far now to stop.

"My father never fired a gun in Vietnam on purpose, but he did fire it once. He had a job that wasn't pretty or glorious or even especially important, but it had to be done. He took the trash from the military base and he ran it to a hole in the jungle to dump to avoid disease. That was my dad. US Army Trash man."

The girl nods. She's looking at him like he's giving her a riddle, and if she can answer it she'll walk away unharmed. Maybe she will. Stranger things have certainly happened, but not very many.

"Every time he made that trip, he took the same kid from the village the base was built on with him. He never told me the kid's name, because he couldn't remember it. My dad wasn't much for stories himself. One night, he and this kid are on a trash run, and it's a big one. The GIs had a party so big you'd have thought the war was over, but it wasn't. It wasn't even St. Patrick's day or anything, they were just bored, and they hated it there, and what the fuck else were they going to do?"

He pauses for effect, and she says, "I don't know," like she's never heard of a goddamn rhetorical question before.

"Anyway this is too much trash for his little shit heap of a van, but my dad's no mechanic so he doesn't know that. He loads her up, and even though she's a little sluggish she runs. Until they get about a mile out of town, when the engine backfires and stops. There's a bang when in it backfires, and then another bang. You know what that was?"

"A gunshot?"

"A gunshot. Right between the eyes of that little kid. My father picked him up, looked around, and dumped him in the pile with the rest of the garbage. Nobody gave a shit except him."

"Is that story true?"

It's partially true, and partially true is close enough. He's sure as shit not telling her how true it is. He runs the blade along her cheekbone, just enough to draw blood. It runs down to her lips, and stains her teeth.

"I'm going to kill you." He tells her. "Do you know that?"

She nods her head, which is not what he expected. He expected a scream, or a cry, or anything else.

"You killed that girl," she says, "the one I saw on the street. The gypsy."

"Maria," Jacob corrects her automatically. Patience eyes widen, and he can see her brain making a series of connections he isn't privy to. This, he isn't so fond of.

"Maria. You killed her just like this. Did you tell her before, too? Did you tell her that you were going to do it?"

"I didn't have to."

"You didn't have to tell me either, but you did."

He supposes that's true. He likes this one after all. She's smart, and smart is better than fat and its better than sexy. Smart makes him feel like a hunter, like he caught a bit of prey that was worthy of his efforts. Smart deserves to be honored.

"What's your name, kid?" He asks her. She shakes her head like he's trying to get her to swallow cough medicine and she can't stand the taste.

"I'm not going to tell you," she says. "I'm not going to be the name you share with the next girl you kill."

"It's not just girls," he says. "There was an old woman, and a nun. Even a man, one man. I'm not a pervert."

"Just a killer."

"I'm a predator."

"You're a coward."

He starts the motions. This one he wants to bleed. He cuts a double helix across her wrists. She cries out, but she doesn't scream. At least not loud.

"I'm a goddamn shark," he says.

"You said that to her, too," says the girl. Weakly, now. She's losing life fast, and she doesn't have much left to give.

"I did," he admits.

"Do you want to know a secret?" The girl says.

His curiosity is piqued, so he risks coming closer. She's too weak to lash out now. She does grab a handful of his collar and pull herself close. Her blood gets on his shirt. He'll have to burn it. He can't walk home like this. He's fucking up left and right with this girl, and he's not really sure why.

"Tell me," he says, "and I'll end it quicker."

The girl smiles. It's a real smile, and she'll still be wearing it, later, when the cops find her body and the blue and red light bathes the market stalls and concerned tourists. It's a pretty smile, and he wants it to stop.

"She knew you were full of shit, and I do too."

She's gone. The blonde's gone and now Jacob's the one shaking. Something's wrong. It doesn't feel the way it's supposed to. He didn't do it right. He couldn't have done it right, because he's still hungry.

That's when he sees the goddamn cat, licking the back of its paw and staring at him with its unblinking green eyes.

It steps gingerly around the pools of blood settling in the concrete and comes to rest beside the girl's head. Never breaking eye contact – is it eye contact if you make it with a cat? – with Jacob, it places a single paw on the girl's face. Her eyes close. If it weren't for the bloody cuts he'd made across her wrists, she'd look like she was sleeping.

"Is that what you want?" Jacob shrieks at the cat.

It hisses back, but he knows better than to try and catch it. This isn't an ordinary animal, he can see that now. It's something like Tony's dog, and if he went so far as to touch it he'd be changed irreversibly. There is a way he can win this, still. A way he can satisfy his hunger. Jacob grabs the knife. He takes her long, blond hair and he cuts it to ribbons. It doesn't satisfy him the way he wanted it to, but it's something. The cat can't stop him, and it's not even trying. He's still got the power here.

"Fuck you," he tells the cat. But it's already gone. Somehow, he knows he'll see it again. Next time he'll bring a goddamn cage

THE TEARS
Paolo

PAOLO KEEPS THE LIGHTS OFF and the heat on while he works. It doesn't take him long to pack. There's very little of him to put away: two weeks' worth of clothes, a couple of dime novels, a bottle of scotch. It all fits in one bag, or at least it did on the way in. Paolo's never been one to accrue material wealth, despite his best efforts. Anyway, he can't afford much these days.

It's quiet now. He had waited until classes started for the girls before making a break for it. In an ideal world he'd slip out quietly and no one would be the wiser. To be sure, there were things he would miss, but no one could convince him to stay. That wouldn't stop them from trying of course. Nor would it make them feel any better. He decides to snatch a toothbrush. They won't miss one in all the mess.

He's zipping up his bag when he feels a chill in the air. He hadn't heard the door open but he knows she's there. She's standing in the doorway. How long had she been there? He doesn't want to speak, but she's not going to move unless he does. Maybe not even then. She's got one arm blocking the doorway and another holding her pants. She must have started to strip right outside the door. Paolo shoulders the bag and starts to move in her direction, but the expression on her face stops him.

"You weren't going to tell me, were you." It's a question, but she makes it sound like a statement.

Her voice is louder than the situation calls for, like she'd been someplace with loud music, or come in from the subway, but that isn't it. She's just figured it out. Paolo shakes his head. The bag's heavier than he expected.

"Why?" She asks. It's a fair question, but one he's not sure he can answer.

There's any number of reasons he could give, but he doesn't. He's pretty sure the answer's a matter of pride. He could make a break for the door, but she wouldn't get out of the way. A single tear, black and oily, begins to snake its way down her face.

"I can't stay," he blurts.

"Ok." She says. "But do you have to leave?"

She's really crying now. The porcelain tint of her face has flooded to pink. Each tear strips away a little bit of her carefully constructed façade, and each tear diminishes her. The Girl with the Egyptian Eyeliner: Paolo's never seen her without it, but he's never seen her put it on either. She's always up hours before him, and it's always already there. He'd never thought about how long it must take her to apply. How much effort must go into its preparation. Now it's gone, in just a minute of quiet sobbing.

"I've already found a place," he says at last.

She nods, biting her bottom lip.

"Can I come with you?"

It's about then that his eyes start to sting. He shakes his head.

"I don't know anyone else. I don't have anyone else."

"You live in an apartment full of people who hang on your every word. You're literally never alone. Some of these girls would probably kill for you, with a bit of convincing."

"I hate these girls, Paolo."

He doesn't say anything to that. He'd never thought about it but he realizes that it's probably true. He takes a few steps closer to the door, and she clears the frame to come closer. Her pants fall in a sad little heap just inside the apartment.

"So why do you do it? Why do you talk to them the way you talk to them? Why do you act like you do?"

She turns her head. Was that too much? He wonders, but it's already been said. She's inches from him now. There's no more makeup left, only darkened streaks. Her face is flushed, but underneath's a grey sheen like a layer of ash. She looks like a survivor of Vesuvius. This is the sort of description she would love, he realizes suddenly, and he almost shares it with her.

"Put your bag down." She says quietly. "Put your bag down and I'll tell you why."

He drops the bag beside him. She opens it, pulls out a pair of his jeans sitting close to the top, and steps into them. She zips it closed afterwards.

"I wasn't always like this," she says. "Back in the states I was… quieter. I don't mean just that my voice was quieter, but that what I was saying was quieter. How I dressed was quieter. I was… I was like Patience. I was a quiet girl. I was a good girl. But I was alone. I got into the program to come here, and I realized I didn't have to be that way anymore. I could be anything; I could be anyone I wanted to be. And then the first night I was here… I was just walking down the street and I saw this man, it looked like a priest or something. I saw him get hit by a taxi. I mean really hit, he flew through the air like a tennis ball. I was scared, Paolo. Really. But the next morning, I put my face on. Just like you've always seen it. I became someone else, because I didn't want to be scared anymore."

She stops her story there and looks at him, glassy-eyed. She's still crying, but the tears aren't black anymore. There's nothing left of the rings around her eyes. Without them she seems younger. Looking at her now, Paolo can see that she really is only twenty-two years old. He often forgets.

"What changed?" He asks.

"I got tired. I got scared. People would do anything that I

said. Anything. Jessica lost her virginity because I told her to. Sonya dumped her boyfriend in the states because I said so. I don't even know where some of them came from. People would buy whatever I bought, eat whatever I ate. And they'd follow me wherever I went. The night I met you I ditched them. I went to the restroom at a nightclub and I walked out an emergency exit. I just wanted a night to myself."

"So why did you talk to me? Why not just drink alone."

She shrugs her shoulders. She genuinely doesn't know. That night she'd seemed so confident, so sure. He thought she'd come there to hunt, not to hide.

"The next morning they all looked so lost. They looked hurt. They looked... sad. Every day since then I've been watching them. Watching Patience take notes. Watching Cara flip her hair right after I do. Listening to Catrina's voice sound more and more like mine. Paolo if I told them to fuck you one by one, they would do it. If I told them to shave their heads they would do it. If I told them to go out into the street and blow the first man they saw they'd do it. How could I not hate them?"

It's a fair point, and not a question he can answer. He doesn't try. The story is over now, he knows her well enough to know that. He picks up his bag and starts for the door. She doesn't try to stop him. He ought to say something. She's still crying, but it's slowed down.

"I'm sorry, Nadia," he says, and shuts the door behind him.

Paolo sits on his bag on the sidewalk waiting for a taxi. The air smells like coffee and sweat. It's a smell he's used to. The kebab shop a few doors down from their apartment building is blaring Middle Eastern pop music. The owner of the shop is on the street dancing his ass off with some American college girl. She's not one of Nadia's, but she might as well be. The heavy eyeliner, the intricate leather sandals, even the dance moves – all of it could have been lifted straight from the Cult of the Girl with the Egyptian Eyeliner. In that moment Paolo understands that the truly terrifying thing about Nadia isn't the twelve disciples she has wrapped around her finger. It's the fact that each of those girls goes out into the world and influences others. Every trip to the grocery store, every night out dancing, every walk to class made another whole new convert. Slowly but surely, the girls were turning the whole city to their way of life. If even one of them kept up the act when they got back to wherever they came from, there was no telling how far the word would spread.

Paolo starts to walk. The market's roaring with people buying leather wallets and rabbit-fur gloves, Africans selling scarves and Korean immigrants selling watches and postcards. There's so much noise that for a moment he can't hear the siren. But then he sees the lights, and it's all he can hear. Red and blue, flashing out of an alley at the very end of the last row of vendors. The light pools in all the cracks in the cobbles, scattered around uneaten sandwich bread and the little paper cups that all the gelato places around town serve with. Paolo starts to walk toward them, and with every step he becomes more certain. It's her. Whatever he saw, whatever was wrong with her, she's gone. Kitsune is gone.

It's hard to make out beyond the fluttering of the *polizia* milling around, and the flashing of cameras, but from the way they've got the street cordoned off and the way they push onlookers away, he knows that whatever it is has got to be brutal. He pictures her skull shattered against the cobblestone, blood fanning out in an arc running down to the closest drain. Please don't be her, he whispers. Please.

It doesn't take Paolo long to realize he's going to get his wish. He gets a glimpse of the body, and it's not hers. There's no little foxtail tattoo on her calf, no hawk feather in her hair, and the dress is wrong. The dress is all wrong. It's a black number, V cut deep enough to get her burned at the stake in some countries and Paolo recognizes it twice over. He saw it first on the Girl – on Nadia – the first time they met. He saw it crumpled on the floor, and later hanging in a closet. Later still, he saw it on another girl, someone who must have snuck in when she wouldn't be noticed to borrow it, just for one night. Just to have camouflage. Just to fit in.

"Patience," he says. "Holy shit."

He walks back up the block in a daze. At least three vendors move like they want to pester him, but the look on his face stops them. His feet carry him up the stairs, and with each step he relives the night before. He didn't go after her, he just came back and sulked. No. He came back and thought about Kitsune, and about Nadia. He made plans and decisions and he knew that Patience might be in trouble and did nothing.

"It's my fault," he says, on the wrong side of the door. There's no one to hear him here and no one to say it to. On the other side he can hear someone blaring what honest to god sounds like Joni Mitchell over a pair of cheap speakers. It is. It's "Big Yellow Taxi". The door isn't locked.

"Nadia?" He says, and she steps into the living room. She's still crying, but not as much. Her face is pink as a newborn baby and all he wants is to be able to sustain the small flush of happiness she gets when she sees him.

"You're back," she says, and is he?

There are so many ways to tell this story, and he can't begin to start with any of them. It's all too much. This shouldn't be happening. It can't be.

"Aren't you?" She asks.

Paolo nods. He crosses the room slowly, stepping over bras and belts and a handful of scarves. He stretches out his arms as he gets close and she slides into them. He realizes, as he completes the embrace, that this is the first time he's ever just hugged her. She's warm.

"What's wrong, Paolo?"

"What do you mean?"

"You're crying. You weren't crying when you left, but you were crying when you came back in."

Raising a hand to his face, he sees that she's right. The easy thing to do would be to say he's crying about her. That he's sorry. That he never meant to hurt her. She'd find out what happened eventually, it didn't have to be from him.

"I still have to go," Paolo says. She nods slowly, waiting for him to finish. "But I was thinking maybe we could. That we could do dinner? I guess? Sometimes? I just, I want to see you, you know? I don't want to not see you."

She's smiling and trying not to laugh and if he didn't say anything this happiness would stretch on forever. She'd stay, and he'd start his job, and they'd be happy. Maybe they still can, but it'll be different once he tells her. He takes a step back and sits on the ground. She joins him. He takes her hand, and this is another first.

"There's something more important we have to do, though."

"What's that?" She asks.

"We need to talk about Patience."

THE BUCKET
Tony

TONY BUYS A HANDFUL OF BUCKETS from a local florist and gets to work making bombs. It isn't what he planned to do with his Thursday, but at this point he doesn't have another option available. His friends have deserted him. His family is too dysfunctional to be an option. His dog sleeps on a bed of skeletons and, lately, refuses to be touched. This is what it's come to, Tony thinks. Making bombs out of cow shit in my living room. He packs each bucket tight, and goes over the plan in detail. He'll need one to take out power to the Hospital. One each at key supporting beams throughout the building, he's counting eight of these. Another throughout to keep the explosion even, call it four. And one or two in the bishop's room to ensure his body is thoroughly destroyed. There can be no survivors. There can be no more like Jacob.

Every headline Tony reads brings a splash of bile into his throat. It's not that he's surprised Jacob would do it, it's that he's surprised at the targets. The Gypsy Girl – Jacob seemed to think the Roma walked on water after all the research he'd done. Tony wasn't sure Jacob was even Jacob anymore, at least that he was entirely himself. He can see Carrera's hand in this, or what he imagines his hand to be. He remains embarrassed that he had noticed the man so little while he was walking among the living.

All told, Tony has sixteen buckets. It's a lot of cow shit,

enough to get the job done. All he needs is the right opportunity. By his observations, the hospital staffing is most sparse on Tuesday afternoons, so that will be his target. That gives him a little less than a week to sit on this. To change his mind, maybe. But it's hard to change his mind when every time he leaves the house the dog's pile of bodies grows bigger, and fatter, and ranker. Tony's got to figure out something to do about it, but not tonight. Tonight he's going to sleep.

When Tony wakes up, the Angel is inches from his face. Her face invites panic. Not because she is panicking, but because she is concerned, which is close enough to it. She waits for him to put on pants, and they meet in his living room.

"Tony," she says, "There is something you need to know."

There are lots of things he needs to know. He needs to know if the formula he'd read was accurate enough to support his calculations for a demolition of the building. He needs to know if it's possible for him to survive this, or if he's doomed to be the vector of whatever spirit is attached to Crosby now when he kills the bishop once and for all. Something tells him none of these questions are the ones she's ready to answer.

"When we met, I told you that your dog was possessed of a malevolent spirit, you remember?"

"No, I've forgotten."

He hasn't, but evidently he has forgotten that she doesn't understand sarcasm.

"That was a joke. Yes, of course I remember."

"I led you to believe that the only spirit here was the bishop, but it's more than that. Do you believe in demons, Tony?"

He didn't believe in demons, of course. But he didn't believe in angels not too long ago and now he's got one sipping tea in his living room most nights, so what difference did it make?

"I would have said no before, but I'm willing to be open."

"I believe, in the infancy of his career, that Carrera tied his fortune to the actions of a demon. As long as he could keep its hunger satiated, he would remain in power. The Roma were Carrera's obsession alone. The demon could have gotten his blood anywhere. The Roma were not missed, and not wanted, and they made it easy. That is all."

Tony thinks about the dream he used to have, and the doorknocker with the engraving that hung on the door to their home in Porto.

"The demon," he asks her, "do you know its name?"

"It is called Azazel," she says.

Of course, it would be the same. Why would it not be the same? He had traveled for miles and miles, and lived for years, and never left that horrid room.

"I believe," says the Angel, "that when that man, Jacob, made contact with your dog, the demon found a new place to make his home. Carrera resides in your dog, of that there is no doubt. But Azazel has gone elsewhere."

Would that change his plans? Could it? It was one thing to set off a bomb, and another entirely to kill a man one on one.

"I don't think I can kill Jacob," Tony says.

"I will not ask you to," says the Angel, and she steps towards the window. "Azazel, I will destroy myself."

And then she's gone. Tony's left in the dark, thinking about demons, and he's sad to say it's not for the first time. It takes a few seconds for him to process her words, but when he does they hit him like a lightning bolt. She's going to kill him. The Angel is going to kill Jacob.

THE RING
Jacob

JACOB WANDERS THROUGH THE CEMETERY at San Miniato, crunching the sparse gravel underfoot and interrupting the chanting of the monks announcing five o'clock in moans from their shuttered cloisters. A new sun throws a festive pink blanket over the silent mass of indignant gravestones, huddled together like pigeons over spilled seed. He wears black: a sport coat, a silver stripy tie. An observer would think he was here to bury a friend. The chanting stops.

In the courtyard there are two kids – charges of the monastery, maybe – chasing a soccer ball with a tree branch. Jacob wonders if they're re-enacting the martyrdom of their decapitated saint and patron, or sampling playing a game of their own design. He watches them from a distance as they trip over wildflowers grown from the graves and taking turns attacking each other's necks with their improvised swords. They ignore him. The sky turns blue.

Beneath them the city spreads out like a picnic, wool-white and brick-red blotches wafting with foodborne odors; the butterscotch burning of unclean ovens; bakery-goers with pan-singed pastries; honey; cream; lemon; street after street of steam-dampened produce; plums and melons and chicory, filling the air and settling sugar-heavy in his lungs like sediment from the river. Jacob's mouth starts to water, and he smiles.

He told the girl at the jeweler he'd always thought, when he was younger, that he'd grow up and marry a girl who loved the Strokes, who kept her hair in a double braid, who wore plaid and bleached her asshole, even though he didn't know what that meant back then. When he told her that she blushed until her head looked like a little red balloon that would float all the way away from her little shop on the Ponte Vecchio, over the city, out into the country, out into nothing. She didn't respond. Anyway, now he's here with Kita – with Ana. She couldn't tell you shit about the Strokes but she can recite the lyrics to any song by the Clash and probably tell you the chord progression while she's at it. The shop girl doesn't care about any of that, and really Jacob doesn't either. All he cares about is her. He's done with playing around, done with kicking girls to the curb and starting the hunt anew. The hunt's changed, so the girl can stay the same. He wants her to.

The ring itself is like something out of a magazine. It is the very definition of a wedding ring, and there's no room for debating it. The main setting is a beautiful square cut diamond, it's maybe twelve, thirteen carats if that's your measure, but Jacob's more interested in the other stones. Fanning out from the centerpiece is a swathe of tiny rubies, garnet, and pearls. The way they spread, they look like seafoam washing in. That's what most people would probably say. To him they look like blood, shooting through the air after he spills it. The girl at the jeweler had told him its value was seven thousand, but he'd held her to six. Something in his eyes let her know not to haggle back. He'd been kind to cut the price so low.

Part of him wants to mend fences with Tony, first, just so he can see the look on that little shit's face when he sees his 'Kitty' with Jacob's ring. Tony would melt into the earth like someone had dropped gelato. He'd never speak again. The mental image is almost enough to make him call, but he keeps his phone tight.

He's thinking about that dog. Something about it wasn't right. It was afraid of him, but not in the way he'd expect. Not in the way he's used to, and getting more used to all the time. The dog was afraid the way a caveman would fear fire, or the sight of their own reflection in a mirror for the first time. He saw something he recognized in that dog, and he didn't want to see it again. Nothing was worth that.

The kids are still at it, and Jacob's had his fill. He starts heading away, because if he doesn't he really will kill one of them. Now that he knows he can, the temptation is so much harder to resist. As he walks he passes by the gravestones, and he sees something familiar. It's in a cluster of newer stones, wealthy citizens of recent decades rather than the fortunate of the Renaissance days. It's got two names on it, and neither of them are Italian:

In-Tak Lingo, 68
Kita Lingo, 7

Kita. Of course. And In-Tak must be her father's birth name, as well. That they're buried here is a surprise, but a fortunate one. All of a sudden her reaction to that name is explained. All of a sudden her nickname, her desperate defining of her identity, her occasional flashes to that far-off look; all of it makes sense. She was looking for her sister, even now.

There's another grave up here he came to see, but he has to scare the kids away first. It isn't hard to do. He just furrows his brow and looks their way, and pops their soccer ball with the blade of his knife.

"That's one more thing I owe you," he says to the grave.

Maria Magariet, 17

Jacob checks around to make sure he isn't being watched, then gets a little closer. He takes his knife, and chisels one word into the side of the stone, shallow but legible. Shark. If he was a shark, then so was she.

"I'm not going to stop," he tells her, and for the first time, the thought almost terrifies him. "I think you were the only one who could have stopped it."

The monks stop chanting, and that's his cue to leave. He can't afford to be seen here, at least not by adults. There's one thing he wants to do, though, that he has to do, before he can go. He leans close, and presses his lips to the stone.

"You were right," he said, "I am a liar. But you, I never lied to."

With that he's done. He puts the ring back in his pocket and heads back down to the city proper. Tomorrow is going to be a big, big day.

THE FUNERAL
Paolo

THIS IS ONLY THE SECOND TIME IN Paolo's life that he has worn a suit. When his mother died, he was six and his suit would have fit a teddy bear. He spent what felt like an hour standing on a stepstool in the bathroom trying to tie his tie the way the man at the store had taught him. He'd done it so fast, but try as Paolo might, he just couldn't recreate what he'd seen. This time, he's got Nadia to help him.

After she stopped with the makeup there was about a week of Cara trying to be the ringleader, but it couldn't last forever. Sunday morning, the day before the funeral, Catrina fluttered into the kitchen in a plaid shirt and blue jeans and just like that the spell was broken. Cara put her hair back in a braid, Megan slipped back into her New Jersey accent, and after a bit of cajoling even Sonya's boyfriend agreed to take her back. They're doing their best to pretend that all is right with the world, and if it weren't for what happened to Patience, it would be.

"I feel like it's my fault," he says to Nadia as she tightens his tie. She kisses him on the cheek. This is a new thing that she's started to do to show him that she's okay and that he's okay, and he's learning to appreciate it. The tie knot is a perfect Windsor. They're ready.

Nadia rents them all a limo and it's their last hurrah as an ensemble. This time, they follow her not because they're watching her every move for instructions, but because she's the one who's composed. She's the one who's stable. She's naturally a leader, and sometimes that's what you need. They each tip the driver on their way out, and he looks absolutely floored at the stack of cash in his hands.

"Don't get carried away and leave us here," Paolo jokes. There's no danger of that.

The funeral's happening at the main chapel of the *Santa Maria Novella*, a more modern-looking cathedral closer to the train station. The location had been Sonya's suggestion. She'd ridden in a taxi with Patience their first day in Florence, on the way from the airport. The ride had taken them by the building, and she'd practically squealed. It was her favorite, Sonya insisted, and no one wanted to argue. Paolo escorts them to their seats, one by one. At Nadia's suggestion, he's a pallbearer. He's the only one who knows her, but the others offer their condolences genuinely, and with real compassion. He's amazed how heavy it is. He'd thought she would be lighter.

Inside the church the girls have placed all of the flowers Patience kept in their apartment, plus another twenty or so bouquets gifted from god knows where. The death was high profile, and it got enough attention to merit a larger funeral. Somehow, though, the little African Violet they've placed by the coffin outshines the rest. It was the first thing she brought in when the idea hit her, and even though it was on its last legs when she got it she wouldn't let it die. The girls have honored her memory well. None of them have the green thumb she did, but they haven't let a single thing so much as yellow on its stem.

At Paolo's insistence, the casket is closed. He's the only one among them that saw the body before it was taken away, and he can only imagine how it would affect them, even cleaned up. The girls all agreed that it was best to remember her as she was. So that's what they did.

They each get up to speak, one by one. They share stories of their time with Patience. Some are sweet, and some are embarrassing, and some are, frankly, vapid, but it's the portrait of a life. Nadia, uncharacteristically, speaks neither first nor last, but summarizes herself well.

"Patience was real," she says, and a crowd full of strangers nods along with her. "She is real. Most people, they don't get to have that. She was lucky she did. I just wish she'd stayed lucky." Honestly, Paolo's too worried about what he's going to say to catch most of the rest of her speech. It must be a good one though. There's not a dry eye anywhere in the house.

Looking around the room, Paolo can still see a few girls in black with winged eyes. Even if she's done with the show, the ripples are still spreading. He wonders if she notices. He wonders if she feels pride. The priest calls for anyone else to speak and Paolo realizes her family hasn't come. He'd called them, and they wanted to make it, but they didn't think they'd be able to afford it. What a horrible thought, to not be at your daughter's funeral. Nadia looks at him, and nods. He gets up to speak.

"Patience was a hell of a chess player. She never met a plant she couldn't be a mother to, and she never met a person she couldn't at least try to like. She could tell you a story about calving her family's horses, and ten seconds later grab a guy and get on the dance floor and make anyone in the room, I mean anyone, raise an eyebrow. Whatever she was doing, she wanted to do her best at it, and her best was always very, very good. Patience always tried, always. That's what made her special.

That's what made her who she was.

A month or so ago, Patience saw another girl, who'd went the same way she ended up going. She was walking back home after a long night out with a guy she'd met the night before and didn't bother to get the name of, and if any of you want to judge her for that you can go straight to hell. Sorry, father. The thing is, Patience didn't do that just to fit in. She didn't do it because some of her friends were doing it, or because it's what the girls on television did. She did it because she could. Because she wanted to, because she liked him and she liked how it felt. And if she was going to sleep with a stranger, god dammit she wanted to be the best at that too. Sorry, again, father.

I saw her picture, in the paper. It was almost a month exactly before she died, and I saw her there. She had a dress on that she'd borrowed out of a friend's closet because she couldn't afford to look the way she wanted to, the way she could. She had the same dress on, the night she got killed. She caught my eye in that picture not just because she was pretty, which she was. Not because she was sad, which of course she was. Everyone was. She caught my eye because she was praying, and she was the only one who thought to do that. She was the only one who thought that poor little Roma girl was worth the time. Who thought she was worthy of her prayers. It's kind of funny, when you think about it. Actually, it's mostly just sad. There's maybe ten of us here that knew her, that really knew her, and yet the crowd for her funeral is filling this church. That girl that Patience prayed for, she didn't get a thing. No service. No crowd. Just a little plot and a couple of paragraphs in the paper. Patience told me that when she saw her lying on the ground, she looked peaceful. She wasn't afraid. I hope she remembered that when her time came. I hope she found that same kind of peace. And wherever they are, I hope they're together.

And you, Patience. I want you to know I'm sorry. I'm sorry I didn't watch you better. I'm sorry I didn't tell you what to do, and where to go, and who to trust. I'm sorry I couldn't save you. That none of us could. You deserved better, kid. From all of us."

When he sits back down, the girls are all crying, and Nadia kisses him on the cheek again.

"I'm sorry," she whispers to him.

"For what?"

"For everything."

Cara gets up and grabs her rose. There's a stem for each of the girls, and they each take one. There's one for him too. One by one, they walk up and lay their flower on her coffin. Some of them say a prayer, in passing. Some of them cry. When it's Paolo's turn, he lays his hand on the mahogany and whispers.

"I'll do better next time. That's a promise."

THE WILL
Kitsune

WHEN ANA'S FATHER DIED, HE LEFT her three things. He left her an apartment above the restaurant her family had once owned, where she lives today and, realistically, will probably soon die. He left her a small sum of money which she had used to purchase, among other things, the guitar she can no longer play with her shaking hands and weakened arms. Lastly but most importantly, at least to her, he left her his bookshelf. In the weeks and months leading up to her parents' escape from North Korea, her father had taught himself English from some of these books. He had studied them in translation and learned most of them by heart, and though reconstructing a language from their flowery verse and exaggerated dialogue was difficult, it was within his power to achieve. Her father spoke beautiful English, but it wasn't always totally accurate. He believed form mattered over function, always. They had that in common.

To Ana's mother, her father had left the remainder of his fortune, which was no paltry sum, given the success of their restaurant and his other investments. She had been instrumental in the earning of the money in her own right, so this was only fair as far as Ana was concerned. The money didn't really matter to her anyway, she had as much as she felt the need to have. He had also left her their apartment on the *Borgo Ognissanti*, and its contents, most of which she had since sold or given to a thrift store run by a family friend because she couldn't bear the painful remembrance they forced upon her. She had kept only two things. The first was a book of poems that her husband had written, most of them for her. Ana knew few of them well, as her mother shared them only sparsely with others, but one line had always stuck in her mind:

> *the lotus on the water*
> *does not float*
> *for the lightness of*
> *its pink petals*
> *but the green root*
> *snaking to the earth.*

This, her mother had kept, and one thing more: the picture of Kita that Ana holds in her hands now. She had taken it from her mother's house years ago, weeks after her father's passing. Stolen, she had stolen it. Her mother thought it was missing, and had nearly lost herself in guilt at its absence. Ana had almost returned it, but she couldn't bear its loss any more than her mother. It was the only thing they had of her. Of Kita. It was the only way she could remember her sister's face.

It's only fitting, then, that she return it to her mother in her own will. Ana had started to write it this morning, and it hasn't been making itself easy. After several false starts, she settled on a method she felt was fair. She wrote down all the names she could think of, crossed most of them off the list, then began the task of assigning her possessions to each as she found a good match.

To her mother, Ana left the photo. She left the feather, and the beads, and the copper wire from her first broken guitar string – all of the things she kept in her hair, even now. She left her father's bookshelf, and the apartment she was living in. She returned as much of herself as she could give to the woman who had birthed her, and who would soon see her family come completely to an end so many miles from home. Her father had wanted his ashes to return to Korea, but the request had been denied. There was no way to achieve it through proper channels, and no one they knew had been willing to take the risk of doing it illegally. Ana could hardly blame them.

She left a handful of items to her handful of friends. A notebook filled with lyrics and ideas for riffs and chord progressions to one of her bandmates. A bottle of liquor that at this point was more nostalgic than alcoholic to a roommate who probably wouldn't remember her name anymore. At the end of the list there was only one item, and in a way it was the only thing that mattered: her guitar. She knows she ought to give it to Jacob. He lives with her, and whether he realizes it or not, he's keeping her alive. She can barely take care of herself most days, and she hardly feels like moving if he doesn't make her. Without him she'd most likely have died before she'd written a will to begin with. The thing is, when she thinks about giving it to Jacob, all she can think about is the face in the mirror. The thing is when she thinks about giving it to Jacob, she thinks she'd rather smash it into splinters first, and she's not sure why. And Tony has been to more of her shows than anyone alive. He'd been an ass on the phone and she'd been one back at him but at the end of the day with the exception of wanting more from her than she'd ever wanted to give him, he was her most loyal friend. Her guitar would mean something to him. It would hurt him not to have it, if she was going to be gone.

"Fuck it," she wheezes, "I'll be dead anyway."

She gives the guitar to Tony. The list is done now, and with that decision made, Ana realizes something. She's left nothing to Jacob. She knows this ought to bother her, but it doesn't. Suddenly, it's back to being simple. Suddenly, it's not so complicated. Not anymore.

THE PRESENT
Tony

TONY'S FILLING UP THE LAST OF HIS buckets when the phone rings. No one calls him anymore, so whoever it is must know something about what he's doing. Right? He almost doesn't answer, but he's far too anxious to just sit and let it ring. What if they know where he lives? What if they're already outside, waiting? He picks it up, takes a deep breath, and answers. Whoever it is doesn't speak at first, and he can't take it. He breaks the silence himself.

"Hello?" He says, and honest to god his voice cracks. It cracks exactly like it used to do all the time when he was twelve, and it pisses him off to hear it. He can't think about that now.

"Hello?" He repeats, and this time he sticks the landing.

"Tony," says a voice and he feels an uncharacteristic sense of relief to realize that it's only his mother.

"Oh," he says, collapsing in a heap onto his couch, "it's you. What do you need, mother?"

She laughs a dry, shaking laugh that somehow even from the other side of the phone reeks of booze.

"You're drunk," he says, and feels a guilty pang of déjà vu.

"I am," she admits, "but that's not why I'm calling. Well it is in a way, I guess. I wanted to call you earlier, but I couldn't. I guess I had to drink first."

It's such a comforting thought to know that his own mother

needs to line up shots to summon the mental fortitude necessary to talk to him for any length of time. It's exactly the boost of confidence he needs right now, when his life is falling into jagged shambles he's using as shrapnel for fertilizer bombs. He takes a deep breath, and tries to relax. Really, he should just be grateful it's not the cops.

"Is everything alright?" He asks her. He does some mental math and figures there's only a handful of tragedies left that would motivate her to call him. "You're alright? Are you sick?"

There's that laugh again. It's the sound a bird would make on its death bed, just before it asked you for water.

"No, Tony, I'm alright. Just this once I'm not calling for myself. I'm calling for you."

Even with all of the possibilities that had crossed his mind for his life since he had first learned of the possible reality of Angels and Demons, this was not among them. What could she possibly think he needed, or at least that he would need from her. Tony hasn't needed anything from his mother in years, and that is very much by design.

"I'm not sure I know what you mean," he says.

He's not going to fall into the trap his mother is so good at setting. She's always saying things in an effort to get him to finish her sentences for her, especially if she has something less than kind to tell him. Mostly, he goes along with it because it's easier to take when it comes from him, but this time he's making an exception. If she wants to make a point she'll have to do it herself. She sighs.

"At first," she says, "I was hurt you didn't tell me. Really. I mean I know we don't speak much these days, that we haven't for a long time. But I thought that was one of the things you would tell me"

"What?" He pulls at the line, but she doesn't bite.

"When I thought about it, though, it made sense. And I'm

surprised I didn't see it. No, that's not true, I know why. I guess we both do."

"What are you talking about, mom?"

Tony hears the familiar sound of whiskey pouring over a single giant ice cube and he wonders how many this is for her, and how many she can handle these days. If she's changed as little as it appears, this would have to be at least her sixth.

"When you were home. For Magritte. You remember that?"

"Obviously, yes."

"Well you remember a lot of it, but you probably don't remember that I went into your room while you were out to iron your shirt. I wanted it to be pressed and clean for the funeral."

"Of course you did."

"Tony, I saw the hairs all over your suitcase."

Hairs? Tony looks around the room, and sees the only possible culprit. Crosby doesn't shed much, but what little he does sticks to Tony like a magnet. Like he's absorbing the dog's essence little by little, which in context is a sobering thought.

"Mom, I didn't tell you because I didn't think you'd want to know about it."

"Does it make you happy?"

What a strange question. One he only has to answer because of the peculiar circumstances of his life, circumstances she only knows half of. For most people, just hearing the word dog is enough to crack a smile big enough to serve a meal on.

"Most of the time, yea."

To his surprise, Tony realizes he isn't lying. Not this time. His mother seems satisfied. It's only when he hears the sound of her blowing her nose into a tissue that he realizes she's crying. He's only seen it a handful of times, but it's always silent as rain at the edge of the horizon.

"Tony, I want you to know I got you a birthday present."

Tony's hands clench on the edge of the table, but he holds

back the flurry of curses that rise to his lips. The possibilities are endless. Maybe it's anti-freeze. Tony reaches around for his own bottle of whiskey, but it's in the cabinet.

"Do I want to know what it is?"

"Well that's the thing, Tony. You've already gotten it."

Tony's certain he hasn't. He hasn't even gotten mail in a week, and he tells her as much. Once more with that damn laugh. Crosby looks up every time he hears it, and his ears perk like he's heard something from the street below.

"What kind of dog is it, anyway?" She asks.

"It's a Puli. The kind of medium sized dogs that look like mops, or like they've got dreadlocks."

"Bob Marley dogs."

"Sure, Bob Marley dogs."

That's exactly what he'd thought of on that first night, but that's not what shocks him. He hasn't heard his mother made a joke in years. When he was a little kid, he thought she was the funniest person he'd ever known, but given he could count the people he knew on the fingers of one hand back then, that wasn't saying much. He wonders what she thought of him as a child. Back then she was so caught up in the divorce, and her job in Portugal, and her friends, and her life. Did she even know what kind of kid he had been? She must have. Whatever he thought of her, she wasn't a monster.

"Tony," she says, and she's really slurring her speech now. Either she's more than six deep or something else is going on. "Tony, I wasn't a very good mother, was I?"

"Don't talk like that, mom."

"You only call me that when you're lying to me. Do you know that?"

He's never thought of it, but she's probably right.

"You don't have to say it. I won't make you be cruel to me if you don't want to."

Tony's starting to put the pieces together, and now he's really wishing he had that whiskey. Out of the corner of his eye, he sees the Angel.

"Mom... Mother, I think you're lying to me, too."

"When?"

"When you told me you were alright."

She laughs that laugh again and this time Tony knows. Some things are hereditary.

"Jesus, ma," Tony says, and he hasn't called her that since he was a kid. Since their little flat in Porto.

"Language, Tony."

He's crying. Why is he crying?

"I didn't want you to do this, you know that, don't you?"

"Maybe," she says. "Maybe I'm just using you as an excuse, I don't know. The truth is, it's something I've wanted to do for a long time. But I couldn't leave him alone."

Tony holds back the flash of ire he feels at knowing she's talking about Magritte, because he knows what he'd do for Crosby. What he's going to do.

"I understand," he says, and this time they both know he's telling the truth. "How long do you have?"

"Not long," she says.

"I could call the cops, you know." He says, and his voice cracks again. The Angel rests a hand on his shoulder. He hadn't even heard her coming closer to him. Did she know that this would happen? Did she know that his mother was going to die?

"It's too late for that, I'm afraid. You can't stop this Tony, even if you wanted to. And it isn't your fault. I'm sorry, Tony. I really do love you. I always have, even back then. Even-"

She trails off, and Tony knows what she means but he doesn't want to think about it. Instead, he thinks about the apartment in Porto and his big wide bed. He was too small for it. It was Queen sized when he would have felt like he was drowning in a twin. He can remember, albeit fuzzily, a night when thunder threatened to tear their roof from its hinges. When the sky shuddered under the weight of the rain it was dumping down on their city, and their very building trembled with each peal of lightning. Tony lay awake, an island in a sea of crimson sheets, clutching a pillow. His mother came in, and took his tiny little hands in hers. She didn't say much, just 'shh-shh', barely a whisper, a couple of times. But each time she said it the city felt further away. After a while, Tony fell asleep. That morning when he woke up she was still there, on the outside of his covers, staring at him. Her eyes were red and tired.

The Angel touches his forehead, and Tony feels lighter, calmer. He feels like he's ready.

"Shh," he whispers into the phone, and again, "shh-shh." He hears his mother choke down a sob. The Angel's gone now. This moment is for him to live on his own. On some level, he's always known that this was coming. Maybe he'd even thought about it, when he was in darker places. Sometimes, in his darkest moments, he had even longed for it. But however he had envisioned it, there was one thing he hadn't predicted. He didn't expect it to hurt.

JACOB'S DREAM:
The Snake in the River

DOWN BESIDE THE ARNO, ON THE RIVER'S bank, where the rats – the giant rats, the nutria – build burrows and cavort and float in the murky water like bloated brown buoys, where the city's solitary egrets hoard away their fish like aging misers and seagulls circle in unchallenged predatory packs, where the only reeds growing are bent and arthritic from the weight of their thorns and even the pigeons are wild, there is a girl being swallowed by a massive albino serpent. Jacob has fallen in love immediately. They could be Orpheus and Eurydice, Icarus and the sun. He consults his watch. It is twelve twenty-three.

She is too beautiful for him; like one of Giotto's pale frescoes thrown out across church walls amidst the bits and pieces of burnt-up bibles, her physical form seems cursed by the jealous reality of a mediocre universe. She has blonde hair, buttery and delicate as rising custard. She is being eaten by a snake.

He arrives at the bank and his shoe is engulfed by the cavernous squelch of soggy beach-mud. Everything is in retreat; the rats and the snake and the girl in its belly. He ask the reeds and the cat-tails, 'where can she have gone' but their bitter inanimate stalks lack the will required for speech. There is an egret.

"Egret," he asks, "what shall I do?"

And either the bird responds or Jacob imagines him saying,

"If the river is your problem, talk to Poseidon."

Where is Poseidon? In the stone sprawl of the *Piazza della Signoria*, that purgatory and picnic ground for great and mediocre works of art, there is a statue – or rather a fountain – dedicated to Neptune, that Roman corruption of the sea god in question. He stands before it. What once was a gushing display of falling water has slowed to a quiet drool. His trident is absent, driven off by the stoic disapproval of the *Palazzo Vecchio*. At one time this was a god.

Neptune, Jacob begins, but he corrects himself. Poseidon. Where has that snake gone? There is a myth that this statue can dance, or that at night when the moon is petulantly bright and hanging fat in the sky it walks around attempting conversation with the other mute masterworks, the mad monarch babbling to his terrified court. It has nothing to say to him now.

Where will he go? A pet shop, a library, a bar. The crinkled red hump of Brunelleschi's dome. Digestion, Jacob knows all too well, is a rapid process. He is fleeing begging gypsies on a sweat-flushed street when he bumps into a glass-paneled Madonna with its eyes sprayed black, clutching her deformed Christ with a pride that fades with the color of her paint. His little robe is red as a slab of raw beef, and his chubby finger points skyward. Jacob looks up. The sign announces that a tarot reading costs thirty euros. The stairs are worn in the center.

Sprawled across the table, the Queen of Cups straddles the Hanged Man and the Devil and the old woman keeps pulling cards – the Page of Swords, the Empress, the Tower, the King of Wands – this, she informs him, is a bad hand. Lust and chaos, corruption and beauty. Is the Hanged Man a portent of good or of ill? A journey, a struggle, a knife in the darkness. Blonde hair on the High Priestess, sitting on top of the deck. Jacob starts to weep and the old woman comforts him by asking for money. Begin at the beginning she says. Where is the beginning?

Down by the water Jacob addresses the nutria in their burbling hordes, hair slick as an oil spill, uncountable heads bobbing in the water, a chorus of Angels or unpardoned souls. Please help me, he asks them. Where is she? The watch pressed cool on his skin tinkles the opening notes of its grating alarm. It is two forty-one. The rats want him to sing.

What will he sing? Something from Dylan, Boccelli. Too much confusion. *Con te partirò*. This is the way the gentleman rides, the gentleman rides, the gentleman rides. Nursery rhymes and nonsense verses bubble from his lips, fluttering faulty in the air like wind-torn butterflies. The rats are hissing at him. Jacob begins to hum.

The rats say that there is a place where the white snakes swim, yes. The underworld. The hell place. The dark place. The cellar. They say there's a bar called Osiris where the dead take tea, and a river or a forest or a fountain or a spring where the raindrops or the water or the bucket or the well down in the blackness stirs the silence with echoes of the ending of the world. Jacob is confused. He asks for directions, for a sign, for anything. They tell him that in the city there is a street. In the street is a bar. In the bar is a well. In the well is a snake.

Jacob is in a graveyard, now. The church of San Miniato al Monte stands bone white and gold-soaked at the highest point of the city, the smug parent of a wayward child. Stray cats crawl around its ankles wailing for meat. Jacob looks out across the mossy swathe of city below him – ceramic-capped buildings, blind, deaf, and dumb. A soccer stadium. A synagogue. Disembodied structures heaped haphazardly, or carefully arranged in an archaeologist's wax-veined vision of antiquated life. Towering over everything, Jacob sees the steel skeleton of an unmanned crane.

The bar is at its feet. Jacob knows this because the cats know this, he thinks. They expect things from him. Save the girl, they say. Feed us. The machine hangs a right angle in the empty sky, a rusted hook dangling like a tooth on a tendon from its vast perpendicular. Does it know him? Does it care to? Does it take tea with the Hanged Man while the snake swims circles in an old stone well?

The voice of the crane is barren as a blind man's pupil, monotonous in its apathy, its breath hot as a steam engine, its solitary hook-tooth affording a sinister lisp. It speaks to no one. The cats alone acknowledge its presence. It stands hunched over Florence, a bulldog chained to a garbage bin. Jacob is wasting time, thinking.

He could climb it, drive a jackhammer into its heart, but he has no jackhammer. He could try the levers. He would need holy water, or a bible, or a crucifix, or a wrench blessed by John the Baptist to pull the thing apart, screw by soldered screw. He could take up the flute. He could chop it like an oak tree, or gnaw it into splinters with his own eye teeth. On the great crane's corner, a pigeon turns in slow circles, trying in vain to attract a mate. He is out of ideas.

Jacob's breath resumes beneath the neon blinking of a non-descript bar, dull beyond the blue-green buzzing a sign and the skeletal looming of the silent crane. He has survived. He suppresses a shudder, and repeats his mantras.

The world hates a whiner.
Everything happens for no reason.
This is the way we wash our face, wash our face, wash our face.

He takes a deep breath, and enters the bar.

Osiris is a holding pen for drowned cats, a way-station for slaughtered swine, cows, meat for the Central Market – in the corner a teenage girl with bloodied wrists takes tea with a fledgling pigeon, crushed up from collision with a fourth-floor window – the bartender sells beer at two euros a pint.

There is a dance floor, off in the corner. A conga-line of lamp-posts, the sort lined along the river, tripod tiger legs scraping bronze-on-bronze and scratching away at the warped wood beneath them. A solitary seagull, flapping in the rafters, settles, tired, to earth. The last lamp in line waddles over and, with a muffled thump, comes to rest over the ruffled bird. A squeak, a puff of feathers. It is four forty-three.

Jacob approaches the bar. The bartender is a bloated individual; a man with an eye-patch, purple in the face, with a water-logged noose draped around his neck. This must be The Hanged Man. The All-Father. Jacob has questions for him. Where is the girl with the blonde hair? Where is the well, and the snake? Does that hurt? What exactly am I doing?

He says:

"I think you should leave, friend."

Wait. There is a door. A cold hallway lit by the invisible moon. Paintings of eight-legged cats, fish with human arms, Christ after Christ after malformed Christ. The sound of water dripping, pooling, sliding slowly down a gently curving stone. A well. A snake. A girl.

"I have come from the river," Jacob says, "with the sea god's blessing to take the girl. The city loves me. I have spoken with its birds. I have kissed its painted women. I have stood among its dead and buried heroes, and screamed at the silent skeleton of the crane your cousin. This is my right. I will leave with the girl."

The snake uncoils from his well, one muscle after another, a waterfall of protein and tendons, coiled-together fibers and fangs and eyes and sand-white scales. This is Jacob's moment. He imagines St. George and his dragon, Sigurd and Fafnir, Apollo and Python – he could be Perseus and she his Andromeda. Jacob would give his kingdom for a sword, or a shield emblazoned with a cross. Winged boots. She stands there dripping with gold hair and water from the Arno. She is his prize. This is his right.

The snake wraps himself around her, lovingly as a flag covering a coffin, natural as the double helix on the wand of Hermes. She offers no protest. Her arms slide along his scales, her white arms, muscular arms, a musician assessing her instrument. She speaks. Who does Jacob think he is, she wants to know, to come into her home like this? Her voice is soft as an over-ripe plum. The snake's massive head leers over her shoulder. Who does Jacob think he is, she wants to know, to begin with? She turns to the serpent and presses her lips to its face, or maybe its nose, or its mouth. Her eyes closed, her blue eyes, wild as a bramble erupting from concrete. The kiss lasts for what seems like hours. It is four fifty-two.

To no one in particular, Jacob says;

"Perhaps there has been a mistake."

Part 5

You know I lose,
you know I win
You know I call for
the shape I'm in.
It's just a game you
see me play,
Only real in the way
That I feel
from day to day.

Although the answer
is not unknown,
I'm searchin', searchin',
and how I've grown.
It's not all right
to say goodbye,
And the world on a string
Doesn't mean a thing.

No, the world on a string
Doesn't mean a thing.
It's only real in the way
That I feel from day to day.
No, the world on a string
Doesn't mean a thing.

from "World on a String" by Neil Young

THE RAIN
Paolo

IT'S RAINING FOR MAYBE THE FIFTH DAY in a row and all Paolo wants to do is stand out in the street with his mouth open until he drowns. He's done the math. He figures his lungs hold about two gallons each, and it's probably coming down at a rate of a couple liters an hour. It would take him the better part of the afternoon to drown, but he'd get there eventually if no one stopped him. He sighs, and returns to reality. Nadia's got her face pressed against the glass probably doing her own calculations, and the other girls are nowhere to be found. It's been hell here since the funeral, a dead silence whose only virtue is productivity. In lieu of conversation, the girls have finally gotten the place clean. Spotless, even. There's no more socks on the floor, no more empty bottles lining the countertops. It even smells clean, with that fake-lemon smell of Lysol. He slides closer to Nadia, and she rests her head on his shoulder. Paolo's dated before, of course, but his relationships have until now been purely exercises in sex and convenience. In the past week he's learned an entire new language of affection and caring it's been hard for him to master, but he's starting to get the hang of a few phrases. He puts his hand on her head and scratches lightly. She's been crying, he can tell from the damp patch her face left behind on his shirt. He doesn't know what to say to her just yet, so he says nothing and hopes for the best.

They'd gotten a letter from Patience's family a few days after the service. They were so kind. They said their daughter had told them over and over about her friends, and how close everyone was. She said they had always hoped she would find people like that, and they were glad that she had people to be there for her service when they couldn't. That had been the last straw for Nadia, whose guilt on the subject of Patience was different and considerably stronger than Paolo's. Since her little cult had disbanded, she had apologized to each girl in turn for the things she had said, and most of them had forgiven her. The whole thing felt like something out of a dream to them, he could see it in their faces. They remembered what she was talking about, but it was like it had happened to someone else, like they had read about it in a newspaper. There were no hard feelings but the group, since the funeral, had felt like strangers rather than friends who had known each other for nearly a year. Paolo had decided to let her do her apologies alone. It seemed better that way, more proper. But it made it hard for him to understand what she was going through. And he didn't really know how to ask. Now though, with her tears soaking through to his chest, he knows he needs to give it the good old college try.

"What's on your mind?" He asks. This he knows the answer to, at least broadly speaking, but he doesn't know enough to be more specific than that. She looks up at him and her eyes are glass. They're like the surface of a pond he could jump into and send out a perfect set of ripples.

"I keep having this dream," she says, and this is not what he expects to hear. He expects her to say 'I keep thinking about Patience' or 'I feel so lonely now that everything's changed' or something obvious like that, but he doesn't let his surprise register on his face. "It's the strangest thing. It's such a complete dream, not fragmentary at all. And it's always the same. Does this ever happen to you?"

Paolo thinks about his dream of the bar. He'd always figured it was born from reading too many of his mother's crime novels, but it had seemed like more than that lately. Like something prophetic, or at the very least seriously ominous. "Yea," he says. "It does." But he doesn't elaborate. That dream is not for sharing, at least not yet.

But hers is, and she shares it. As she talks, Paolo's eyes widen, and his stance changes. She takes her head off his shoulder and he holds both of her hands, periodically squeezing them show support or whatever that's meant to signify. It really is a fucked up dream. But it also makes a lot of things make sense.

Nadia has had the same dream every night since she ceased to be The Girl with the Egyptian Eyeliner. Every night, exactly the same.

It is Florence, but not as she knows it. The streetlights are candles burning foul-smelling oils, and the few shop windows are for butchers, spice merchants and apothecaries hawking nothing of any real medicinal value. The people dress in either opulent silks or rags, with very little in-between. There's more of the rags, though, much more. And the ones in the rags have formed a group hundreds strong, marching through the street. She follows them as they move, not quite part of their number but too close to be fully separate. They are chanting, but it's not Italian she recognizes. Some have torches. Some have sharpened implements and tools she doesn't recognize the function of. Most, though are carrying, for lack of a better word, Art. They hold small-sized sculptures, paintings, books, and icons. Some have formed teams for larger items, some struggle under the weight of objects well beyond their capacity but still manage to keep pace. The procession, if appraised, would likely be valued in the millions if counted today. Judging by the attitudes of the mob, she guesses they'd value their goods considerably lower. Finally, they come to a place she recognizes. It's the *Duomo* and the *Battistero* but not quite as she knows them. The dream's too murky for her to identify how they've changed, but they're not quite the same and she's moving past them too quickly for her to analyze. The mob gets louder as they move past the cathedral, and she starts to hear the echoes of other groups coming from other streets. There are hundreds of them, thousands even, all converging on one place: the *Piazza della Signoria.* In the square, her group and the others fan out in a massive circle around the outskirts of the square. In the center are two men, by their robes clearly priests of some sort, shouting in the same bizarre half-Italian the crowd had been using. They move in unison. They speak in unison. The assembled swarm dumps their priceless artifacts one at a time in the square before the men, and they each take a torch from the crowd.

This is so familiar, and Paolo almost interrupts her storytelling to give her a history lesson, but he doesn't. He's transfixed by the fact that someone with no knowledge of this story could dream it so perfectly. She must have heard about it or read about it somewhere and forgotten, yes? Do they tell Americans about the Bonfire of the Vanities?

There's no time to wonder. Dream Nadia is screaming herself hoarse as she watches painting after painting and book after book fall into the fire. There's something strange though, that stops her voice. She feels a chill, like a cold wind blowing over the enraptured mob. It's not possible, because the fire raging in the *Piazza della Signoria* is massive, all-consuming. But it is. And that's when she realizes that it's daytime. The whole dream, it had been so dark that she'd thought it was nearly midnight, but when she looks up she can see the sun. But there's no light coming from it. The city is in full shadow, and no one seems to question this but her.

She's just wrapping her head around this when another figure steps out of the crowd. It's a woman, dressed in a full suit of armor and carrying a sword of fire. Joan of Arc is her first thought but the age and the country are all wrong. No one but her and the priests seem to acknowledge the woman, and the priests are terrified. Well, that's not quite true. One is terrified, and the other looks... excited? It's hard to read his expression. One thing is clear, he knew she was coming, and now that she's here, he's ready. It's the first time the priests separate and in separating, Nadia begins to see the flaws in their illusion of sameness. The priest who was frightened – who is frightened, he's almost cowering now – looks like you'd expect a priest to look. An older man with sharpened features, deep sockets around his eyes, and a permanent sneer make him sinister, but he is nevertheless a man. The second is something else. His skin is blackened, ashen. His eyes glow like embers, but give no light. Nadia doesn't know what to call it, but the one thing it isn't is human. The woman in armor seems concerned only with the beast, sparing no attention for the cowering priest. The crowd is unaware of any of this. They're just dumping their shit on the fire like its charcoal instead of art and literature. It occurs to Nadia that maybe no one else can see the woman and the thing masquerading as a priest. As if to confirm her theory, they begin to charge towards each other.

Nadia sees their fight as though she's catching it frame by frame between the flashes of a strobe light. In one flash the thing's arms have swelled to twice their size and grown giant, obsidian claws. In the next, the woman's flaming sword has separated its arm from its body. In the next, it's grown it back, and is swiping with both jagged hands at the woman's face. It's difficult to follow, and the longer she watches the more she feels a sense of dread. In the dead space between frames she fears for the woman. Each blow she lands on the beast it seems to heal, and each blow it lands she wears, until her steel plate is sticky with her blood and a black, oily, substance that must come from her enemy. At the last, she seems beaten. The priest, the real one, has regained his composure and driven the crowd into a frenzy. Nadia hides her face in her hands, and the world goes grey. And then she feels heat, slight at first but growing in intensity. It's like the sun on her skin, but closer somehow. Hotter. The grey fades and she peers between fingers. The light nearly blinds her. Pinned beneath the creature, the woman glows with an incomparably bright light. Even dreaming, Nadia fears it will blind her. But as badly as it hurts her – and it feels like it will burn her eyes from its sockets, it does worse to the thing. It shrinks from the light like a wolf from a fire, and releases a screech like some primordial nightmare from the world before people. The woman stands tall now and Nadia would swear her form was flanked with wings, wide and spread and powerful, but it's impossible to tell. As she moves closer to the beast, he begins to decay, rapidly – like the light has turned him to dust and a strong wind is carrying him away. The woman grabs him, and it smiles.

"Farewell, Azazel," she says.

"Until we meet again."

It's last words are a hiss and an echo and its already gone. The light fades and the mood of the crowd begins to shift. The priest looks uncomfortable as first one rock, and then another, is tossed in his direction. He begins to run. Nadia doesn't follow him, and neither does the woman. They stand in the square, facing each other, as the crowd disperses and leaves them alone with each other. The feeling of dread starts to return, little by little, as the woman comes closer. She's still got that sword, and she's raising it in anger. Nadia can't move. She can't do anything, anything except wake up. So that's what she does.

Paolo doesn't know what to say about Nadia's dream, so for a while he says nothing. He waits for her to say more, and for a long time she doesn't. She seems to feel better, though, having told him, and despite the strangeness of it he feels a bit better for hearing it. He feels like a weight has lifted from them, somehow, and in spite of himself he starts to smile.

"Listen, Nadia, there's something I wanted to ask you."

She puts her finger to his lips, and kisses him. It's a soft kiss, sweet and light and full of real affection, not lust. In that moment, he knows the answer to his question, but he waits for her to finish with whatever's on her mind. Whatever it is it's hard for her to express. She looks like she's searching for the words like they're buried in a stack of paper on a messy desk, and it's not a look he's used to seeing on her. She's usually so confident in her speech, so assured. It's almost a relief to see her struggle, but he keeps that thought to himself. Whatever's making her feel this way, it's got to be hard for her, and he needs to be present for that. Being a boyfriend is hard work, it turns out.

"The thing is, Paolo, I had this dream again last night. It's always the same, the dream, it never changes, but last night it did. Last night it was different. When the woman came to me at the end, I saw her face. For real, like I was seeing it for the first time. It was Patience, Paolo. I think it's always been Patience."

Paolo grabs her and pulls her to him and waits for the tears to soak his shirt again, but she's dry. He doesn't let he go, just strokes her hair lightly and watches the sky. A stray thought passes him, and he almost says it out loud but thinks better of it. After a bit, Nadia wriggles free, and he kisses her again, matching her affection in kind.

"Maybe it was," he says. "Maybe you knew she was different."

"She was, wasn't she? I don't know, it's just weird that she's gone. That I didn't notice until she was gone how much I..."

She doesn't finish the thought, just stares out the window.

"When was the last time you saw a pigeon, Paolo? Those things used to be everywhere, I feel like I haven't seen one in days. Do they migrate? They don't, right?"

Paolo shrugs and tries not to shudder. Had she read his mind? It's exactly what he'd been thinking. She wriggles free and he kisses her, matching her affection. First on the lips, then on the nose, then on the forehead. The last one makes her blush, and this is new too.

"So," she says. "You had something you wanted to say?"

"Yea, I did."

Paolo almost changes his mind, but he knows he's come too far for that. And the thing is, he doesn't want to. He's ready for this, as ready as he's going to be.

"I wanted to ask you if you'd thought about staying. Here. With me."

Nadia looks at him with a blank expression, and for a moment he feels a real twinge of fear. And then she smiles, and everything else is gone.

THE KISS
Tony

THE STREETS BETWEEN THE BAR AND his apartment
are no grayer than usual. There's no rain, not even a cloud worth
mentioning, but you could have fooled him. Not for the first
time, Tony wonders why he even moved to Florence to begin
with. A new life, he'd said at the time. Some life. Wherever he lay
down roots, the same weeds always grew to choke them. That
was probably his fault.

As expected, the apartment is occupied upon his return.
Crosby sleeps on a mattress of dead birds. At this point, he's
outpacing Tony's ability to throw them out without drawing
attention. Just another problem he doesn't know how to solve.
The Angel is there, too, standing in the doorway to his bedroom
bone-white and bird-beautiful. He's pretty sure she isn't real to
anyone but him, but hers is a madness that clarifies reality, rather
than obscuring it. At least that's what he tells himself. Anyway,
he muses, existence is overrated.

When he comes toward her, she starts to step away. She's
trying to show him something. The dog, probably, asleep by the
window – the little murderer always sleeps soundest after a busy
day. She's saying something, but Tony isn't listening. Not this
time. He puts his hand over her mouth and just looks into her
eyes. They're blue, the eyes: a wet blue, and a bit glassy, but with
an uncommon feeling of depth. Tony's not sure he could

describe his own eyes half as well. He's forgotten them.

Gently, he pulls his hand away from her face. She doesn't say anything. Her lips are the shade of red most women apply layers and layers of colored wax or whatever the fuck to maintain. He wants to kiss her, so he kisses her. He puts his lips against hers, and pulls her close. The armor is cold and bulky, but the skin underneath is warm -warmer than he expected, almost uncomfortably so. She doesn't struggle, but she doesn't reciprocate. Whatever she was prepared to hear from him tonight or any other night, this was not part of it. She tastes like powdered sugar and smells like nothing and Tony realizes that if he didn't stop himself, no one else would stop him. He opens his eyes. She's watching him with no trace of confusion, or expectation, or pity. It must be so easy, he thinks, to be an Angel. To have no questions. To have no will. He starts to put his hands on her hips, and then Crosby starts to snore. Tony laughs.

"Is something funny, Tony?" She asks.

Whatever had come over him, it's gone. He leaves his hands in place, and holds her tight. He rests his head on her shoulder, and starts to weep. Slowly, her arms raise from her sides and wrap around his back. It's not a tight embrace, but there's no question that's what it is. She begins to pat him on the back. His tears turn to sobs. Tony's not sure how long he cries, but it's the longest the Angel has stayed in his apartment.

"I'm sorry," he whispers at last. "I know you have to go."

"It is alright, Tony." She says, with real kindness. "You must not apologize to me. You are doing more than should have been asked of you, more than is asked of most men and women. It will not kill me to comfort you."

Is that actually what she's doing? Should he feel comforted? Tony's surprised to find that he does. He releases her, and she takes a few steps back.

"You must have had something to tell me," he says. "That's

why you're here, isn't it? To tell me something?"

The Angel smiles, and there's real sadness in it. It's the smile his father made when he left him at the airport in Portugal with his mother. It's the smile his teacher at the school in Porto made when he told her they were moving back to the states so his mother could re-marry. It's the smile his stepfather had when his mother brought Magritte home. Tony's pretty sure he's seen that smile from everyone in his life, at one point or another.

"This time, Tony," she says, "I just came for you. Are you alright, now?"

Amazingly, the answer to that question appears to be yes, for the most part.

"I'm afraid," he says. "But the fear's getting smaller."

"That's good, Tony."

With that she steps towards the window. Either it's his imagination, or her footing's less sure across the hardwood than usual. For once, it seems like she's struggling under the weight of the armor. She presses a hand against the windowsill, and takes a deep breath in preparation. She wasn't lying, Tony realizes. Whatever it is, she can't be around the dog this long.

Still, her wings unfold from their hiding spots, and she takes flight. It's a shaky start, and it seems for a moment that she's not going to make it, but she does. Tony goes over the window to close it, and the dog starts to stir. It's amazing that the Angel can literally burst into flight an inch away from him without disturbing him, but Tony wakes him up right on cue. Tony's startled to hear a low growl coming from him. Crosby usually reserves that for birds, or strangers, or heavy children. For whatever reason, skinny kids and heavy adults don't bother him, but the combination does. Tony can't figure it out. He follows the dog's eyes to the floor.

"Holy shit," he says, even if only the dog can hear it.

It's a feather. The Angel's left a single white feather behind.

THE GHOST
Kitsune

THIS ISN'T THE FIRST TIME JACOB'S BEEN gone late into the night, but it's the first time he hasn't been back by morning. She would worry about it if she weren't so weak, and if she weren't so worried about that weakness. When he had left, she had been on the couch. She was still there, but she'd managed to get herself into a more comfortable position. She knows she's here for the long haul. These days, any time she lays down she's worried that this will be the time she doesn't get back up. These days, she knows it really could be.

Flat on her back, she thinks of her family. Of her mother, who she could call at any moment but seems always to choose not to. Her father, who she could visit at the gravesite just outside of town, but never does. As she does every time she wants to sleep, she thinks of Kita. She has one memory of her sister, but it's vivid. They were young. Kita was not quite two years her senior, but older enough to know things Ana didn't, and old enough to feel responsible for her younger sister. Kita wanted to go canoeing with their parents, and their parents would not let her. They thought Ana was too young to be her partner. Kita took her by the hand, and showed her how to do it. One stroke after another, they went down the river for nearly an hour. The only problem was their parents had gone the complete opposite direction. They were lost for nearly three hours, but returned no worse for wear. Ana can remember looking up at the sky and seeing shafts of light filtering through her sister's hair. She would have been so beautiful. She could have done anything, anything she wanted. Ana had always known that.

She had taken the name Kitsune because of her sister, though she never told anyone. Kitsune was Japanaese, and not Korean, so her mother did not process the connection. Or perhaps she did, and said nothing. Regardless, the name was for Kita. She had had a little doll, a red and white stuffed fox that was her constant companion. She had tattooed the foxtail on her leg when she was seventeen, in a fit of mourning that could be overcome no other way. The name stuck from then on. She wonders what Kita would think of it. What she would think of her. Would she want an unlicensed, lazy, punk guitarist for a sister? A sister who couldn't even stay in her band? Who wasn't sick as far as any doctor was concerned, but was wasting away of some invisible disease anyway? She wanted to believe that Kita would love her no matter what. That was the sister she knew, that she remembered, but it's hard to be sure.

"I can help you," says a voice, and Ana knows it's not hers.

"Let me help you, won't you?" It repeats.

"Who are you?" She calls.

"You know who I am. Come and find me. There is something I have to tell you."

With effort, Ana drags herself to her feet. Her legs feel like they would rather break than bend to move her to the other room, but she needs to return to the bathroom mirror. She knows that, somehow.

"I cannot carry you," says the voice, reading her thoughts once again, "but you must come."

Ana maps out the room by furnishings she can lean against, and carefully makes her way to the bathroom. She almost falls through the doorway, but she steadies herself, and pulls herself against the mirror. For a few seconds, she has no reflection at all. But she's just late. It's not her reflection on the other side at all, this time, that much is clear. It's her sister. It's Kita.

Their father had had the first flaring of the cancer that would ultimately consume him while the family lived together in Korea. It was one of the things that made him feel the need to flee. He was concerned that he would not survive in North Korea with the medical care available, and he was even more concerned at what his family might have to do without him to support them. Ana was old enough to know that her father was sick, but not why his being sick had made her mother and sister so sad. She had asked Kita and Kita told her they were sad because it meant they had to leave, to run away.

She had not understood it then, but she understands it now. There are times when treating the disease is not the issue. The issue is something you cannot see, something you cannot hear. But sometimes seeing or hearing will be worse than the disease. Sometimes all you can do is hide.

It was a few weeks later when her mother and father put her sister in the trunk of their car and started to drive. They drove slowly, following the speed limit and staying steady. She couldn't see, but she could feel it from the way the car shook. They stopped three times. Ana could not hear what her father said, but each time they were able to keep moving. As an adult she understands that money must have changed hands, or paperwork. She cannot imagine how many favors had to be called in to make the escape possible. She knew so little about how it happened, she and Kita had been bundled under layers and layers of tarp and fabric. The whole ride, Kita held her hand and told her that it would be ok. Until she stopped. Ana could remember the feeling of loneliness when she lost her sister's hand, but she had said nothing. She was too afraid. Afraid that if she screamed, she would be heard. That they would be caught. So she rode in the dark and the silence for hours. When the trunk opened, it was her mother who unfolded all of the fabric and found Kita blue and breathless, a knot tangled tight around her neck. They had never spoken about it since then.

"Ana," says her sister, and presses her hand to the glass of the mirror. Gently, Ana matches the gesture. She can feel warmth from the mirror, for the first time in god knows how long.

"You must listen to me, and you must be strong. Can you do that?"

Ana nods, but she doesn't feel strong. She feels like sleeping, and she knows that if she lays down she will sleep and maybe never get back up again.

"Ana, you have to run. You are in horrible danger. You understand that, I know that you do."

"Danger?" She asks. She wants to say more but her brain can't form the words. The cough splits her open like a walnut. Each time this happens it lasts longer, and each time less of her returns. "How?"

"That man is not what he seems. He is dangerous, sister. He will take the life force from you, and he will only get stronger. He will suck you dry until there is nothing left, and he will only continue to feed when you are gone."

"A parasite," Ana whispers.

"Yes," Kita says, "and a shark, too. You were right, both counts. But what he is does not matter. You have to run. You have to escape. If you do not, you're dead."

"I'm not strong enough," she whimpers, and she knows that

it's true.

"You are," says Kita. "And if you are not, I will make you stronger. Come here."

She leans against the mirror. It's cold everywhere her sister isn't. Her sister's lips graze against the glass on her side of the mirror and it's hot. Ana feels the warmth all the way through her, and for the first time in weeks she feels healthy. She feels alive. But Kita's starting to fade.

"I do not have much time," Kita whispers. "Remember what I said. I'm sorry I couldn't be there Ana, I never would have let this happen."

"I know," Ana says, and that's when she realizes that she's started to cry.

For a moment, her reflection is gone, but slowly it fades back into view. This time, it's no different than her reality. This time he can see exactly how far she's come. The sunken pits in her eyes leak dark grey spider web veins across her face. Her cheeks are hollow, and her lips are dry, and her eyes are red. There's a film of blood around her lips. Her belly is distended, as though she's malnourished. She doesn't look like someone who is ready to fight. What she looks like is Death. Maybe that's what she needs to be.

THE CONFESSION
Jacob

"FORGIVE ME FATHER FOR I HAVE SINNED," Jacob says into the darkness. "It's been seven years since my last confession."

He's in the booth at the Santa Croce, the last place on Tony's old list of tourist traps he's yet to visit. It's a beautiful church. Tony might be an idiot, but he's an idiot with good taste. After walking around the place and taking in wonders including Gallileo's tomb and severed finger, if sign is to be believed, Jacob locates the confessional booth. Some things, you just can't resist.

"Seven years is a long time," says the priest. From the man's voice, Jacob can tell he's old. He can't be less than seventy unless he's a smoker. No less than sixty, even then. Either way, he'll be dead soon. There's no need for Jacob to take an active role in it, he'll get there on his own.

"Yes, father. I do realize that."

"Have you been to church in your absence from the booth, my son?"

"On occasion." This is the truth. He'd been raised a Catholic but was what you'd call lapsed. He went, but only once in a blue moon out of nostalgia, or obligation. Those were his excuses at least. Really, he just wanted to reassure himself his lack of conviction was secure. He has never failed in this.

"What is it that brings you to confess, my son?" The priest

asks. He's keeping his voice neutral, but something tells Jacob he's heard enough by now to know whatever it is will be juicy. The truth is, neither man has any idea what they're doing here.

"Father, I've committed the greatest sin I know to commit, and I've done it in full foresight of the lord's judgment."

The priest sits silent, waiting for the story.

"I do not confess for forgiveness. I don't want forgiveness. I don't need it."

"We all need forgiveness, my son."

"You might. Your congregation might. But I don't. Or if I do need it, I don't want it."

"The lord grants us free will that we may turn our back on him, but we do so at our peril."

Bullshit, it's all bullshit. Jacob tamps his anger down in that deep well where the hunger lives. After all, he initiated this conversation. He knew exactly what to expect from it.

"I believe, father, that I am a source of peril and not its victim."

"I don't understand your meaning, child."

"This is my sin, father. I have taken a life. To be truthful before god, I have taken six."

The priest sits in silence as Jacob tells the stories, each in their proper order. Maria, though the first, remains his favorite. The girl with the blond hair is a close second. The worst was the nun he had hunted from the apse of this very cathedral. She had cried for her life before he took it. Offered him things he wouldn't expect her to know how to make good on if he let her live. Six stories, and six lives. The priest sits in silence for each, and remains in silence when Jacob has finished.

"So." Jacob is satisfied with his performance, all things considered, "what shall be my penance? Will it be seventy Hail Maries or eighty? Hm?"

He gets no response. No amount of goading will disturb the

priest. If Jacob couldn't hear his breath and see the glint of his glasses through the screen, he'd have thought the man had gone to fetch the police. He still could, though it would violate his ethics. Something tells him the penance for turning in a murderer is considerably less than the penance for murder. He feels his anger boiling over. He can't kill this man, but he can put the fear of god into him. Better yet, he can put the fear of Jacob into him. There's just one problem.

He gets up, walks around to the priest's door, pushes it in, and finds the chamber empty. There's no sign of the priest – if anything the room doesn't look as though it's been used in weeks. Where the fuck had he gone?

Jacob stalks the grounds for fifteen minutes at least. He finds paintings and frescoes and statues and altars, but no priest. Not so much as a soul other than him is anywhere within the cathedral, now, which is strange. The place ought to be swarming with tourists. There had certainly been no shortage of them milling about outside of it. He returns to the confessional booth. He examines the priest's booth again, more carefully, looking for any sign of anything amiss. This time, he finds it. It's a little burnt scrap of paper, small enough it had avoided his attention before. It doesn't say much, it's just a name, but it's one he recognizes.

"Giancarlo Carrera," Jacob says. The name echoes in the empty chambers of the cathedral like a moan from a mourning mother. As soon as he sees the name, the hunger returns. It's stronger than it's been before, even stronger than the night he killed Maria. He's got to sate it, if that's even still possible. If he even can. When he killed that blonde, he felt nothing, even as her blood cooled on his knife. The kills after that hadn't been much better. He needed more. Somehow, there needed to be more.

Jacob crushes the burnt paper between his palms. What

ought to feel like charcoal or ash feels thick, and black, and viscous. It clings to his fingers like oil, but it smells like ink. As if in a daze he walks with his hands outstretched to the fresco sprawled across the closest wall. He'd paid it no attention when they first came in, but it's clear as day now. It's the ruins of a city, burnt and bloody. It looks like Florence, but it's not – the Duomo's missing, and a few other landmarks. There's pieces of the usual medieval horror-show scattered throughout, with beheadings and flayings and murders of every sort imaginable on display, but they're just set dressing. The main event is at the center; an Angel stands, wings splayed, over a terrified priest. It's got to be some historical figure – Savagnarola, maybe, or some lesser-loved pope – but the face is familiar. It could be his father. It could be him. Jacob realizes then that his hands are moving. They're stretched out, inching closer to the painting. He watches, in fascination, as his fingers gouge into the eyes of the angel, leaving them black. When he's finished, his hands are completely clean again. The priest is gone from the painting, and the hunger's gone too. At least for now.

THE ACQUAINTANCE
Paolo

IN THE RAIN THE CITY IS A JUNGLE, and the rooftops a canopy. Women with tiny dogs scurry from shelter to shelter on the back of black stilettos that ought to trip them at every gap in the cobblestone. Businessmen with umbrellas the size of car bumpers bulldoze the streets, writing off all casualties as collateral damage. Even the nuns seek reprieve, grey habits sodden and black from the soaking they've taken. It's a shitty day, as far as the weather is concerned, but that isn't stopping Paolo. He's got a calendar, and appointments, and places to be. It's all very new to him, but so are a lot of things. So is Nadia. So is most of his life, since he managed to turn it around.

Thanks to Nadia, Paolo smells like incense and gasoline. He hates the new cologne she insisted he wear – it's all the rage in Paris, she assures him – but be kept his head above the fray and lets her choose it for him. Rubber-shod schoolkids fly by hunting for puddles to ruin, but he stares them down and they give him a wide berth. He's got his only good pair of shoes on and he intends to keep them dry. There's not a lot that could get him down today, but that would sure as hell do it. They're new, these shoes. Things of beauty: black and red oxfords with immaculate stitching. They'd set him back a couple hundred, but that's alright too. Everything's alright, today. It would be the perfect day to quit smoking if he still smoked. Maybe he could start back up.

Paolo's taking it slow. There's a briefcase slung over his shoulder that once belonged to his father, returned to him courtesy of Claudia. Mostly, it's empty. There's a good pair of headphones, some bad pens, and a shitload of crumbs. The big ticket item, though, is a piece of paper. What's amazing, thinks Paolo as a little French Bulldog splashes by with some trash in its mouth, is that a piece of paper can actually make or break a man's life. It's not a deep thought, or an original one, but who cares? It's a true one, and today this piece of paper has made his life a good deal better.

He stops for coffee at a little shop across from a square where his father used to play from time to time. His old man had always loved the acoustics here. He claimed he could tune a string on his guitar and halfway across the square you could hear it well enough to describe his fingerprints. In retrospect, that didn't make much sense. Waiting on his cappuccino to cool a little, Paolo cracks open the case to admire his paper. The object in question is a lease, good for a year. The flat's a little spot on the Oltrarno with a two minute walk to the Boboli and a three minute walk to the best pizza in town. He hasn't told the girls yet, or not all of them. He's hoping Nadia will decide to stay.

She's been different, since the funeral. Quieter, but happier, once the mourning wore off a little. He's learning things he never expected about her. She plays the violin, and cooks, and can recite pi to its twenty-fourth digit. He's trying to show her things about himself, too. He's trying to make them a life. Every now and then, he still thinks about Kitsune, but it mostly just makes him sad. He hopes she's alright. He hopes, whatever he saw that night, that it was temporary. If there's anything he's learned, anything he trusts, it's that that's what life's great unhappiness is – temporary.

The cappuccino is safe to drink, finally, so he downs it foam and all. It's good. Not great, but good enough. Case closed, he gets to work. Paolo's got a job, now, after all. And when you've got a job, you've got to work. It's time for him to get to it.

Paolo's on his way back from the showing when he decides to walk by the old apartment just to see if that girl's shoe is still there. Of course it's not, and he knows that, but wouldn't it be a laugh? The couple he'd shown the apartment to were lunatics, but they were lunatics with money. They spoke in hushed whispers between themselves in response to every single thing he told them, but he must have been saying something that they liked because they signed it. It's not the first deal he's made in his new gig, but it's the first one he's done alone. It feels good. He doesn't love it, but it's real. It's safe. It's adult.

The old apartment window's in one piece, and the shoe is still there. It's only been, what, four months? Somehow Paolo had expected to see the place burnt to the ground. To see Franco's obituary in the paper. Anything. How disappointingly uneventful. With that out of the way, Paolo's got the whole day to kill. Once upon a time, he'd have just started drinking. Today, though, he wants his head clear. Which is good, because he's pretty sure he knows the guy sitting alone on the hospital steps. Someone he's seen, but not recently. A friend of Kitsune's? A fan? Someone she always talked to, but never introduced him to.

"Tony," he says, and he knows he's right. He makes a beeline for him. Tony starts to squirm when he figures it out, but at this point Paolo's committed. It'll be fine once he introduces himself, right? Right?

"Ciao," he says to Tony, who mutters it in return. "I don't think you know me."

"I don't," Tony says, and this looks like it concerns him, greatly.

"Well we haven't met, but I know who you are. You're Kitsune's friend."

"You know Kitty?"

Paolo nods. Tony's mood brightens when he says her name, but he looks sad right on the heels of that happiness. It's then that Paolo starts to worry. Maybe Kitsune's not alright. Maybe it wasn't a temporary thing this time. The thought unsettles him to say the least.

"I do," he says. "Or I did. We used to, um. Well I guess you'd say we lived together. Or dated. Or something."

There's a flash of recognition. Paolo wishes they could skip this part and cut to the chase, but he knows he can't justify that when he's the one who started this conversation in the first place. The rules of conversation have to be observed, like it or not.

"You're Paolo," Tony says, and Paolo nods.

"Listen, is she alright? Kitsune, is she doing well these days?"

Tony shrugs his shoulders. He's hugging a briefcase a lot like Paolo's tight to his chest. Maybe there's a piece of paper in there. Maybe his life's just changed, too, and not as much for the better. Paolo feels a pay it forward moment coming, but he's got to get this line of questioning done first, to get a bit of closure.

"I'm honestly not sure," Tony says, "It's been a long time since we talked."

Paolo feels a sense of relief. Maybe she wasn't better, but she couldn't be worse if no one knew about it. At least not the people she still kept close. It's not certainty, but it's enough.

"The last time I saw her," Paolo says, "she seemed sick. Do you know if she got better?"

Tony laughs a dry, rough laugh.

"She's still dating the prick she started seeing after you, so no, I doubt she's doing very well at all."

Paolo doesn't like the sound of that, but maybe it's not his business. He tries to put it aside. Something in Tony's face has got him convinced he needs to try out his newfound sense of self. Everyone needs a pick me up every now and then.

"Listen, Tony."

"I've got to go soon."

"This won't take long. Whatever you've got going on in there, or whatever it is that's happening to you. It's going to be ok, you know? This too shall pass and all that?"

It's not his best motivational speech, but it must work because Tony gets up and reaches out a hand.

"Thanks," Tony says. "I really hope you're right."

With that, he turns and starts to walk towards the hospital doors.

"Paolo," he calls over his shoulder. "You're not heading in here too, are you?"

Paolo shakes his head, and there's honest to god relief on the other man's face. There's happiness, even.

"Good," Tony says. "Don't."

THE HOSPITAL
Tony

SOMEWHERE, THINKS TONY, SOMEWHERE there is a fish on a hook with more control over the direction its life is going than I have.

The hospital is frigid despite the record-setting summer blistering the cobblestones just outside its doors. The layer of sweat Tony earned carrying his heavy briefcase filled with explosives all the way from his apartment isn't doing him any favors. He can feel it cooling and congealing against his skin. Nurses and orderlies mill around with focus and determination, but absent an explanation for their actions he can't help but compare them to bees at a hive. Or, as Jacob would have said, ants on an anthill. He tries not to count them. He tries not to look at their faces. He tries not to look at his watch. It's eleven thirty. He's set the first charge on a timer to go off in a minute's time. He has only a short while to get into position before the power is cut to the building, and only a short time after that to set the rest of the charges. Not for the first time, Tony feels a strange sense of pride at the thoroughness of his plan. Not for the first time, this makes him want to go home, get in bed, and never get out. It's too late. It's eleven thirty one.

The lights flicker off unevenly, but almost in unison. They're down for maybe three seconds before they start to cut back on. Not all of the overhead lights return – the generator doesn't power the building in full, only what it needs to for the patients to stay alive. It takes another thirty seconds for the alarm to go off. It's longer than he expected, but it's within the acceptable range. Tony's hiding in what amounts to a janitor's closet. The room smells like bleach and condoms, hopefully because of the boxes of latex gloves on its single shelf. From its little window, he can see people start to mill about. He can hear muffled voices. They're going to start moving patients. He's got another ten minutes before he can move.

Tony told the Angel it would take him fifteen minutes to get the charges set, and five to clear the building before he blew them. That gave her twenty minutes to get the other people out of the building. He wanted to see their faces, he said, before he pulled the trigger on this. He wanted to know they would be safe. He tries not to think about the other coma ward patients. Most of them are dead anyway, he tells himself, but he knows it's not true. Just like it's not true that this is alright, that this is the only sane option in a sea of bad choices. If there is a hell, that's where Tony's headed, but there's no turning back now. It's time. He clears the closet.

Tony finds his way to bishop Carrera's room. For a moment he has to duck into a broom closet to avoid an orderly dragging a straggling junky out of the recovery ward, but that's the only hiccup. It's all going smooth, smoother than he thought it would. Maybe the Angel's decided to interfere, after all. It takes him three minutes to find the room. Three hundred and thirty-three, says the number on the outside. He's been here before, of course, but he hadn't focused on that detail. There's no time to do that now, either, so he doesn't. He just steps inside, closes the door, and gets to work.

He sets two charges. One at the foot of the bishop's bed, and the other at the head. He's already had time to lay a few in key locations throughout the hospital proper over the last week, which should go off when the bishop's room blows. It should be just enough to take the building down. He still doesn't want to think about it, even while he's doing it. He still thinks about turning back.

"You're a piece of shit, you know that?" He says it to the bishop, but he's talking to both of them. Maybe Jacob's right, and the whole city's full of shit. Maybe the whole goddamn planet is.

"I had a shit life before you went and got hit by that taxi, but it was mine." He continues. A monologue isn't part of his plan, but he's ahead of schedule so there's time for a short one, even if his audience won't appreciate it.

"Why do you hate them so much?"

He's talking about the bishop, and he's talking about the gypsies, but in that moment he thinks about Jacob and the ants. The night after that apocalyptic fight in his living room, Tony had run out to the park looking for ants. He found a hill and its network of tunnels in the shadow of an oak tree. It was a wide-set mound, low to the earth and dotted with unkind footprints, trailing sand in all directions through the jagged grass surrounding. Tony had grabbed them in great itchy clumps and dropped them into a cardboard box he'd used to move into his apartment. Once it had held his records, but that day he turned it into a terrarium.

Back inside, Tony built a little obstacle course to prove his point, should Jacob ever get the chance to hear it. He put a sugar cube at the center of a tap water moat and put the ants on the big island, with a little sandcastle he made with a thimble for good measure. He waited for the promised bridge of corpses, the sacrifices for the greater good. Jacob believed in it so securely, so certainly. Tony believed they would starve to death. They were both wrong.

Tony could almost hear them, but that was impossible. That

microscopic clicking and chattering of their brittle pincers and buzzing of their sandy wings, it was his imagination. There was chaos, but it played out in silence. Red ants swarmed over black and large over small. The ones with wings were surrounded and destroyed by those without, their unique portions removed forcibly and dragged away in pieces. At the peak it was impossible to discern amongst the confusion where one creature began and another ended. Tony wasn't sure he wanted the dust to settle. It would end in trumpets and horse-hooves and the Battle Hymn of the Republic, and oh Christ, he regretted getting it going. Eventually it ended. Only one ant had survived, but somehow, it got to the sugar cube. Tony put the box outside. Jacob would have been proud of him.

"I've got to go now," he says to the bishop.

Carrera doesn't respond.

It really is time to go. The plan was for him to wait for the Angel to give a signal, but she hasn't done it and he can't wait anymore. Somehow he trusts her to make it right. Somehow he trusts her to make it worth it.

"First, though, I've got a present for you."

Tony produces two bottles of pills from his pocket, and leaves them on the bishop's bedside table. No one but him will ever see them, but he knows, and that's enough.

"Fuck you," he says, and walks out.

THE AMBULANCE
Kitsune

AFTER MINUTES OF WAITING, the keening siren of an ambulance pierces the silence. Waves of red and blue light cascade over the room; first one and then the other, like the tide going in and out. Ana stands by the mirror, battling her reflection. She's only a shadow now; a whisper from a voice that screamed itself hoarse long ago. The bags under her eyes could hold all she needs for a weekend retreat. Maybe I should go, she thinks. Maybe I should just go someplace quiet for a while. Wait for all of this to go away. But it wouldn't go away. Not in a weekend, not ever. She wouldn't be going to recover, or to weather the storm. She'd be going to die.

Jacob is still sleeping. His breath rises and falls in rhythm with the emergency lights. He could sleep through anything, she had discovered. Nothing woke Jacob but Jacob. She had never been like that, even when she was healthy, and now she barely sleeps at all. She takes her eyes off the mirror. Better to look at anything but her sallow reflection. Better to count scratches on the dresser - thirteen, there are thirteen. She decides to get dressed. Little by little, she makes it. She's looking through his drawers for a shirt when she finds it: a black velvet box. She doesn't need to open it to know what it is but she does anyway. The diamond catches the red and blue and throws it out into a million tiny points. It's then that she knows for sure. She really can't stay. It's that simple, and it's that hard.

Ana grabs a suitcase as the last wails of the siren fade into the morning. She tries to remember that Neil Young song about the ambulance. Tony would know it, if he were here. He knew them all, down to the most arcane detail. Thinking about him, the words came in a flash:

> *an ambulance can only go so fast*
> *it's easy to get buried in the past*

It was one of the only lines in the song that wasn't just a nonsense rhyme. Did it mean anything? Did it matter if it did? A coughing fit begins, and she can't stop it. She tries to hold back the noise, tries not to wake Jacob. She wants to be gone when he wakes up. But then what?

Ana throws the last of her things in her suitcase and takes a long last look at the bed. She could see it so clearly now. That 'something' that lay beneath the surface with Jacob was so evident when he slept. Most people look peaceful. Most people smile, or drool, or snore. Jacob does nothing. He *is* nothing. When he sleeps, it's just like he turns off the lights. Everything is darkness. Or at least, it is until it isn't. Jacob's face turns from a blank slate to a snarl in a moment's notice. His teeth are blunt instruments, but they look like fangs the way he bares them. The expression holds too long, refuses to fade. What is he dreaming about? What could possibly cause him to make that face?

His eyes shoot open, and he gasps. He makes eye contact with her, briefly, but his eyes are different. The pupils are darker, larger. They're like pits – like black holes in the center of nothing. They hold that moment for so long she starts to think she should say something, but then he breaks it and stares up at the ceiling. He's shaking, and twitching, and a low moan that sounds like the whistle on a train is coming from the depths of him. Then it stops, as suddenly as it had started, and his eyes close. Somewhere in the distance, there's the sound of an explosion.

"What the fuck was that?!" Jacob asks.

It's the obvious question, but she doesn't answer. How could she?

"Seriously, what the fuck was that?"

"I don't know."

He's panicking. A column of black smoke slowly rises against the horizon, expanding into a cloud behind Brunelleschi's dome. Now comes the time for the less obvious question.

"Wait. Is that a suitcase? Did you pack a suitcase?"

A sick feeling comes over her. Her body feels like Jacob's snarl, twisted and harsh. Out of the corner of her eye she swears she sees a girl. She sees Kita; young and beautiful, and sweet - something Ana never had the chance to be, and never wanted to be. It isn't dread she's feeling now, not anymore. It's something else entirely. Something physical.

"Are you packing a fucking suitcase right now, Ana?"

"I packed it already," she says, "it's packed."

"Why? Can I ask that? Can I ask you why?"

"You can ask."

She doubles over. The pain is increasing. It's like a force moving in her belly. Like something growing faster than her body can adjust to, something she couldn't possibly hope to contain.

"So why? I thought-"

"Shut up for a second."

"Jesus Christ, can we at least talk about this? You can't just leave without telling me."

"I said shut the fuck up and let me breathe, Jacob."

Jacob looks over at the dresser and sees the little velvet box, out and ready. His expression shifts. He understands now, but it doesn't matter. Ana's head is spinning. She feels like she's going to throw up. She is going to throw up. Jacob looks concerned but he doesn't get out of bed, doesn't rise. He can't. He's cuffed to the bedposts, she'd made sure of that. She slams her hands down on the tile floor. The pain is only getting worse.

"What's going on? Are you ok?"

She's doubled over on the floor nearly screeching. Her face is drawn, and pale, and bony. How does he not know that she's ill? How did he never notice?

"I'm not, no. I haven't been for…"

Silence. Another ambulance siren – this time it has company. There's a whole damn fleet. They'd be headed to the smoke. She could see it through the window, a black mass wrapping itself around the city. It would settle soon, and dim the ruddy brilliance of Florence's crimson tile. At least for a time.

"I'm sick, Jacob. I've been sick almost the whole time I've known you."

What was it Tony had said? He's sick, he's a sickness. Maybe he'd been right, after all. There had to be a first time for everything.

Ana begins to cough. The first few are shallow, quiet, but they get deeper and louder as the fit continues. There is no light at the end of this tunnel, no end in sight. The coughing accelerates and crescendos into a full cacophony, and then it stops altogether. She begins to gag. The smoke rises over the city like a cobra stretching its cowl before it strikes. She throws her head back. She has a moment to think *I'm going to vomit*, but she's wrong. She heaves, but what comes out isn't something that's hers to dispel.

It emerges slowly, carefully. It is thick and viscous, and it smells like the river – like algae and rat shit. It falls all at once and settles into a puddle, but it doesn't stay there. It's a living thing.

"What the fuck is that?" Jacob asks. He's always ready with the tough questions, a real go getter.

There's no time for her to answer. The thing is taking shape, or rather shapes. She shuffles back away from it, but it's slithering towards her. It's black mostly, the thing. The kind of blackness that absorbs light, that devours warmth and stifles sensation. She can't look away. It's moving closer and closer, but she's too weak to do anything about it.

On the bed, Jacob is thrashing and screaming. She can tell by the motion of his lips that he's calling her name, telling her to move. She knows that she should, knows she should stand up and run, or try and smash the thing, but she can't. She has a moment to think 'this is it' before the sound of shattering glass breaks the spell. She screams.

By the time she's gotten it processed, it's already over. The black oozy thing is ruptured and splattered across the floor. There's a little white cat in the midst of the mess, its fur matted in patches with black goo. It had torn the thing up in a flash, without noise or fanfare. She could swear it was watching her, looking into her eyes. Whatever it sees there, it seems satisfied. It begins to clean the goo out of its fur. Is it – is it purring?

Jacob looks at the cat like he's watching a ghost rearrange the furniture. He's white as a sheet. Ana's never seen him like this. Nothing rattles him, nothing bothers him. How had that appealed to her? Why had she stayed with him?

"I've seen this cat before."

"The cat."

"Yes, the cat."

"That's what you want to talk about here."

He's completely terrified. Odd that he's scared of the cat and not the puddle of sentient goo it had just obliterated.

"Will you please get these damn cuffs off of me?"

With the thing dead she feels stronger. Her legs are wobbly, but she can stand. She gets up and moves over to Jacob, clutching the key. He's still staring at the cat. Why would it bother him so much?

"Where did you see it before?" She asks.

"The cat?"

"Yes, the cat."

And then it's clear. Then the truth becomes obvious. 'What's the matter with you?' She'd asked him once. 'I don't care much about people,' he'd said in return. 'I'm people,' she'd said, and she'd been right.

"Never mind, Jacob."

She takes the key, dangles it in front of his face, and then throws it out of the shattered window. The cat hops up onto the bed and settles on his chest. The weight of it seems to deflate him. His breathing stiffens and slows – it seems to be somehow heavier than a cat, as it settles on his stomach.

"What the fuck!" He tries to scream this, but it comes out as a wheeze.

"You know, Jacob, in the time since I've known you you've taken nearly everything from me. I don't play guitar anymore, I don't talk to my family, I don't even see anyone but you. And I let you do that. I let that happen. I let you take Tony, and the band, and even my house."

He looks horrified. He has no idea what she's saying and he starts to say so. She raises a hand to shut him up.

"The fucked up thing is you don't even know you're doing it. You're not trying. You just take. You're a black hole, Jacob. You absorb feelings, and people, and whatever you want. Whatever you need."

Slowly, his expression shifts. He transforms from the dumbfounded man with the cat on his chest into something sinister and bleak. The expression leaves a pit in her stomach that reminds her of the black ooze that had emerged from it only moments before. The cat begins to arch its back and hiss.

"You're wrong," he says. He's smiling now. "I'm not a black hole, I'm a shark. I kill people, Ana. I killed a girl the night you told me your real name. I killed another the night I had that fight with Tony. I've killed others, and I'm not going to stop."

And this time, for the first time, she knows that he's telling her the truth. He wants her to respond. He wants her to love him for it, somehow, or if she's not capable of that to revile him. She won't give him the satisfaction. Apathy is all that Jacob deserves, and it's all that she's willing to give him.

Ana watches the last traces of red and blue light fade from the room. Stepping around broken glass, she makes her way to her suitcase. In the distance the black smoke is fading into the ether, and the sound of sirens dims. Would this have been Kita's life? She wonders, not for the first time. If I had been left to die, and not her, would she be standing here looking at this man? Would she be trying not to cry? It isn't the first time she's asked questions like this, but it's the first time she's been grateful for the answer. For the first time she feels relief that Kita did not have to see this, to have the life she gave her sister. For the first time, Ana wonders if maybe it had been her who had made the sacrifice after all. There's a minute's silence as she gathers the last of her things and makes for the door. The cat's still there, still holding Jacob in place. It's like it's waiting for her to leave. Like it's protecting her from him. Ana has a moment to be grateful, and to wonder where she'll go, now that all of this is over. Then the cat starts to change.

The first sign anything is different is the shadow. It grows and contorts and spreads itself out, towering over Jacob's prostrate form. Ana's thinking about the inky monster the cat had killed, but there's no sign of it. Even the black that had clung to its fur has faded away. As the shadow gains clarity the cat seems, slowly, to grow. Before her eyes, Ana can see a pair of wings stretching from its back. It grows longer, and sheds its fur, and trades paws and claws for hands and feet, and a tail for a decidedly feminine figure. She's beautiful, truly. Much as she might want her to be, though, she isn't Kita. At least not this time.

Jacob watches the transformation silently, with a look that could only be described as desperation. His eyes beg Ana for help, but she doesn't know how to help him and she isn't sure that she would if she did. When the change is over there is a woman Ana can only describe as an angel, naked, straddling Jacob on the bed but not in the way that he likes.

"It's you," he says, and a single black tear begins to streak down his cheek.

Ana can just barely a glimpse of the angel's face. She'd seen it before, but only in the papers. It was the gypsy that had died, killed in the streets by – had that been him? Of course, of course it had. Tony was right.

"I am not what I appear, Jacob. And neither are you."

In the Angel's hands is a sword. It wasn't there before, but it's there now. She raises it high.

"Go on," Jacob says. "You know I can't stop it."

"I am truly sorry," says the Angel. "The fault is my own."

She swings the blade down. It cuts cleanly into Jacob's chest, but it isn't blood that spurts out in an arc from the moment of impact. It's that same black goo, and it sizzles and steams where it hits the wall. At each point of contact, each droplet, a single grey feather appears. They fall, slowly, to the earth. When the first one lands, a pigeon appears. And then another. And then another. Before long her room is swarming with the birds, cooing and flapping, and slowly finding their way out the window. They form a massive cloud as they hit the air, and an immense cacophony of sound. As they disperse, they pass through the smoke billowing from the site of the explosion, and it dissipates. Ana feels lighter. Stronger. Something has changed. The Angel stands. Jacob's dead, really and truly.

"Is it over?" Ana asks.

The Angel clears the room in slow, clean strides. She takes Ana's face in her hands and kisses it, tender and soft. It isn't the sort of kiss she's used to getting. It isn't hungry, and it isn't demanding. It's giving and it's generous and it's sweet, and when it's over she realizes that she's crying.

"It's never over," says the Angel, and then she's gone.

Ana feels a wind whip through the apartment, and she knows there's one thing left. From her pocket, she produces the picture of her sister. She scrambles for a pen. On the back are two names, and a date so far in her past it shouldn't have the meaning it does, not anymore. But that can't be changed. She sees that now. Instead, she lays it flat on her dresser and adds two more names. When it's over, it reads:

Kita Lingo, 1993
Maria Magariet, 2015
Patience Etheridge, 2015

She's not sure where the names come from, but they fit, and she puts it back in her pocket. Now it really is time to run.

ABOUT THE AUTHOR

Chris Parthemos used to live in Florence, Italy, but he doesn't anymore. For the curious, this is not the story of why that's the case. These days, Chris lives in his home town of Richmond, Virginia where he happily enjoys the city's thirty plus breweries, and a much more reasonable cost of living. Plus most of his family lives there. *Furball* is his first novel, and he very much hopes it will be viewed for what it is: a recognition and cynical depiction of the darker side of humanity one sometimes encounters, particularly where one doesn't expect to.

This book was born from a dark place.
Expect lighter things on the horizon.

AUTHOR'S NOTE ON MUSIC

Music is a very important part of my writing process. I'm always listening, and the music I tie to a character is a part of how I build them for myself. If you've enjoyed this book, you may also enjoy the playlist linked to in this QR code, which you can also find on Spotify as the Official Furball Playlist. Everything mentioned by name is there, as well as quite a bit more.

www.ingramcontent.com/pod-product-compliance
Lightning Source LLC
Chambersburg PA
CBHW022135170626
46807CB00005B/1951